Books are to be returned on or before
the last date below.

2 4 MAR 2014

2 1 FEB 2017

LIBREX-

STAR TREK:
THE NEXT GENERATION NOVELS

STAR TREK:
THE NEXT GENERATION GIANT NOVELS

STAR TREK®
THE NEXT GENERATION

THE PEACEKEEPERS

GENE DEWEESE

TITAN BOOKS

LONDON

STAR TREK **THE NEXT GENERATION 2:**
THE PEACEKEEPERS
ISBN 1 85286 070 7

Published by
Titan Books Ltd
19 Valentine Place
London SE1 8QH

First Titan Edition November 1988
10 9 8 7 6 5 4

British Library Cataloguing-in-Publication Data. A catalogue
record for this book is available from the British Library.

Printed and bound in Great Britain by Cox and Wyman Ltd, Reading,
Berkshire.

For Becky Bontreger.
You were there when I couldn't be,
and you did more for her than I could
ever have done . . .
Thanks.

THE PEACEKEEPERS

Chapter One

"IT WAS A wild-goose chase, Number One, but I have to admit I am not at all displeased at that."

In fact Captain Jean-Luc Picard looked more than just "not at all displeased." A slight smile gave his normally stern features a decidedly relaxed look as he settled his wiry frame into the comfort of the captain's chair. In the main viewer, the sparse stars of this remote section of the Orion Arm slid smoothly past as the *Enterprise* warped toward the nearest Starbase, hundreds of parsecs distant.

Seated at Picard's right, Commander William Riker smiled. "The Ferengi are not the most pleasant people to deal with, even under the best of circumstances."

Picard nodded, the shadow of a memory hardening his features briefly. "You're developing a gift for understatement, Number One. Personally, I would have no objections whatsoever to serving out the rest of my career without ever having to hear the name again."

"Look at it this way, sir," Riker said. "We didn't find any evidence that the Ferengi had been active in this sector, but we did discover two previously unknown class-M planets, both of which may be ready for Federation contact in a few generations."

"Yes, Captain," Lieutenant Commander Data volunteered helpfully from the forward station, "any mission that results in the discovery of more than three billion sentient beings could not be considered a 'wild-goose chase.'"

Riker smiled as he looked at the android. "I'm surprised you're familiar with that phrase, Mr. Data."

"On the contrary, Commander, I'm not. I was quite puzzled when the captain first made use of it. My information indicated that the Ferengi, though their values do not coincide with those of the Federation, could not be considered 'wild' in the sense of their being uncivilized, barbarous, or primitive. Nor are they of avian ancestry. I therefore concluded that the phrase must be a figure of human speech not included in my programming. However, the subsequent exchange between yourself and the captain has, I believe, enabled me to deduce the approximate meaning."

Riker laughed. "And that meaning is?"

Data pulled in his breath and straightened in his chair, as if he were a student who had been called upon to recite. "A project that fails because the information that caused the project to be initiated was false or misleading in some way," he said, finishing with a questioning glance at Picard.

"Very good, Mr. Data," the captain said with the ghost of a chuckle. "I've never heard it defined more precisely—particularly by someone who first heard the expression only minutes before."

"Thank you, sir, but I was designed to—"

Abruptly, Data fell silent, his luminous golden eyes widening imperceptibly as the displays on the panel before him flashed a tentative message. His fingers danced briefly across the panel, confirming and enhancing the information.

"Captain," he said, "scanners indicate the presence of an artifact of considerable mass, bearing zero-one-two, mark zero-zero-five."

"Another starship?" Picard responded. "Don't tell me it's Ferengi."

"The mass is consistent with that of a small starship, sir, but it is not under power."

"A derelict?" Picard sat up straighter and leaned forward slightly.

"Possible, sir, but at this distance—"

"Then we had better get closer. Mr. La Forge, alter course accordingly."

"Aye-aye, sir." Lieutenant Geordi La Forge, the slim, silvery Visor covering the blank whiteness of his sightless eyes, tapped in the changes unerringly.

"Mr. Data, put the object on the viewer, maximum magnification."

"Already done, sir, but at this distance it is impossible to discern any details."

Picard squinted at the viewer and the indistinct, featureless dot at its center. A flicker of impatience darted across his aquiline features, as it sometimes did on those rare occasions when he was forced to realize that, superb though the technology was that drove the *Enterprise,* it was still not quite magic. It had its limits, and the fact that he could issue an order did not mean that, when it was carried out, the results would be as perfect as he had hoped.

"Lieutenant Worf," Picard said, standing and turning toward the aft section of the bridge where the Klingon monitored the science stations, "any indications of life forms?"

"Nothing yet, sir. But—"

"I know, Lieutenant, 'but at this distance' there's no way of being positive."

"Yes, sir," Worf rumbled in agreement, "but what I was going to say was that, although the sensors can't yet detect any life forms, there are indications of a functioning power source aboard the vessel."

"Now we're getting somewhere," Picard said. "Lieutenant Yar, open hailing frequencies."

"Hailing frequencies open, sir," the blond security chief responded from the tactical station immediately above and behind the command area.

"Mr. La Forge, proceed on impulse power the last million kilometers. Do not approach closer than ten thousand kilometers without further orders."

"Aye-aye, sir, ten thousand kilometers."

"No response, sir," Yar announced as she leaned forward over the tactical console.

"Continue monitoring, Lieutenant, and transmit our own peaceful intentions, all languages, all frequencies."

"All languages, all frequencies, sir."

In the viewer, the central dot was beginning to grow. Picard and Commander Riker stepped forward, flanking Data and La Forge at the forward station, as if by moving closer, they could speed its growth.

The forward turbolift slid open and Counselor Deanna Troi emerged, her dark hair a mass of curls today instead of in the severe, pulled-back style she had been affecting recently. Joining them, she stood next to Picard.

"I sense anticipation in your thoughts, Jean-Luc," she said softly.

Picard indicated the viewer. "There's something out there," he said. "We'll see what in a few minutes."

She nodded, her eyes taking in the scene, then sliding subconsciously from the viewer to Riker— and quickly returning.

The dot continued to grow. Data was the first to speak, his precise voice reflecting the restrained blend of curiosity and puzzlement that gripped him whenever he encountered something new, something not included or explained in his phenomenally massive memory. "I can observe no obvious means of propulsion, Captain. Does it not seem peculiar that a vessel without a propulsion system should be found nearly a parsec from the nearest stellar system?"

Picard nodded, stepping closer to the holographic image.

"Propulsion systems are not necessarily always as obvious as a warp drive nacelle," Riker commented. "Our own impulse engines, for instance."

"Coming out of warp drive, sir," La Forge announced, and a moment later the image in the viewer shimmered and resolidified. The dot, now expanding rapidly, was beginning to show shape and detail even to eyes less sharp than Data's.

And there were indeed no propulsion units. When the image had first begun expanding, it had reminded Riker of a crude, blocky version of the saucer section of the *Enterprise,* detached and floating free, but now he could see it was actually rectangular, little more than a spacegoing box. Not only were there no propulsion units, there were no ports or openings of any kind, nor even a single marking that he could see.

"Sensors indicate total absence of life, Captain," Worf reported from the aft station, "and extreme age."

"How extreme, Lieutenant?" Picard asked, not turning from the viewer.

"At least ten thousand years, sir."

A faint shiver ran down Picard's spine. Despite his decades in space, he had yet to reach the point at which new discoveries, new indications of the true immensity and diversity of the universe could ever be considered routine. There were some starship captains, he knew, who claimed that after a hundred new star systems or a hundred new life forms there was nothing out there anymore that could give them the same high, the same tingling sense of wonder that their first voyage between the stars had given them. He was not one of them. He hoped he never would be. If that happened, it would be time to retire to a desk terminal somewhere, to turn his command over to someone who still felt a tingle of awe whenever he or she looked out at the billions of stars, the trillions of cubic parsecs still to be explored.

"And the functioning power source, Lieutenant Worf?"

"Standard antimatter, sir, and it appears to be supplying power to a number of individual devices."

"And the nature of those devices?"

"Unknown, sir. They are operating at an extremely low level, consuming very little power, as if they are not fully operational."

Picard frowned thoughtfully. "Possibly some form of hibernation device for passengers or crew? To travel between the stars in a sublight ship, the crew and passengers would almost certainly be kept in suspended animation."

Worf maintained his silence, but his sideways glance at Picard hinted that only humans, not Klingons, would require that kind of pampering.

For another minute, the image continued to grow, until it almost filled the screen.

"No sign of any drive, sir, even impulse," Data reported, "nor is there apparently any functioning attitude control. The vessel is drifting at a rate of approximately one arc second per minute. If not checked, it will make a complete rotation in three years, seventy-seven days, nine—"

"Thank you, Mr. Data," Picard interrupted, studying the image in the viewer. Even at this distance he could see no evidence of sensors, no external projections of any kind, nor any obvious openings.

"Ten thousand kilometers and holding, sir," La Forge announced.

"Still no life-form readings, Lieutenant Worf?"

"None, sir, of any level. If any beings were in hibernation, they're dead now."

"The vessel's proper motion with respect to the nearest stars, Mr. La Forge? Does its trajectory give any indication of its system of origin?"

"None, sir. Its linear motion is essentially zero with respect to the local stars."

Picard frowned.

"Internal structure and atmosphere, Mr. Data?"

"It is laid out essentially like a chessboard, sir, with extremely narrow corridors crisscrossing throughout the vessel. The antimatter power source is at the center, moderately shielded, surrounded by—"

"Moderately shielded, Mr. Data?"

"The shielding is a degree of magnitude less efficient than that of the *Enterprise*. The resultant radiation could, over the long term, prove detrimental to the health of any who occupy the vessel."

"It could have killed them? In their hibernation chambers?"

"In ten thousand years, it would be possible, sir."

"But it presents no danger to short-term occupants?"

"Such as ourselves, if we beam over to observe the vessel's interior firsthand? I believe not, sir."

"Very well, Mr. Data," Picard said, nodding minutely. "Continue. Are there any indications of living quarters?"

"No, sir. There is no area with an atmosphere anywhere within the vessel."

"This lack of atmosphere—by design or by mishap?"

"It is impossible to say, Captain, without inspecting the scene firsthand."

9

"Anything else?"

"Near the center, there is a second, lesser quantity of antimatter. Its shielding is even more inefficient than the other, but, because of its lesser mass, it presents no more of a radiation hazard than the larger mass."

Picard frowned. "A weapon, perhaps?"

"Possibly, Captain. It does bear a functional resemblance to our own photon torpedoes, but judging from its position near the center of this vessel, there would be no way of launching it."

"From what I've been told so far," Picard said, "there would be no way of launching anything from *anywhere* in this vessel except by transporter. You haven't found any openings yet, have you?"

"None, sir, but that doesn't mean—"

"I know. Tightly sealed doors or weapons tubes aren't detectable at this range. But even if there were launch tubes, a single weapon on an otherwise defenseless vessel doesn't make sense. Nor does the lack of propulsion. It couldn't run even if attacked."

"It might not have needed to, sir," Worf said. "I have been studying certain readings more closely, and I now feel they indicate the nonfunctional remnants of a primitive cloaking system."

Picard turned abruptly toward the science stations. "Nonfunctional? You're positive?"

"Positive, sir. The readings indicate that the entire final stage of the system—the stage that actually produces the cloaking effect—has either failed entirely or is missing altogether."

Picard turned to again scowl at the image—the puzzle—in the viewer. For several seconds, he was silent, a spark of hunger in his eyes. Finally, sighing mentally, he stepped back.

"Number One," he said abruptly, "assemble an away team to beam over."

Riker smiled. Picard knew he had seen the spark in his captain's eyes, the spark that said, if it weren't for the rules, Picard would lead that team himself.

"Right away, sir," Riker said, gesturing at La Forge and Yar as he moved briskly toward the forward turbolift.

Field-effect suits activated, Riker, La Forge, and Yar stood on the transporter circles. Riker signaled to Ensign Carpelli at the controls.

On the bridge, Picard stood just behind Lieutenant Commander Data, still at the forward station.

"Beaming over now, sir," Riker's voice informed him.

"Good luck, Number One," Picard said with a faint smile. "Keep in touch."

"We will, sir," Riker said. His voice faded on the last word as the transporters took hold.

For a moment there was only silence, and then Worf said: "Sensors indicate away team has arrived on alien vessel, Captain, in the targeted corridor."

A moment later, Riker's voice returned, only slightly fainter than when he had spoken from the transporter room, even though he was now ten thousand kilometers distant. "Deserted, as advertised, Captain," he said, and, a second later: "Tricorders confirm, no life forms on board, no atmosphere and no gravity. And no light except what we brought with us."

There was a brief silence, and then: "We're in a long corridor less than a meter wide. It's perfectly straight as far as I can see in either direction, but it looks more like an equipment access passageway, almost a crawl space, than a hallway. There are panels on the walls that look like—"

He broke off. "Lieutenant La Forge, why don't you take over the descriptive duties? I assume you're seeing a lot more than either Yar or myself."

"Probably, sir," La Forge admitted with a slight smile.

He was silent a moment then as he looked up and down the corridor, absorbing the jumble of wavelengths his Visor fed directly to the visual centers of his brain. To anyone accustomed to normal sight, it would have been sheer chaos, but years of experience had enabled him to effortlessly select the images he wanted, to ignore the clutter of irrelevant wavelengths and their unwanted—for now—information. The selection process had become virtually automatic over the years, requiring no more concentration than would be required of a normally sighted person who wanted to locate a red flag among a hundred green, and then, a moment later, to pick out the only one that was circular, not square.

"The corridor goes approximately fifty meters in either direction," Geordi said. "There are a half dozen intersecting corridors at regular intervals, and at least a dozen doors—panels, really—on each side. But there are no markings of any kind, either on the panels or on the corridor walls. The doors are big enough for beings approximately our size or possibly slightly larger to pass through. The nearest panel—"

"Captain!" Worf broke in, his rumbling voice filled with urgency. "Bring them back, now!"

"What—"

"The device containing the secondary mass of antimatter has become activated! At the present rate, it will reach a critical stage in less than a minute. The explosion will surely destroy the entire vessel!"

Chapter Two

PICARD TAPPED THE insignia on his uniform, activating the communicator. "Transporter room," he snapped. "Bring the away team back, now!"

Another tap. "Will, we're bringing you back! Something is happening over there!"

Turning abruptly, he strode up the ramp to Worf and the science stations. "The secondary mass of antimatter, Lieutenant—do you have its precise coordinates?"

"Yes, sir."

"The instant the away team is safely back, transmit those coordinates to the transporter room."

Tensely, he waited for confirmation of Riker's return. The moment it came, he spoke rapidly. "Transporter room! Lock onto the object at the coordinates Lieutenant Worf is giving you. Transport it as far from the alien vessel as possible, immediately! You have less than twenty seconds!"

"Aye-aye, sir," Ensign Carpelli's voice came back an instant alter. "Locking on now, sir."

"Fifteen seconds to detonation, Captain," Worf

rumbled. "The readings make the object appear very much like a photon torpedo without a drive attached."

"Energizing transporter," Carpelli announced. "Object being transported—now."

"Five seconds," Worf said. "Object gone from derelict but not yet—" A pause as new readings appeared. "Distance of object now five thousand kilometers beyond derelict. Detonation process continuing."

Abruptly, the viewer was filled with the harsh glare of the distant annihilation, blotting out the image of the derelict.

"Detonation process complete," Worf concluded, his back still toward the flaring viewer. "Derelict appears to be intact."

In the viewer, the glare faded and the derelict reappeared.

A moment later, the forward turbolift hissed open and the away team strode in, led by a frowning Riker.

"What happened, Captain? Why were we brought back?"

"Something—your presence, I suspect—triggered an antimatter device," Picard said, gesturing at the screen, where the filmy aftermath of the distant explosion still obscured most of the stellar background.

"A booby trap?" Riker wondered, eyebrows rising.

Data looked up curiously at Riker's words but said nothing.

"Perhaps," Picard said, "but if so, it was a rather drastic case of overkill. If we hadn't transported it out, the explosion would have vaporized the entire vessel."

Riker grimaced. "Thank you for the timely action, Captain."

"Don't mention it, Number One."

"Are we going back?"

Picard turned back toward the aft stations. "Lieutenant Worf? Can you detect any further such devices?"

"Aside from the central power source, sir, there are no indications of further quantities of antimatter anywhere on the vessel. Nonnuclear explosives, however, remain a possibility."

"Not likely," Yar put in. "If such devices exist, they would surely have been designed for use before the antimatter device. In fact, they could hardly have been designed for use *after*."

Picard nodded. "Agreed, Lieutenant. They wouldn't even exist after an explosion of that magnitude. But in a construct as old as this one, the possibility of malfunction cannot be overlooked. The explosion itself may well have been one."

"I do not think so, Captain," Worf said from the science stations. "The readings indicated a deliberate sequence of events designed to end in the antimatter explosion that we witnessed."

"Then what *was* its purpose?"

"Obviously, sir," Worf rumbled, "to destroy the vessel and any beings that had boarded or approached it."

"It makes sense, sir," Yar agreed, "if we assume that this was a military outpost of some sort. Self-destruct devices are quite common in the histories of many worlds."

Picard frowned. "A military outpost? With no means of propulsion, only a cloaking system? And no weapons but a single suicide device?" He looked around the bridge. "Data? Lieutenant Worf?"

"There are no readings to indicate the presence of weapons, sir," Worf said, and then added, "no weapons with which we are familiar, at least."

"There are a number of unknown devices still operating, however, sir," Data volunteered. "They could conceivably be weapons. Though they are not fully activated, readings indicate that they contain some form of subspace circuitry."

"What kind?"

"Unknown, sir. Without a closer examination, it is impossible to tell."

"Are they still operating at the same level as before?"

"They are, sir," Data said, quickly scanning his panel. "There has been no change."

Riker turned to face Picard. "We need a longer look, sir."

Picard was silent a moment, his eyes on the image in the viewer. Then he nodded. "Very well," he said, "but be prepared to have your visit cut short at any moment."

The barren passageway of the alien vessel took shape around the four members of the new away team—Riker, Data, Yar, and La Forge. As the transporter field released them, Geordi felt a moment of disorientation, even dizziness, as the lack of gravity made itself felt. An easy adjustment to his field-effect suit generated a mild magnetic charge, just enough to give him the traction necessary to "walk" rather than swim. The lack of an atmosphere had no physical effect, but the silence that closed in so abruptly on them was unsettling.

"Let's not waste any time," Riker said, his voice sounding oddly thin through the communicators, "and keep your field-effect suits on full. For the time being, we'll stay together. First—"

"Number One," Picard's voice interrupted, "the self-destruct circuitry appears to have been reactivated by your return. Even without the antimatter device, it could conceivably still be dangerous."

"Understood, sir. The energy it's using registers on our tricorders. We'll check it out immediately. Lieutenant La Forge, lead the way."

Studying the tricorder screen, Geordi turned

slowly. "This way," he said, looking up after a moment, "but I doubt that I'll need this," he added, indicating the tricorder. "The radiation leakage from the antimatter core will probably be enough of a guide."

He shivered slightly as he moved off down the narrow passageway and the others followed, single file. The radiation, hard and sharp to his Visored senses, was much like the split-second burst that had pulsed through the *Enterprise* when the distant self-destruct device had detonated, a burst that no one but he—and the *Enterprise* sensors—had seen. It was at times like this, he thought as he walked, that the Visor was both the most helpful—and the most disquieting. He knew that the radiation from the antimatter core was, for no longer than any of them would be exposed to it, essentially harmless, but still its harsh, brittle light had an effect on him that no other type of radiation did. Somewhere deep in his mind, it triggered a visceral response, a fear that he had difficulty controlling. A natural reaction to the inherent deadliness of the radiation? he wondered.

He shivered again, pushing the thought away. Turning a final corner, he found himself facing, not a panel, but a solid bulkhead. To his Visored senses, it glowed harshly, almost blindingly with radiation leakage. Transferring his attention to the tricorder he still held, he saw that it pinpointed the energy sources. One, the main core of antimatter, was a dozen meters beyond and below the bulk-head, beneath the deck and two more layers of shielding. The other, almost obscured by antimatter radiation, was immediately beyond the bulkhead. There did not appear to be access of any kind, almost as if the entire central section were a self-contained unit, meant to be replaced if anything malfunctioned.

"Our sensors show you virtually on top of the device, Number One," Picard's voice came over their communicators. "They also show the radiation level increasing. Are you all right?"

"So far, sir," Riker said, studying his own tricorder. "But I don't think we're going to be able to check the device out, at least not directly. We'd have to use our phasers to cut through a bulkhead, and that doesn't appear wise at the present. As you said, the radiation level is increasing, and the level beyond the bulkhead is reaching the danger point."

Riker paused and manipulated his tricorder. "But the core activity has increased only slightly. Why is the radiation—"

"I believe I understand, sir," Data broke in as he looked up from his own tricorder. "When the device that was about to detonate was transported out, some surrounding material was transported as well, including part of the thickness of the deck on which it stood. Because that deck was itself part of the core shielding, the leakage has increased. It is also possible that what remains of that layer of

20

shielding, because of the molecular stress associated with having a portion of itself sheered away by the transporter field, is deteriorating."

"I suggest you remove yourself from the area, Number One," Picard said in a tone indicating more than a simple suggestion, "now!"

"Yes, sir," Riker responded hurriedly, "but there's no cause yet to beam us back to the *Enterprise.*"

"Perhaps not—*if* you move quickly enough on your own."

"On our way, sir," Riker acknowledged, gesturing at the others.

With a sense of relief, Geordi turned his back on the glinting radiation. He knew it was not deadly, not yet, but its harshness grated on his nerves nonetheless.

"If our time aboard is to be limited, Commander," Data volunteered before they had covered more than a half dozen meters, "perhaps it would be more efficient to split up."

"My thought as well, Mr. Data," Riker responded after a split second's hesitation. "From what we've seen so far, we have roughly a kilometer of passageways here. You and Lieutenant LaForge take everything to the right of the passageway we're in. Lieutenant Yar and I will take the left."

After five minutes, however, it began to look as if every part of *every* passageway was as featureless as those they had seen during their first minute after beaming over. Even Geordi's Visor couldn't distinguish one panel from another, one wall from another, and the tricorders revealed identical but indeterminate activity behind each door. *Something*—dozens of somethings, perhaps hundreds—were operating at extremely low power levels, power levels so low that, even at this distance, the tricorders could not provide a reliable circuit analysis. There were intimations that subspace circuits were involved, hinting that the machines were simply large subspace radios, but there were other indications of transporter circuits, so closely intertwined with the subspace circuits that they seemed to be a single machine rather than, as they must be, two separate ones.

The only circuits the tricorders were able to analyze fully were those in the panels themselves—circuits that would respond to any attempt to breach a panel - by sending a massive surge of power through the machinery behind it, probably turning it into little more than a pile of slag.

Geordi was turning dispiritedly from the third seemingly identical panel when the deck beneath their feet shivered slightly. An instant later, a faint vibration could be felt. Abruptly, he turned toward the core. Despite the half dozen or more solid walls that lay between him and the core, he saw the antimatter radiation pulse higher, flowing through the walls as if they didn't exist.

"We're bringing you back!" Picard's stern voice erupted from the communicators. "Stand by!"

Then there was Carpelli's voice from transporter room. "Locking onto Yar and Riker, now."

Then silence, followed by Riker's voice as he and Yar stepped off the transporter platform in the *Enterprise:* "Where are La Forge and—"

"Getting them now, sir," Carpelli's voice said, and Geordi felt the tingle of the transporter beam as it locked onto him.

But suddenly, the tingle was gone.

There was only Carpelli's voice: "Sir, I've lost them! Something—"

And from the bridge, Worf's bass rumble: "Deflector shields around the derelict, sir, blocking the transporters!"

Chapter Three

"DEFLECTORS?" PICARD'S VOICE was a mixture of incredulity and anger. "Gawelski!" he snapped at the lantern-jawed young ensign who had taken La Forge's place at the conn. "Take us in to direct visual range, now!"

Gawelski's fingers responded almost as quickly as Geordi's would have, and the *Enterprise* leaped forward, covering the ten thousand kilometers under impulse power in seconds.

"Data! La Forge!" Picard said sharply. "Can you hear me?"

"Quite well, sir," Data's imperturbable tones came back. "We do not appear to be in any difficulty as yet. Something is causing the vessel to vibrate, however, at a frequency of twelve-point-four-eight cycles per second. Our tricorders also indicate that the antimatter core has increased its energy output dramatically."

"And its leakage," Geordi added. "It's not dangerous at this distance from the center—yet—but I would appreciate anything you can do to get us out of here, sir."

"We're doing all we can, Lieutenant," Picard assured him.

"Analyzing the deflector field, sir," Worf reported. "It appears to be designed primarily to block transporter operation. Its resistance to phaser fire would be minimal. I suggest a pinpoint phaser burst directed at the generators."

"Can you locate the generators, Lieutenant," Picard asked.

"Now that they've been activated, yes, sir." Worf tapped a control. "Feeding coordinates to tactical station now, sir."

Lieutenant Brindle, occupying the tactical station, looked questioningly at Picard.

"Don't fire quite yet, gentlemen," he said. "Mr. Data? Lieutenant La Forge? Our sensors indicate you are in no immediate danger from the radiation. Do you concur?"

"At the current level," Data responded, "I am in no danger at all. It will begin to have adverse effects on Geordi, however, in approximately twenty-seven hours."

"Very well," Picard said. "Lieutenant Brindle, lock phasers onto the coordinates Lieutenant Worf supplied. Hold fire, but be ready."

"Phasers locked on, sir, ready to fire."

A moment later, Riker and Yar emerged onto the bridge. Brindle stepped aside as Yar hurried to the tactical station and made a quick survey of the controls.

"What I want, gentlemen," Picard said, "is as much information as I can get. Specifically, I want some kind of assurance that if we *do* fire at the vessel's shield generators, we will not be treated to another surprise, something even nastier than those we have already been subjected to. And this includes you, Mr. Data, Lieutenant La Forge. Take advantage of your situation to learn what you can—but cautiously."

"Of course, sir," Data acknowledged. "We will endeavor to locate a control center. Our tricorders, I believe—"

"Radiation level increasing again!" Geordi broke in. "I can see it."

"Stand by to fire on shield generators, Lieutenant Yar," Picard snapped.

"Standing by, sir."

"How much of an increase in radiation level, Lieutenant Worf?"

"Approximately ten percent, sir," Worf responded. "It appears to be a result of increased energy output, not further deterioration in the radiation shielding."

"And where is this new energy going, Lieutenant? Do any weapons register yet?"

"No weapons, sir, but a new area has begun to function." Worf paused, studying the science station readouts. "It appears to be a hibernation unit, although that particular area is so heavily shielded against sensor probes, the readings cannot be considered reliable."

On the apparently awakening derelict, Data's luminous golden eyes widened as he looked up from his tricorder screen. "Captain," he said, "if I am not mistaken, we are less than thirty meters from the newly functioning area Lieutenant Worf has described. With your permission, we will investigate."

"Granted, Mr. Data. I don't need to tell you to be careful."

"No, sir. Thank you. Geordi—" Data broke off, looking again at his tricorder screen. "I believe an atmosphere is returning, sir."

"He's right, sir," Worf put in instantly. "Thirty percent oxygen, the rest inert gases. At the present rate, it could reach Earth normal in less than five minutes."

"Four-point-six-eight minutes," Data, still monitoring his tricorder, supplied helpfully.

"I'll bet it's all tied in with whatever's in the hibernation unit," Geordi said suddenly. "The ship's waking it up and getting the place ready for it. If we get a move on, we can get there before it's fully awake, which might be the safest time."

"Mr. Data, be—" Picard's voice began, but abruptly was cut off.

"Captain?" Data glanced at Geordi, then tapped his communicator insignia. "Captain?" he repeated, but there was still no response.

Geordi grabbed his elbow.

"Come on, Data," he said, "let's go. It looks like our communicators are being blocked now, too, and that's all the more reason to get there before that thing, whatever it is, wakes up."

Resisting the impulse to dive headlong down the gravityless corridor—what would happen if gravity suddenly returned, as the atmosphere was doing? —Geordi shuffled awkwardly in Data's wake. The android, following the readings on his tricorder, managed to look, if not graceful, at least efficient. Monitoring his own tricorder, Geordi saw that the air pressure continued to increase. The percentage of oxygen, however, began to drop, finally leveling off at twenty-four percent.

"The radiation level's still increasing," Geordi said as they rounded another corner in the passageway. "What's my time limit now, Data?"

"Approximately twelve hours at this level until adverse reactions begin, Geordi. But I'm sure the captain will have extracted us long before then."

"I hope so, but the way things have been going lately—"

He broke off as they came to a stop before a

massive door. It was twice the width of the other panels, the first thing they had seen that would justify the term "door," but it was just as featureless as all the others. Geordi shook his head. "Whoever these people are, they sure don't believe in room numbers."

"Would the assignment of numbers be beneficial?" asked Data, already running his tricorder scanner smoothly up and down the door.

Geordi laughed as he checked his own tricorder. "No, Data, I doubt that it would. But in case you hadn't noticed, the air pressure has leveled off, approximately seventy percent of Earth normal."

Without warning, the ceiling panels of the passageway pulsed into life, taking on a pale, yellowish glow, dim to human eyes but not to those of the android. A moment later, the door shuddered and slid sideways, vanishing into the featureless metal wall. Beyond the opening were a dozen waist-high platforms, topped with rectangular, vaguely coffinlike shapes.

"Looks like they were just waiting for us to knock, Data," Geordi said uneasily.

"Or for the air pressure to reach the necessary level," Data said, alternating his attention between the room itself and the readings from the tricorder. "Doubtless those are the hibernation devices Lieutenant Worf's instruments detected. However, there are still no life-form readings."

"Whatever's in them died?"

"Perhaps, but even then, at this range there should be enough residual organic material—"

As abruptly as the door from the passageway had slid sideways, the near side of the closest coffinlike structure slid downward, revealing a darkly cushioned compartment, more than large enough to contain a single human body.

But it contained nothing but a cluster of a half dozen dangling wires and tubes.

Data's eyes widened imperceptibly. "Curious," he said. "Even though the occupant is obviously no longer present, the machinery continued to attempt to perform its designed function."

Geordi shrugged, still feeling vaguely uneasy. "That's just the way machinery is," he said, but then, as he realized how his words could have been taken, added hastily, "Present company excepted, of course."

Data was motionless for an instant, as if processing the statements. "Ah, yes, I see. Your second remark was meant as an apology, in the event that I had chosen to take offense at the first."

Geordi smiled sheepishly. "But all it really did was call attention to it. Sorry."

What might have been an experimental attempt at a smile pushed at the corners of Data's pale lips. "No apology is necessary, Geordi. That is just the way humans are."

Abruptly, Geordi laughed, much of the uneasiness vanishing. "How right you are, Data. Are you *sure* you want to emulate us as much as you say? We tend to get our feet stuck in our mouths far too often for comfort."

Data underwent another instant of motionless thought, and then said: "I assume that is just another figure of human speech, since the possibility that there are those among you still violent enough to tear an offender's extremities from his body seems—"

"Just a figure of speech, Data, so far as I know. But before we get too far off the main track—another figure of speech—maybe we should check the rest of these." He gestured at the other boxes, presumably also hibernation chambers.

Data quickly consulted his tricorder. "No activity and no life readings," he announced. "And the activity in the first has ceased as well." He paused, turning toward a door in an otherwise featureless wall. "However, there is considerable electrical activity taking place—"

Like the door to the corridor, the smaller door shot abruptly upward, revealing a smaller room.

But this room, unlike everywhere else they had been in the vessel, was far from featureless.

"Bingo!" Geordi said, a grin almost as wide as his Visor lighting up his ebony features.

Occupying most of the upper half of the far wall was a viewscreen of some kind. Beneath it stretched a double bank of controls, discrete physical controls, each with its own indecipherable marking, not the programmable panels of the *Enterprise*.

And in the middle of the upper bank, an amber light was flashing urgently. As he watched, a map appeared on the viewscreen—a map, apparently, of the vessel they were on.

In the center of map, at a point Geordi assumed coincided with the antimatter core, a bright green circle appeared, flashing on and off in time with the amber light. A string of symbols, obviously a message of some kind, took shape immediately under the green circle.

"The radiation leak!" Geordi exclaimed, his mind racing as the events of the last few minutes suddenly fell into a pattern. *That's* what this is all about! We weakened the shielding when we beamed that bomb out! There must be a computer still keeping an eye on things here, and it noticed the increased radiation, so it decided to throw up a shield and keep people out. And now it's trying to wake up the caretaker so he can repair it. Only the caretaker's been gone ten thousand years, and nobody ever got around to telling the computer." He shook his head. "Data, any chance you can figure out how to respond to this thing?"

"It is highly doubtful, Geordi. The possible responses, while not infinite, are impossible for even me to calculate quickly. If there were some way of linking it to the *Enterprise* computer . . ." He shook his head.

Geordi sighed. "I was afraid you were going to say that. If there were just some way of decoding all this, *maybe* we could talk it into lowering the shields before we're fried."

Experimentally, he tapped his communicator, but there was no response. "Still cut off. And I assume the shield that blocked our communicators also blocked the *Enterprise* phasers. Otherwise, the captain would have blasted the generators and had us out of here by now. I heard Worf feeding their coordinates into the tactical station before we were cut off, and Tasha was ready to go."

"I had made the same deductions myself, Geordi. However, since we are inside the shields, perhaps we could disable the generators ourselves."

Geordi nodded. "Just what I was about to say." He scanned his tricorder screen briefly, then looked up. "This way, I think," he said, gesturing toward the center of the vessel as he started to shuffle from the room.

Before he reached the door, Data's hand fell on his shoulder, the android's grip gentle but unbreakable.

"I will go, Geordi," he said. "As you just now indicated, the generators are apparently quite near the antimatter core, where the radiation is strongest." He darted a look at his own tricorder. "And its rate of increase accelerated once again approximately forty-five seconds ago. While you will be safe for several minutes at this distance, the radiation levels near the core are becoming too high for you to withstand for more than the briefest period without a heavy-duty radiation suit. I, on the other hand, can not only move more rapidly than you but am capable of enduring much greater levels of radiation without substantial harm."

"Data—"

"It would not be logical for you to accompany me, Geordi," Data said, maintaining his grip on the young lieutenant's shoulder.

"I know, Data, but—"

"But it is human to wish to do so, even when you know it to be counterproductive?"

Geordi was silent a moment, then nodded. "Something in our screwed-up collective psyche, I guess." He pulled in a breath. "Get going, before it gets too hot even for an android."

"I will try," Data said, taking his restraining hand from Geordi's shoulder.

As he turned to leave, a second light, this one a brilliant yellow, began flashing on the panel.

On the viewscreen, the green circle blossomed out momentarily and then vanished. In rapid succession, all in a matter of a second or less, a hundred other circles, all brilliant yellow like the light, flickered into being and vanished.

All but one.

Then the map itself vanished, and, for an instant, an image of the *Enterprise* appeared, but then it, too, was gone.

Dozens more lights, scattered everywhere on the panel, began to flash intermittently, randomly as far as Geordi could tell.

Suddenly, the room was bathed in light, and both men felt the paralyzing grip of a transporter.

"Mr. Data! Lieutenant La Forge!" Picard slapped uselessly at his communicator, unable to reestablish the link to the derelict.

"Full shielding now in place around the vessel, sir," Worf rumbled. "No contact possible."

"Can our phasers penetrate?"

"Given enough time or power, yes, sir, but the vessel would almost certainly boost its power to strengthen the shields. The resultant increased radiation levels—"

"We may not have any choice!" Picard snapped. "Lieutenant Yar, keep phasers locked onto the coordinates of the shield generators. Dr. Crusher, report to the transporter room immediately with everything you'll need to treat cases of severe antimatter radiation."

"Right away, Captain," Beverly Crusher's voice came from her office in sickbay.

"Number One? Lieutenant Yar? You were there. Is there anything, any detail at all, you can remember that could help?"

"Sorry, sir," Riker said, shaking his head. "There were just passageways and doors, no controls, no markings of any kind, nothing on the tricorders that we hadn't already gotten from the *Enterprise* sensors."

"Nothing, sir," Yar concurred. "However, if it comes to using the phasers, I would make two suggestions. First, get as close as possible before firing, right on the fringe of the shields themselves. And second, target all phasers on the generator coordinates, set them for maximum power and minimum dispersion, and fire them all simultaneously."

"Make it so, Lieutenant," Picard said, nodding in grim agreement. "If it works, if you can punch through the shield fast enough, the resultant antimatter radiation increase will be extremely rapid but also very brief. Ensign Carpelli, be prepared to lock onto Mr. Data and Lieutenant La Forge the instant the shields go down. Get them out, fast!"

"Ready, sir!"

"Lieutenant Worf, the radius of the shields."

"One-point-three kilometers, sir."

"Ensign Gawelski, take us in to one-point-four kilometers."

"Aye-aye, sir."

"Lieutenant Yar, double-check those coordinates."

"Yes, sir. The field is spherical, and the coordinates coincide precisely with the center of that field, approximately ten meters from the antimatter itself."

Picard grimaced. "The phasers' dispersion—"

"At this distance, we can keep it to less than a meter, even with all phasers firing simultaneously."

"Dr. Crusher, are you in place yet?"

"Not quite, sir, the decon units are bulky, and I'll want them set up, ready to receive the men the instant they appear. For Geordi, especially, seconds could count."

"I am quite aware of that, Doctor!" Picard snapped.

"I'm sure you are, Captain, but also be aware that it is not the time between now and the assault that will determine the radiation damage he suffers. Until your phasers begin their work, the radiation level, while high, will undoubtedly be tolerable as long as Geordi and Data keep their distance from the core. It will be the radiation during those seconds between the phaser firings and the moment they are transported out of there that is critical!"

Picard was silent a moment, and then he nodded, though there was no vision hookup to sickbay. "You're right, of course, Doctor," he said. "Notify me when you're ready."

Tensely he paced, alternately eyeing the image in the viewer and glancing at Worf's implacable features and Yar's equally tense ones. Waiting had always been hard, but now, when he felt responsible for what had happened, for letting the four return to the derelict, for not reacting quickly enough at the first signs of danger, it was especially difficult. But he had no choice. If he had taken a second longer with those earlier decisions, if he hadn't allowed his own curiosity, his own impatience to cloud his judgment—

"Ready, Captain," Beverly Crusher's voice informed him.

The tension in his body tightened a notch and then released as Lieutenant Yar nodded her preparedness.

"Ensign Carpelli," he said.

"Ready, sir," Carpelli's voice came back from the transporter room.

"Lieutenant Yar, when you're ready."

Another moment of silence, and then: "Firing—now, sir."

For less than a second, the space around the derelict vessel flared with blinding light.

Then it was gone, and the derelict, defenseless, filled the viewer.

"Shields down, sir," Yar reported sharply, the brief words edged with triumphant satisfaction.

"Radiation still intensifying, sir," Worf rumbled. "We will need to put up our own shields if it continues."

"Do you have them, Mr. Carpelli?" Picard snapped.

But there was only silence from the transporter room.

"Carpelli! Do you hear me?"

Another moment of silence, and then: "They're not there, sir! They're gone!"

Chapter Four

RELIEF FLOODED THROUGH Geordi La Forge as he felt the transporter field grip him. A moment later, his Visored senses were overwhelmed by the familiar envelope of kaleidoscopic dematerialization energies closing in on him, changing and shifting so rapidly that he could focus on nothing.

But even as the energies swirled around him, he realized there was something different, the energies somehow duller, less intense. But they were never completely the same, he told himself. Like snowflakes, no two trips through the transporters were ever identical. The important thing was, Captain Picard had come through—as Geordi had known he would. When the field released him, he and Data would be safely back in the *Enterprise* transporter room.

For an instant, there was the nothingness of the transport itself, then another blur of chaotic energies, virtually a negative image of what he had experienced a moment before.

But then, before the flaring energies faded, before the world could re-form around him, it started all over again.

And this time the differences were dramatic, frightening.

If the energies had been duller, less intense, the first time, now their intensity was almost blinding.

And they extended into frequencies and wavelengths Geordi had never before experienced during transport, perhaps never before under any circumstances. Whirling and flaring, beating at his senses, they twisted into seemingly impossible, mind-warping patterns, patterns that, as they persisted and intensified even more each instant, made him long to rip the Visor from his face.

But, gripped by the transporter field, he could not move.

Suddenly, eerily terrified, he wondered: Had the antimatter radiation interfered with the operation of the transporter? Had the radiation become so intense at the moment of transport that it had somehow become intermixed with the energies into which his own body had been converted? In trying to reassemble him on the platform in the *Enterprise,* had the transporter machinery not been able to separate the two forms of energy? Was the antimatter radiation now somehow being incorporated into his own body? Was that the source of these mind-shattering patterns?

But even as the thought took hold in his mind, he

felt the sudden release, the nothingness that came with the moment of transport, and then the maelstrom of energies was reversing itself, withdrawing from him like a receding flood.

And, finally, the world re-formed around him.

Limply, he began to absorb the information that flowed into his Visored senses.

The first thing he noticed was that, as expected, the harsh, brittle glare of the antimatter radiation, so intense in his last moments on the derelict, was gone.

And the palely glowing, distinctively nonhuman form that was Data was still before him, where it had been when the transporter field had gripped them both.

But beyond the android—

Fleetingly, impossibly, his conscious mind couldn't make sense of the chaos of wavelengths that washed over him. Trying to match the shapes and colors to those of the *Enterprise* transporter room only distorted his perceptions, momentarily subjecting him to a dizzying disorientation, which only added to the physical weakness the unprecedented trip through the transporter had already induced in him.

Then, suddenly, he felt Data's powerful hands on his shoulders, steadying him, and the android's face was peering worriedly into his.

"Geordi, are you all right?"

His own hands reached up and gripped the

solidity of Data's arms, drawing strength and stability from them.

For a moment, he focused only on Data's form,
letting the rest of his surroundings settle into
whatever pattern they wanted.

And as they did, as the pattern cleared and
steadied, he realized with a disbelieving start that it
was an unfamiliar pattern.

Only then did the glaringly obvious fact that he
was still weightless penetrate his mind. And it was
that, even more than the seemingly unfamiliar
surroundings, which brought home the fact that,
wherever they were, they weren't on the *Enterprise.*

Nor were they anywhere on the derelict, he
realized abruptly. Despite the continuing lack of
gravity, they couldn't be. There wasn't even a trace
of the harsh glare of the antimatter radiation that
had virtually swamped his senses during those last
moments.

But where else *could* they be?

Releasing his grip on Data's arms, he made a
complete turn, letting his Visored senses take in his
complete surroundings.

Wherever they were, he and Data were sharing a
single, large transporter circle in the middle of a
very plain room. The upper portion of one wall was
a viewscreen, in front of which stood a chair, hard
and utilitarian with flat, sharp-edged armrests, but
there were no controls, anywhere.

But suspended from an invisible support immediately below the screen was what could only be described as the skeleton of a helmet—a small, silvery sphere atop five incurving strips, like fingers that would grasp whatever head they were fitted to.

A meter out from another wall was a single hibernation chamber, identical to those in the derelict, except that this one had no external controls. It was open and empty.

Built out from the wall opposite the viewscreen was the only thing that didn't fit into the sterile plainness of the room: a primitive airlock, looking very much like an artifact from Earth of the late twentieth or early twenty-first century at the latest. The material, Geordi's spectrographic vision told him, was a simple alloy of steel, nothing like the complex, immensely more durable alloys of which every other surface, even the chair, was made. A good three meters high and slightly more than that wide, the airlock took up over half the wall and extended a good two meters out into the room.

"Geordi?" It was Data, concern plain in his normally flat voice. "I can detect nothing physically wrong with you, but your behavior—"

"I'm all right, Data," he said abruptly, turning back to the android. And then, with a nervous laugh: "It just took me a minute to realize that we aren't in Kansas anymore."

"Kansas?" Data looked at him with quizzical concern. "I have never been in Kansas, Geordi. Are you quite certain your faculties have not been adversely affected by our experiences?"

"I'm fine, Data, all things considered," he said with an uneasy smile. "I was just making a bad joke. And an obscure one. *The Wizard of Oz.* Just be glad I didn't call you Toto."

"Toto? But why should you—" Data stopped in midsentence, and Geordi could almost see the connections being made somewhere behind the golden eyes. "Ah, yes, I comprehend the references now, including what I assume you intended to be a pun on my name—but I must admit that the thought process by which you arrived at them in the first place eludes me."

"I'm afraid they weren't the results of anything as logical as a thought process, Data. When I'm scared, things like that just sort of—come out. It's hard to explain."

"I suspected as much," Data said, sounding almost wistful. "I fear that whatever the process is, it remains one of the mysteries of being human that I have yet to fully understand."

"If I ever figure it out myself, I'll let you know," Geordi said, straightening and scanning the room once again. "In the meantime, we have a few mysteries more important than human nature to work on. Like where are we, and how do we get back?"

Abruptly, he tapped his communicator insignia. *"Enterprise,* this is Lieutenant La Forge. Come in."

45

But there was no response, not to his first attempt nor to his tenth, and Data had no better luck. Even after determining that the air was safe to breathe and turning off their field-effect suits to eliminate the slight bit of interference the fields might generate, there was not even a hint of a response. Wherever they were, they decided, they must be enclosed in another shield that blocked the communicators, just as the shields on the derelict had blocked them those last few minutes.

Or they were out of range, Geordi thought, but he dismissed the idea almost immediately. Considering the fact that they had been put here by a transporter—a decidedly peculiar and energetic one, but a transporter nonetheless—it was virtually impossible to be out of communicator range. Even allowing for differences in alien technology, the range of a transporter couldn't be *that* great.

Therefore, they were enclosed by a shield. Get rid of the shield, and they could contact the *Enterprise*.

But first they had to find what was generating the shield.

"Gone?" Picard scowled, his stomach twitching uncomfortably at Carpelli's words. "They can't be gone!"

"But they are, Captain!" Carpelli reiterated. "I don't understand it any better than you, but they are gone. At least they are now. I *think* they were there when the derelict's shields first went down, but—"

"Carpelli! What the blazes are you trying to say?"

"As ordered," Carpelli said, his voice stiffening defensively, "I had the transporters set to automatically lock onto their communicators the instant the shields fell, no matter where they were on the derelict. And they did. They locked on. Data and La Forge had apparently moved nearly thirty meters from where they had been when the shields cut us off, but there was no trouble locking onto them. But before we could energize—it couldn't have been more than a second—before we could energize, they just vanished! Their communicators no longer registered. Nothing registered."

"Their communicators must have malfunctioned because of the radiation!" Picard snapped. "You could have still picked them up at the coordinates you had already locked onto!"

"I tried, sir! I energized immediately, but there was no one there to pick up! No one and nothing!"

"Sir," Lieutenant Worf broke in from the science stations, "the readings I've just analyzed indicate that another transporter, this one apparently located on the vessel itself, was already going into operation at the moment the vessel's shields failed."

Picard whirled toward the Klingon. "Is it still in operation?"

"Negative, sir."

"Can you pinpoint its location?"

"No, sir, but it must have been one of the devices we noted previously, one of those that were in some kind of standby state. Apparently at least one went from standby to full operational status sometime while the shields were up. The moment they went down, it must have automatically energized."

"And sent them to what destination? What do the sensors show within transporter range?"

"Nothing, sir. Except for the alien vessel and the *Enterprise* itself, there are no material objects larger than interstellar dust grains within sensor range."

"Then where—? Scan for life forms, anywhere within sensor range."

"Already done, sir. There are none except those on board the *Enterprise.*"

Abruptly, Picard tapped his communicator insignia. "Commander Data! Lieutenant La Forge! Respond!"

But there was no response.

"Computer!" Picard snapped. "Are Commander Data and Lieutenant La Forge on board?" Could the alien transporter have beamed them aboard, to some part of the ship other than one of the transporter rooms?

"No, Captain," the computer's flat tones came back a moment later, "neither one is aboard."

Picard cut off a curse, his mind racing. Where

could they be? He had been prepared, once they were safely on board the *Enterprise,* to pull back and leave the derelict to its own devices, to self-destruct or not.

But now he didn't dare.

Wherever the two had been taken, whether it had been done by transporter as Worf's instruments suggested or by some other, unknown method, it had been done by something on that blasted vessel, which was looking more like a trap than a derelict with every passing moment.

And without that vessel, without its still-functioning equipment to examine, there was simply no way to find out where—or how—they had been taken.

No way to get them back.

"Lieutenant Worf, what is the status of the derelict's antimatter core? Is it in immediate danger of overloading?"

"No immediate danger, sir, but it is unstable and virtually unshielded. Our phaser burst appears to have taken out all but a fraction of the inner layer of shielding and may have damaged the central power control circuits."

"Engineering!" Picard snapped. "I assume you've been monitoring the situation. I need to know if the vessel's power source can be—" He broke off, shaking his head sharply. "I need to know how *soon* the vessel's power source *can* be stabilized!"

"Yes, sir," Chief Engineer Argyle's gruff voice replied an instant later, "we've been keeping on top of things the best we can from this distance, but there's no way to determine exactly what damage has been done without looking a lot closer. And even then, there's the problem of alien technology—"

"Mr. Argyle, I do not want to know what you *can't* do! I want to know what you *can* do!"

"Sorry, Captain, but no one can make promises —honest ones, at least—under these conditions. All I can promise is that we'll do our best. And that *nothing* can be done about actually repairing the alien power controls, no matter what we find out, until the core shielding has been put to rights. From the readings we're getting now, even our heaviest radiation suits wouldn't get anyone close enough to the core to tighten a stove bolt, let alone do complex repairs. What we have to do first is send in one of our own remote repair units, along with some decent shielding to replace that cheesecloth you people have been punching holes in."

"Very well, Commander Argyle," Picard said, realizing reluctantly that the chief engineer was right. "Make it so."

"At once, Captain. Assistant Chief Engineer Singh is already on his way to storage to fetch one of the remote units."

It was less than five minutes before the first remote unit was beamed into the midst of the deadly radiation, but to Picard and many of the others, tensely monitoring the still-erratic core activity and the level of surrounding radiation, it seemed like hours.

Geordi and Data searched futilely for evidence of the shield that Geordi was certain was blocking their communicators, but there was nothing, not the faintest trace of a confirming reading on their tricorders, no matter how they manipulated the controls.

Finally, more puzzled than discouraged, they turned their attention to the room they found themselves in.

And their first discovery only increased their puzzlement. The airlock didn't go anywhere. It opened easily enough, but a quick scan with the tricorders revealed that the door at its rear wasn't functional. Its controls were frozen solid, and beyond it, again according to the tricorders, was only the exceedingly solid wall of the room itself.

And there were no other doors, no openings of any kind, anywhere in the room. In that respect, it was just like the original derelict. The only way in or out was by transporter.

Abruptly, then, they turned to the problem of the transporter itself and the total lack of controls. Unless it was totally automated—or they were in what amounted to a prison cell—there had to be controls. There was, of course, the helmet, which

51

implied that whatever controls existed were operated mentally. Neither of them was yet prepared to simply snap the helmet on his head, even though nothing the tricorders could determine about it indicated any immediate danger.

Instead, they turned their tricorders to the transporter, assuming—hoping—that it contained circuitry not totally different from that used in Federation transporters. With a great deal of luck, the transporter would be in a standby mode of some kind rather than shut off entirely. If so, the minuscule amounts of power still flowing through the circuits would generate patterns that their tricorders could pick up and recognize. With even more luck, they might be able to locate—and then influence—the circuits that allowed the transporter to switch from receive to transmit.

But, although there was enough power flowing through the circuits for them to register faintly on the tricorders, Geordi and Data quickly discovered that the circuits they had hoped to find didn't exist. Or if they did, they were either dead or totally powered down, with no standby power flowing through them.

This transporter couldn't send. It could only receive.

"It's crazy, Data!" Geordi half shouted in an uncharacteristic explosion of frustration after a final recheck of a reading he'd already taken a half dozen times. "Just plain crazy! What good is a transporter that can't transmit?"

"It works quite well as a receiver," Data said reasonably, "which is all it was apparently designed and built to do. That in itself is remarkable, considering its age."

"One thing I *don't* need," Geordi snapped, "is a testimonial to the superb craftsmanship of whoever built this—this rattrap! We'd be a lot better off if it were a little *less* remarkable!"

Data looked at Geordi for a moment, his eyes widening in mild puzzlement at the outburst. "I was merely making an observation, Geordi. Is there something—" He stopped, as if a thought had just occurred to him.

"Ah, I see," he went on after a moment. "If I am not mistaken, there is a term in human psychology that applies to your present state of mind: hostility transfer. Your annoyance is really with the predicament we are in, perhaps with the devices that sent us here, or even with yourself for having allowed us to be captured, but you have transferred that annoyance to an object that—"

"Data!"

"Yes, Geordi?"

"Another thing I don't need is a lecture on human psychology!" he said testily. But then, noticing Data's eyes looking directly into his, he pulled in a breath and lowered his head sheepishly.

"Especially when it's probably right on the money. Sorry if I snapped at you."

"That is quite all right, Geordi. I am always interested in observing the peculiarities of the human mind firsthand."

Geordi laughed. "And pretty peculiar it is at times, too," he said, but then, abruptly, he sobered.

And turned toward the viewscreen and helmet. "I guess we can't put it off any longer."

Pulling in his breath again, he reached for the silver-fingered helmet. After all, he told himself, it's the only logical thing to do at this point. Whatever the helmet did, it couldn't make their situation much worse than it already was.

As his hand closed on one of the fingerlike prongs of the helmet, whatever held the helmet to the wall released it. Carefully, he examined it, first with his spectroscopic and microscopic vision, then with the tricorder, but his examinations revealed only that *something* was going on inside the silvery sphere and the five flexible prongs. Small amounts of energy were flowing in complex patterns through every millimeter, but what those patterns meant, neither he nor Data could even guess.

Finally, gingerly, Geordi lowered it onto his head, distorting two of the prongs to avoid their touching his Visor. Data, keeping a continuous watch on both Geordi and a tricorder, stood close by, obviously poised to react.

But nothing happened other than a steady, almost imperceptibly faint glow from the silvery sphere atop the helmet.

For several seconds, Geordi stood motionless except for a slight zero-gravity swaying.

He felt nothing.

Until—

Deep in his mind, something tickled.

His hands twitched toward the helmet, but he resisted the momentary impulse to snatch it off.

The tickling increased, spreading outward in all directions, turning to a faint, barely detectable tingle as it spread to his body. To his Visored senses, there appeared a filmy, all-pervading glow that reminded him of the effects of a sensor probe, except that this was somehow more delicate.

And then it was gone.

And the viewscreen came alive, filled for those first moments only with a swirling rainbow that occupied the entire human visible spectrum and a few extra angstroms on either side.

A test pattern? Geordi wondered, but before he could determine any intelligible pattern, it vanished.

And was replaced by a planet that filled almost the entire screen. For an instant, just an instant, he forgot everything in a spurt of exultation.

Earth! Somehow, they were orbiting Earth!

Then the instant passed, and he saw that, though the swirls of clouds, the blue of the oceans, even the solid masses of white at the poles, could have been Earth's, the land masses could not be.

A class-M planet, obviously, but equally obviously not Earth.

Abruptly, the momentary euphoria faded, replaced by a new wave of apprehension. Wherever they were, they had been taken against their will, in all probability by the inhabitants of this planet, who were even now probably on their way to capture or kill—

But the planet could not be real, he told himself sharply. The computer—or whatever it was that putting on the helmet had awakened—had picked an image of Earth from his mind, and then had matched it with the closest thing in its memory banks. It couldn't be real any more than they could be out of communicator range with the *Enterprise.*

The derelict, after all, had been nearly a parsec from the nearest star, he told himself once again.

They had been brought here from the derelict by a transporter. The energy fields that had swirled around him during the process, no matter how unusual or how energetic, had proven that.

And the range of a transporter, even an alien transporter, had to be measured in tens of thousands of kilometers, not tens of trillions

And yet—

Experimentally, he conjured up a vision of Saturn and its rings, expecting a similar but not identical image to form on the screen.

56

But his efforts produced no change.

Turning from the viewscreen, he passed his Visored vision over every object in the room.

"Data," he asked, "does your tricorder show anything new happening since I put this thing on?"

"Many circuits within the wall behind and beneath the screen are now active, but their functions cannot be determined."

Geordi centered his attention on the transporter circle. "But nothing's happening with the transporter? No new circuits becoming active there?"

"None, Geordi."

Geordi shook his head in renewed frustration. Obviously, putting the helmet on had done *something*. But not what he wanted done, which was probably impossible anyway. If transmitting circuits didn't exist, he certainly couldn't create them.

But if they did exist . . .

Frowning, he visualized the circuits as best he could, imagining power flowing into them.

But still no evidence of such circuits appeared on either his own tricorder or Data's.

Abruptly, he snatched the helmet off and held it out to Data. "Here, you take a crack at it," he said, explaining briefly what he had been trying to do. "Somewhere in your memory banks there must be a more accurate representation of a transporter circuit than I've got in mine," he finished, "so maybe you'll have better luck."

"I will of course try, Geordi, if you think it will help."

Geordi shook his head. "I haven't the faintest idea if it will or not, Data, but at the moment I can't think of anything else to try. If you can, be my guest."

"I see," Data said, nodding as he took the helmet. "I believe what you are suggesting is called a 'shot in the dark,' is it not?"

Geordi smiled faintly as Data lowered the helmet onto his head. "You could call it that. But whatever—"

Abruptly, Geordi fell silent, his attention riveted on the helmet. As the first of the prongs touched Data's forehead, the silvery sphere atop the helmet began to glow, not the almost undetectable glow it had given off when Geordi had put it on, but a respectable shimmering.

"Data! Take it off! Something's happening!"

"It is all right, Geordi," Data replied calmly as he lowered his hands from the helmet. "I am aware of the brightness of the light. But I feel no ill effects as yet. In fact, I feel nothing except the physical pressure of the device."

But as he spoke, the glow brightened even more and began to pulse, picking up speed as it went.

"It didn't act that way when I was wearing it," Geordi said, still uneasy.

"Perhaps it is because I, too, am a machine and am therefore more compatible with the device."

"Maybe, and maybe not. When I had it on, I felt something like a tickle, down inside my mind somewhere, and then a sort of tingle, spreading all through my body. Are you sure you aren't feeling *anything?*"

"Not yet, Geordi." Data paused and turned his eyes upward as the pulsing grew still stronger and more rapid. "However, if your human intuition is causing you to be alarmed, perhaps I should—"

Suddenly, Data froze, as if turned to stone, and new and powerful readings began flashing across the tiny screen of Geordi's tricorder.

Chapter Five

W<small>ITHIN AN HOUR</small> the first of the new shields around the antimatter core of the derelict were in place, bringing the radiation leakage down to a tolerable level in the outer reaches of the vessel. During that same hour, the power control circuits that Chief Argyle had feared damaged by the phaser fire appeared to recover. Either they had not been damaged and the power fluctuations had been due to "normal" demands, or the derelict included a sophisticated and very fast-acting self-repair mechanism.

But either way, it was only another five minutes before Riker, Yar, and Worf beamed over to the coordinates Ensign Carpelli had recorded during the brief moment the transporters had locked onto the communicators of the two vanished men.

"Twelve hibernation facilities, Captain," Riker reported moments later, "none active. One is open and empty. The others are also empty."

"Can you see inside them all, Number One?"

"No, sir, but the tricorders—"

"Find a way to see inside, Number One. This whole affair is impossible, so one more impossibility—Data and La Forge being inside one of those devices despite their not registering on your tricorders—is not beyond belief."

"No, sir. But there's virtually an entire wall of controls here. Whether any are connected to the hibernation facilities, I don't know. And before we start pushing buttons, I would strongly recommend that Chief Argyle and a team of alien technology specialists beam over and do as thorough an analysis as possible. Considering what's already happened, Captain, it's virtually a sure bet that this place has a lot more surprises waiting."

Riker could hear Picard's not-quite-suppressed sigh of frustration, but he knew the captain would not let his impatience overrule his common sense.

"Data!" Geordi half screamed as he lunged toward the android, grasping for the helmet.

But he was too late. Before his hands could grasp the helmet, Data's body twitched violently. His boots, still encased in the magnetic field of the partially reactivated field-effect suit, jerked free of the floor and sent him spinning helplessly through the air. His hands jerked spastically toward the helmet but they could not reach it. His golden eyes, wide with a sudden pleading, touched Geordi for an instant before clicking shut like a pair of camera shutters, and his entire body went limp, as if every muscle had simultaneously turned to water.

Data's distinctive aura vanished.

Desperately, Geordi leaped, sending himself sprawling through the air, and somehow he was able to grasp one of Data's arms. In the next instant, he grasped the helmet and jerked it savagely from Data's head. Hurling it aside, he gripped Data's other arm, and the two of them spun together, Geordi's legs flailing, until they thudded against the ceiling and Geordi was able to anchor his boots to the metal. Carefully, he turned Data's body in his arms until the android's boots were also anchored to the metal.

"Data!" Helplessly, he gripped the android's shoulders, as if he could force life back into him. "Data! Wake up!"

For seconds, the android remained rag-doll limp, not even breathing, and Geordi's own heart was racing uncontrollably.

But then, finally, Geordi could feel the muscles in the android's arms slowly begin to regain their tone, as if the nerve connections between them and his brain were slowly being restored. Data's distinctive aura, faint at first, reappeared, and grew stronger.

Abruptly, the golden eyes snapped open. Then they blinked once, almost as if Data were resetting himself, like a circuit breaker.

"Data!" Geordi almost shouted, resisting twin

impulses to shake the android's shoulders to speed up the waking process and to throw his arms around him in a massive hug. "You scared me half to death! What happened?"

For a long moment, Data was silent, as if running an internal self-check, which, Geordi realized, was probably exactly what the android *was* doing.

Finally, in tones reflecting only the normal, matter-of-fact curiosity with which he invariably reacted to any new experience or observation, Data said, "I do not know, Geordi. I have never felt anything like it before. However, I am almost certain that if you had not removed the helmet when you did, I would have been—" He paused, as if searching for a word. Then, his eyes widening ever so slightly again, he concluded: "I would have been permanently deactivated."

"But you're all right now?"

"My self-check revealed no failures, but it is impossible for me to be positive. I would require a complete checkup by qualified technical—"

Abruptly, Data fell silent, and for an instant Geordi feared the android had had a relapse.

But then he heard something, an extremely muffled clanking, and he realized that Data's silence only indicated that he had heard it first.

And it was coming from the vicinity of the empty airlock.

Even as Geordi turned, Data was already examining his tricorder readings.

"Three humanoid life forms," the android said a moment later, "approximately twenty meters—that way." He pointed directly at the dummy airlock.

Abruptly, Geordi brought up his own tricorder, suddenly wondering why, in all the time since they had been dumped here, he had not thought to check for life-form readings. Just because there hadn't been any in the derelict didn't mean that—

The tricorder readings jolted his thoughts to a momentary stop.

Data had been right, but he had left something out.

There were indeed three humanoid life forms roughly twenty meters away, motionless, but several kilometers beyond the three, scattered throughout a volume of nearly a cubic kilometer—

"Data! There are hundreds out there! Hundreds of humanoid life forms!"

"Yes, Geordi, but only three are nearby and approaching."

Which was right—and logical—of course. Blotting out the hundreds of distant life forms and concentrating on the three nearby, Geordi saw that their motionlessness had only been temporary. Once again they were approaching. They would be knocking on the door—or the wall, since there was still no evidence that a door existed—any second.

But then they stopped, and the muffled sounds from before repeated themselves.

"Geordi," Data said, still watching his tricorder readings, "I suspect there is a similar airlock on the far side of the wall, and that the life forms have just entered it and are closing the outer door. The sounds being made, though severely attenuated by the apparent sound-blocking properties of the wall, seem quite similar to those made when we opened and closed this inner lock."

The sounds were too faint for Geordi to tell one way or the other, but he automatically assumed that Data was right. After all, having an airlock on the outside of a solid wall made just as much sense as having one on the inside. Made things symmetrical, if nothing else.

Shaking his head, Geordi alternated his attention between the airlock and the tricorder readings, waiting.

And wondering.

Were they a welcoming committee?

Or the equivalent of a police squad coming to see who had set off the burglar alarm?

Or, even worse, trappers, come to see who they had snared *this* time?

Reluctantly, Geordi took his phaser from his belt and set it to stun.

"Data," he said in a whisper, "whoever or whatever these people are, they could be friendly, or deadly, or anywhere in between, so it might be a good idea if one of us was out of sight when and if they make their entrance. And since your reaction

65

times are about ten times better than mine, you're the logical candidate."

Data looked blank for a moment, then nodded. "I see. You wish me to 'cover you.'"

"Something like that, yes."

Setting his own phaser to stun, Data unhesitatingly walked down the nearest wall and lowered himself behind the hibernation pedestal. Geordi followed Data down the wall but took up a position about two meters directly in front of the airlock.

And they waited.

Beyond the wall, the three life forms arranged themselves in an orderly, side-by-side line and—

Then, from the floor beneath the airlock, Geordi's Visored vision caught the stray radiation of a transporter circuit.

Of course, he thought. How else were they going to get in? But why the dummy airlocks?

For at least a minute, there was only silence from the three now inside the inner airlock.

Finally, according to the tricorder, one took up a position directly in front of the airlock door while the other two moved aside, one to the left, one to the right. When they stopped, each of the two was pressed into the corners of the airlock. When it opened, they would be hidden from sight. Only the one directly in front of the door would be visible.

Geordi's fingers tensed on his phaser, but still he kept it pointed, unthreateningly, toward the floor. Whoever was out there, they seemed to be acting at least as cautiously as he and Data, and the less threatening the situation looked to them when they opened the door, the less likely they would be to panic and start shooting.

He hoped.

The locking mechanism on the door began to turn, slowly and noisily.

When the turning was completed, another half minute passed in total silence.

Finally, on grating hinges, the door swung slowly to the side.

The being who stood facing Geordi, his boots obviously magnetically attached to the airlock floor, was not wearing a spacesuit of any kind. He looked at least as human as either Geordi or Data. His dark hair was cropped militarily close, and his slim frame was resplendent in a light blue, single-piece uniform with a stylized human face on the chest. What looked like an old-fashioned projectile weapon, against which a field-effect suit would provide little protection, hung from a belt that cinched the uniform in at the waist.

And, as Geordi had expected, the man looked very nervous.

For a long moment there was only silence. Data, waiting and listening, crouched silently and motionlessly behind the hibernation pedestal. The alien's eyes, already wide, widened further as he took in Geordi's appearance, but he, too, remained motionless, making no motion toward his weapon.

Finally, apparently satisfied that Geordi was not about to attack, the alien gestured nervously to each side, and the other two stepped hesitantly into view. Their uniforms were a darker shade of blue, and a similar projectile weapon hung from the belt of each. Their eyes, like those of the first alien, widened as they fell on Geordi and his Visor, but they remained still and silent.

Slowly, making no sudden moves, Geordi replaced the phaser on his belt and motioned for Data to step into view.

Their hands twitched in the direction of their weapons as Data appeared, but the motions were not completed.

"Who are you?" Geordi asked softly, hoping that anything he said would get the others to talking so the Universal Translators would have something to work with.

It took only a moment for him to realize that he had succeeded beyond his wildest dreams. Almost the instant the words were out of his mouth, the center alien began speaking, rapidly but stiffly, occasionally faltering and repeating himself, as if he were a schoolboy suffering from terminal stage fright as he tried to recite a poorly memorized speech.

Within less than two minutes, when the Universal Translators kicked in and began emitting random words and phrases, the speaker became even more rattled, his eyes darting fearfully toward the tiny cylindrical devices. As the phrases became more coherent, Geordi realized that the alien was indeed making a speech.

A welcoming speech.

"We most devoutly hope," the alien was saying haltingly as the Translators began producing complete sentences, "that you will approve of the uses to which we have put the marvelous Gifts that you chose to bestow upon us."

"What gifts do you—" Data began innocently when the alien stumbled to a halt, his eyes now virtually glued to the Translators, but Geordi cut the android off smoothly.

"I'm sure we will," he said, gesturing discreetly to Data and raising his voice to drown out the still slightly delayed translation of the android's aborted question. When, a moment later, the translation of Geordi's words emerged, the center alien twitched, almost as if slapped, his eyes darting between his two companions.

"It's just a translation device," Geordi went on, "so we can understand each other."

For a moment, the three only stared, but then the one on the left, shorter and stockier and even more nervous than the others, blurted out, "Are you the Builders?"

Before Geordi or Data had to come up with an answer, however, the apparent leader of the three gestured sharply at the one who had spoken, then pulled himself up straighter and looked directly into the shimmering silver of Geordi's Visor.

"Come," he said stiffly, perhaps fearfully. "We would be deeply honored if you would allow us to conduct you into the presence of our leader. His lifelong desire has been to be granted the opportunity, before his death, to meet the ones who made it possible for him to keep our world from destruction."

"And we would be most pleased to meet with the one who accomplished such a feat," Geordi improvised, trying to imagine what Captain Picard would do in a situation like this. "Wouldn't we, Data?" he added in a quick whisper that only the android's sensitive hearing could detect.

A look of understanding flickered into Data's golden eyes.

"Yes," he said, "we are greatly interested in speaking with your esteemed leader." And then, as he stepped close behind Geordi, he produced a closed-lip whisper that would have done a ventriloquist proud: "My experience in matters that require deception are quite limited, Geordi, but I will 'follow your lead.'"

"Please come with us," the leader said, and all three stepped aside from the airlock door.

Displaying a confidence he didn't feel, Geordi stepped inside, followed closely by Data. Still moving stiffly, the three aliens entered, the one who was apparently the leader pulling the door shut behind them and sealing it.

Strangely, there were no lights within the airlock, leaving them in total darkness, but the infrared portion of the spectrum provided Geordi with images of perfect clarity. Observing all three, he waited for them to do something to activate the transporter.

But none of them did. Instead, the apparent leader made his way blindly to the inoperative door at the opposite end of the compartment, jostling both Geordi and Data as he, in effect, felt his way past them.

Then, without anyone having touched a control, the transporter energized. Geordi braced himself as he saw the energies building around him, almost obscuring the images of the others.

Even more so than on the derelict, however, the energies were dull and faded to his Visored senses, and he wondered if the second stage—if there was a second stage this time—would be even more blindingly intense than the energies that had brought them here.

But there was no second stage.

As the energies faded, he saw that they were in the outer airlock, essentially identical to the inner.

The leader of the three was reaching for the locking mechanism in the outer door, feeling blindly in the darkness.

But also in the darkness, one of the other two—the overly nervous one, the one who had asked if Data and Geordi were "the Builders"—put his hand slowly, cautiously on the weapon suspended from his belt.

Silently, he withdrew it from its holster, and as it emerged, Geordi saw that it was indeed a primitive projectile weapon. Unlike a phaser, it had no nonlethal settings.

From both the infrared patterns of the man's skin and the trembling intensity with which he gripped the weapon, it was obvious to Geordi he planned to fire it the moment there was enough light to give him a target.

Under cover of what to the others was total darkness, Geordi drew his phaser and fired.

Even before the light from the phaser beam died out, he was turning it toward the other two, his finger tensing to press the firing stud again.

But before he could fire a second time, a new aura pulsed into existence, freezing him instantly in place. For an instant, he thought it was the precursor to the energies of the transporter, but in virtually the same instant, he realized that the aura was closer to that produced by a ship's phaser.

Then his consciousness faded and his muscles went slack, leaving him to hang like a rag doll in the zero G of the airlock.

Chapter Six

"Commencing search pattern under impulse power, sir," Lieutenant Worf reported from the conn.

"Estimated time to complete pattern to twenty thousand kilometers, Lieutenant?" Picard asked.

"Approximately fifty minutes, sir."

Picard nodded and settled back in the captain's chair to watch the viewer and to wait. There was nothing else, at the moment, that he *could* do but wait.

Wait for results of the search. Wait for reports from Number One and Chief Argyle, both now part of the extensive away team on the derelict. Wait, and try to mask his uneasy impatience, his frustration at being stuck here on the bridge and not being in the midst of the away team as it probed for the derelict's secrets—secrets that, he fervently hoped, would lead them to Commander Data and Lieutenant La Forge.

It had taken only minutes to determine that

nothing in the room from which Data and La Forge had been transported was booby-trapped the way the derelict itself had been—the way the panels that gave access to all the other rooms apparently still were. Another few minutes, and the hibernation chambers were open, revealing them to be, as Riker's tricorder had indicated, completely empty.

Now Argyle and some of his men were working to analyze the transporter, to see if they could gain any hint as to where it might have sent Data and La Forge. Other groups, a dozen in all, were fanning out through the narrow access corridors throughout the derelict in attempts to gain entry to the other rooms—equipment compartments, it now appeared—without triggering the power surge that would fuse the circuits of whatever was inside.

And with those efforts under way, Picard had set the *Enterprise* on its own search for whatever object the two men might have been transported to. Once the intricate three-dimensional spiral search pattern was completed, there would not be a cubic meter of space within transporter range of the derelict that had not been probed with everything the *Enterprise* had. If any ship, regardless of shielding or cloaking, existed in that volume, it would be found.

"Captain," Chief Engineer Argyle's voice over the communicator pulled Picard's attention from the continuously shifting star pattern on the viewer, "I *think* we've gotten a handle on where the transporter here in the control room must have sent the men, but I'm afraid it's not going to do us much good."

Picard scowled, tapping his communicator insignia. "Chief Argyle, any information is better than none. Now what have you found?"

"That the destination of *this* transporter was almost certainly somewhere within the derelict itself. But—"

"Then the men are still on the vessel? Regardless of what the sensors and tricorders say?"

"No, Captain, almost certainly not. This transporter apparently sent them on only the first leg of their trip—to one of the hundreds of other rooms, there's no way of knowing which one. The problem is, it now looks as if each of those rooms contains its own transporter. We haven't been able to get inside any of the rooms yet, but the tricorder readings my men have taken from outside indicate the presence of some form of transporter circuitry. We just about have to assume that, whichever room Data and La Forge were sent to, they were simply transported from there to a second destination."

Picard's features hardened as a thought occurred to him. "They—their patterns—couldn't have simply been 'stored' in one of the transporter matrices, could they?"

"We haven't detected any circuitry that would indicate such storage is possible, sir." Argyle paused before continuing, reluctantly. "However,

Captain, I feel compelled to point out that it *is* possible that they may have been transmitted but not—not 'received.'"

Picard suppressed a shudder. From his first days at the Academy, he had heard stories of people who had been transmitted—disassembled, converted to energy, and that energy sent on its way—but never received, never reconverted to matter and reassembled at the intended destination. Officially, of course, all such stories were regarded as unfounded rumors, circulated primarily to scare green cadets. But the possibility of such incidents were, to Picard and many others who so often depended on transporters for their movements, the modern-day equivalent of being buried alive. He had never been able to completely shake off the horror that it still inspired. And now, to think that such a thing might actually have happened to two of his men, two that he liked to call friends—

"Get into those rooms, Mr. Argyle," Picard said, pitching his voice purposely flat so as not to betray the strength of the feelings that gripped him. "No matter what it takes, get into those rooms. Find out what has happened to Commander Data and Lieutenant La Forge."

It was at those times when Geordi awoke—regained consciousness—that he most wished for the ability that others took for granted—the ability to open his eyes as slowly or as quickly as he desired.

But the Visor did not come equipped with the equivalent of eyelids. When he awakened, the moment the visual centers of his brain came on-line, they were assaulted by the full blizzard of wavelengths that bombarded his Visor, and there was no way of shutting them off, no way even of squinting and narrowing the more than one-hundred-eighty-degree expanse of shimmering, weaving colors.

The best he could do was lie still, not adding the extra confusion that would be caused by his own motion, for the time it took his mind to automatically lock onto the shapes that represented solid objects, to sort through the scintillating rainbows that represented inanimate but vibrant energy fields and still other displays that were the auras of living things.

But now, even before the images sorted themselves out, he became aware that he was no longer weightless. He was lying on something luxuriously soft, held there by a gravity very close to Earth normal.

Except—

It wasn't gravity.

The fact that the faint aura that bathed everything in an artificial gravity field was not present was one of the first pieces of information that emerged from the clutter of Visored data, and a moment later he realized that the even fainter but equally distinctive aura of normal, planetary gravity was likewise missing.

That meant, unless he was in the presence of a technology that was capable of a method of gravity generation unknown to Federation science, the weight he was experiencing was the result of centrifugal force. Whatever he was in was spinning, like a twenty-first-century space station, providing the outward sensation of gravity.

Meanwhile, the chaos of wavelengths had begun to sort itself out, and images began to emerge.

Data, his golden eyes alert and concerned, emerged first, standing and looking down at him.

Next came the room he was in, and the fact that the luxurious softness he was lying on was that of a massive couch.

And what he could see of the room itself was easily as luxurious as the couch. On the floor was a reddish-gray carpet, its pile—synthetic, not organic, an automatic spectrographic scan revealed— was as deep as half a dozen of the utilitarian *Enterprise* carpets stacked one on top of another. The entire wall facing the couch—and two other, identical couches—was concealed behind the folds of velvetlike, floor-to-ceiling drapes.

Abruptly, Geordi sat up and looked around, absorbing the rest of the room in a fraction of a second.

Behind the couch, facing the opposite way, were

several chairs, each as soft and body-enveloping as the couch. The chairs were arranged in an arc, at the focus of which was a firmer, more imposing chair. It wasn't quite a throne, but the suggestion was there.

High up on the wall behind the single chair, the wall opposite the drapes, was a meterwide version of the same stylized, circle-enclosed face that had been emblazoned on the uniforms of the three who had come to greet—and kill—himself and Data. Below it was a sliding door, but not one they could easily open. It was perfectly smooth, with neither handle nor indentation.

On the side walls, taking up virtually every square centimeter except for the two-meter-high door at the foot of one wall, were a pair of murals. One was a painting of a ruined city, its streets littered with rubble and shattered bodies, its buildings jagged stumps, while looming in the background was the unmistakable mushroom cloud of a primitive but powerful nuclear explosion. The mural on the facing wall was also of a city, possibly the same one, but here it was glittering in the sun, the streets filled with smiling people. Along one side was a park, and in the distance, in a gap between the buildings, was a countryside that was as parklike as the park itself.

And in the sky, in place of the mushroom cloud in the other mural, was once again the stylized face, this time not quite as bluntly obvious but outlined with at least a degree of subtlety in a series of wispy clouds against a sky that was even bluer than Earth's.

"Are you all right, Geordi?" Data asked.

"Fine, I think, but where the devil *are* we?"

"In the context of your Oz metaphor, I would have to say, 'somewhere over the rainbow,'" Data said solemnly, and then added, looking at the stylized face outlined in the clouds, "and that must be the Wizard, while I could most logically be considered to be the Tin Woodman."

Geordi couldn't resist a sudden grin, despite the less than amusing situation they had obviously fallen into. "Just so we haven't annoyed the Wicked Witch of the West, whoever *that* turns out to be."

"They seem to trust us, whoever our captors are," Data said. "They have taken none of our equipment, not even our phasers."

Geordi glanced down and saw that Data was right. He also noticed that their Translators had been turned off. When Geordi started to reach for his automatically, Data said, "I took the liberty of deactivating them. I thought you might prefer our first waking remarks to be private."

Geordi glanced around the room again. "You think they're listening to us?"

"There is no way of knowing, but I have no reason to believe they are not."

Geordi nodded. "Good thinking. But when someone shows up—*if* someone shows up—let's not let them know that you turned the Translators off deliberately. Let them think our machines fail now and then, so we can have more private conversations later if we need to."

"I will continue to follow your lead, Geordi."

"And I yours." He glanced around the room again. "Do you have any idea how we got here? The last thing I remember is being hit by something like a phaser, right after I had to stun one of the Three Stooges when he took his weapon out and acted like he was about to blast us."

"Since that time, I know little more than you," Data said, apparently either finding the ancient slapstick comedy trio in his memory banks or deciding to ignore the reference for the time being. "I was rendered unconscious as well, and I regained my senses only moments before you, on that couch next to yours."

"I was afraid of that," Geordi said, then turned and moved toward the drapes, looking for the draw cords that would open them. "I don't suppose you know what's behind here, then, either."

"No, Geordi, I felt it more important to assure myself that you had not been hurt."

As Data spoke, Geordi felt for draw cords but couldn't find any. Finally, he gave up and lifted them apart with his hands.

If Geordi could have blinked, he would have, as his Visored senses were suddenly hit by a whole new chaos of information.

Behind the drapes was a window, floor-to-ceiling like the murals.

And beyond the window was an entire world: three valleys filled with trees and fields and half-hidden houses stretched the length of the inner surface of a cylinder hundreds of meters in diameter, and at least a kilometer long. Between the valleys were slots nearly as wide, also stretching the length of the cylinder walls and beyond the slots, only partially visible, massive strips of mirror reflected the light from a G-type sun, only marginally different from Sol, onto the valleys.

It was a space habitat.

Except for the colors of the vegetation—a faint blue tinge to the green—it could have been one of the O'Neill space habitats from the early twenty-first century of Earth. He'd seen holographic images in the Academy and on half a dozen worlds, but he had never seen the real thing.

Until now.

He and Data were in the endcap of a space habitat. Obviously it had not been designed by O'Neill himself, not here in whatever corner of the galaxy they were in, but whoever the designer was had worked on the same principles.

Geordi whistled disbelievingly. "Talk about your basic 'somewhere over the rainbow . . .'"

"Ah," Data said, "this would explain the several hundred life-form readings our tricorders registered previously. We must have been either somewhere along the rotational axis of this structure or on a separate, nonrotating structure."

"Any idea which?"

"From the distance and distribution of the life forms as registered by the tricorder, I must assume we were in a separate satellite."

"Could you find it again if you had to?"

"Not without further information, Geordi."

Frowning, Geordi peered at the spaces where the angled mirrors didn't completely block the view of space beyond. But even his Visored senses could make out nothing. If there were other satellites or even a planet out there—the planet they had seen in the viewscreen in that other place, for instance —none was where it could be seen.

Abruptly, from the ceiling directly above the drapes, there came a humming, and the drapes slid smoothly apart like the curtains on a stage, fully revealing the wall-sized window and what lay beyond it.

An instant later, the door behind the large chair, directly beneath the stylized face, slid smoothly open.

Briskly, a man stepped through, and the door closed behind him. He was old, and he looked as human as the first three they had seen. He was dressed in a one-piece, belted uniform similar to those worn by the others, except it was a brilliant yellow, and in place of the stylized face on the breast was a simple circle of even more vibrant yellow. For a moment, Geordi wondered about the absence of the seemingly ubiquitous stylized face, but then he saw the reason. The man himself must have been, decades earlier, a model for the face. Even now, the resemblance could not be missed.

The man began to speak, but his words, without the Translators, were gibberish.

Geordi started to turn his on, but remembered in time the strategy he had suggested to Data. Putting a puzzled frown on his face, he glowered at the Translator and took it from his belt. Giving it a sharp tap with one finger, he listened a second and then, while looking directly at the man who had just entered, he said to Data, "Jiggle your Translator a little, and then, without being too obvious, turn it on."

Data, also keeping his eyes fastened on the man, said, "I am still following your lead, Geordi."

By then, the man had stopped talking and was looking from one to the other uneasily. Shaking their heads in what they hoped was an indication that they didn't know what was going on, they continued shaking and tapping their Translators until Geordi discreetly turned his on. A moment later, Data followed suit.

"That's better," Geordi said, looking again at the old man. "We have trouble with these things now and then."

The old man's eyes widened momentarily as the

Translators began delivering words in his language, and Geordi could see his entire body stiffen slightly.

"Welcome to the World of the Peacekeepers," he said. "I am Shar-Lon, Chairman of the Council of Peacekeepers. I beg that you allow me to express our boundless gratitude for what your Gifts have made possible. If there is anything we can do to aid you, you have only to ask."

"You could start by telling us why one of your men tried to kill us," Geordi improvised, making his voice stern, "and why you knocked us out and dragged us here."

There was virtually no change in Shar-Lon's expression, perhaps a slight tightening around the eyes, but the infrared portion of the spectrum revealed to Geordi's Visored senses a sudden drop in the surface temperature of parts of Shar-Lon's face and hands, reflecting a change in the flow of blood through his veins. In a human, this kind of reaction indicated increased apprehension, even fear. There was no reason to think it indicated anything different in Shar-Lon.

"I can only apologize that such terrible things were allowed to happen, and assure you that the individual will be dealt with in whatever manner you wish. My deputy Kel-Nar, who personally transported you here, has placed the three under guard, awaiting your command."

"Only one appeared to be involved in the attack," Geordi said solemnly, "but before we decide what is to be done with him, tell us why he behaved as he did. I take it that it was not by your command?"

The old man shook his head vigorously. "I would never—" he began, a pleading tone entering his voice, but then he broke off, as if he had suddenly regained control. "Unfortunately," he continued, his voice once again almost a monotone, "there are a few—a very few—deluded individuals among us who do not share in our rejoicing at your coming."

"Even among your own staff? I assume from their uniforms that the three who came to greet us—and kill us—were sent by you."

"They were. But it is impossible to always predict whom the madness will strike."

"How can we be sure it won't strike *you?*"

"Unthinkable!" Shar-Lon said, trembling. And then, bowing his head: "I am at your disposal. My one desire is to do the will of the Builders. Do with me as you wish. The weapons with which you rendered powerless the one who attacked you are still at your side."

That was true enough. And the phasers were, Geordi could see, still fully charged.

Studying the man again, Geordi wondered: How much was it safe to let him know? Primarily, was it safe to let him know that he and Data weren't the ones he and the others obviously thought they were, the ones responsible for the "Gifts," the so-called "Builders"?

Geordi's normal inclination in almost all situations was to simply tell the truth, but here, there was no way of guessing what the reaction to the truth would be. Shar-Lon appeared to be in awe— or at least in fear—of these "Builders," whoever they may have been, but how would he feel about a pair of lowly imposters? If that fear changed to anger, a lone pair of phasers couldn't hold off the hundreds of inhabitants that the tricorders had shown were present in this cylindrical world, particularly if the majority of them carried the same primitive but deadly projectile weapons that the first three carried. Was it possible, in fact, that the one in the airlock had realized the truth—that Geordi and Data were *not* the so-called Builders— and that was the reason he had tried to kill them?

On the other hand, if they tried to bluff their way through, they would have to keep up a pretense of knowing infinitely more than they really did. Worse, they wouldn't dare to openly ask any of the countless questions that had to be answered before they had even a chance of finding their way back to the *Enterprise*.

And there was the fact that bluffing—lying of any kind—made Geordi acutely uncomfortable. And yet—

Once again, Geordi envisioned Captain Picard in this situation, and he tried to imagine what the

87

captain would do. And, as it always did, the thought seemed to lend him strength, or at least determination.

"Yes," Geordi said finally, his fingers brushing his phaser, "we noticed that our equipment was left untouched, and we appreciate your courtesy. As I am sure our superiors will when we deliver our report," he added, pleased at his sudden inspiration.

Shar-Lon tensed even more. "You have come with a specific purpose, then?"

"Of course. As you might expect, we wish to learn what use you have made of our Gifts."

The instant the final word emerged from the Translator, Geordi realized that, for whatever reason, he must have said something right. Though Shar-Lon did his best to hold his features unchanged, he relaxed visibly, and the infrared spectrum once again revealed an extensive change, this time one that indicated a sudden lowering of tension, almost a relaxation.

"The essence is here," he said, gesturing at the murals. "This," he went on, indicating the ruined city and the mushroom cloud, "is what would have been had we not received your Gifts. And this"—a gesture at the other, the idealized city with the cloud image of his own face hovering in the background—"this is what we have. This is the world that exists."

"Most impressive," Geordi said noncommittally. "If all is as you say, I have no doubt that our report will be favorable, and our superiors will be pleased."

For a long moment, the old man stood perfectly still, and Geordi couldn't read his expression. Even the reactions in infrared were confusing, as if the man's emotions had been cut loose from reality. The relaxation evident only moments before was gone, but Geordi couldn't tell what it had been replaced by.

"Come," the old man said abruptly, his voice now oddly emotionless, somehow hollow sounding, "and I will show you what we have accomplished with your Gifts."

As he turned, the door swung soundlessly open and, with a muffled rustling, the drapes swished closed, abruptly cutting off the panoramic view of the habitat interior.

Chapter Seven

"SEARCH PATTERN COMPLETE to twenty thousand kilometers, sir," Lieutenant Worf reported. "Results negative."

Picard frowned his frustration at the temporarily motionless star pattern on the viewer. "Very well, Lieutenant," he said bruskly. "Expand the pattern to forty thousand kilometers."

"Expanding pattern, sir," Worf rumbled dutifully, not pointing out that the expanded search would take them to a distance that was more than twice the range of any Federation transporter.

"Also plot a course for return to within transporter range of the derelict. Set it to continuously update as we execute the search pattern, and have it laid in and ready to implement instantly."

"Course plotted and laid in, sir."

"Ensign Carpelli, be ready to pull everyone off that vessel as quickly as possible."

"Ready, sir," Carpelli responded from the main transporter room.

"Chief Argyle, Commander Riker," Picard said, tapping his communicator insignia, "we are expanding the search pattern. We will be out of transporter range, but we can be back within seconds."

"Understood, sir," Riker answered for them both.

"Mr. Argyle, any progress?"

"Some, sir," Argyle said uncomfortably. The captain was fair-minded, Argyle knew, but that didn't make it any easier to admit, if not to failure, to only very limited success. "As I reported earlier, it didn't take long to learn how to disarm the triggers in the panels and gain access to the rooms —compartments really. However, I'm afraid our luck hasn't been nearly that good with what we found inside."

"Yes, Chief?" Picard prompted when Argyle hesitated, as if trying to order his thoughts. "Two men are missing, and their lives in all probability depend on what you and your people are able to learn. And how quickly you learn it."

"I appreciate that, of course, sir."

"Then get on with your report."

Argyle swallowed. "We've investigated only twenty rooms so far, Captain, but those twenty appear essentially identical. In the first place,

91

they're not rooms so much as they are equipment compartments—primarily transporters, which we already suspected. The panels are simply access panels for the circuitry, probably to allow easy repair—easy, that is, if you know the secret of getting in without setting off the self-destruct safeguards."

"And the transporter platforms? The controls?"

"So far, we haven't been able to locate any physical controls. We're guessing that everything is controlled by the central computer. And the transporter platforms are *inside* the transporters."

"Inside? Mr. Argyle—"

"I know it sounds crazy, Captain, but that's the way it is. We can't get a direct look at them, of course, but from all readings we've taken, in all twenty areas, there is a cavity almost directly in the center of each transporter. We feel confident that those cavities, each approximately three meters tall and one meter on a side, are the destinations of the short-range transporters. Whatever is sent there is apparently immediately sent on to its next destination."

"The way Mr. Data and Lieutenant La Forge were sent?"

"Yes, sir. We're virtually certain that's what happened to them."

"Then if you can determine which transporter was used, you can reverse it and bring them back."

"I'm afraid not, sir. In the first place, we have so far discovered no way of determining which transporter was used. In the second—"

"Then reverse them all! One at a time!"

"That's probably impossible, too, sir. These transporters appear to be strictly one-way, and—"

"One-way, Chief Argyle?"

"Yes, sir. The best analysis we've been able to make of the circuits indicates that the transporters are able to function only as transmitters, not as receivers."

A new knot suddenly formed in Picard's stomach. "Then Data and La Forge *are* in limbo. Is there no way—"

"No, sir, that's not what I meant," Argyle said hastily. "These transporters appear to be capable of transmitting an object and reassembling it and setting it down at whatever destinations they're programmed for, the same way our own transporters do. What they're *not* able to do is reach out and bring that object—or any object—back in. Whatever is transported, stays transported."

"That doesn't make sense, Mr. Argyle," Picard protested. "Is it possible that the receiving circuitry is disabled? Whenever starships visit prison planets, locks are put on the receiving circuits so that no one can beam up without the operator entering a special code. Perhaps this—"

"Unlikely, sir. Though we can't get a perfect fix on every circuit, it appears that the receiving circuitry is simply missing, not locked out."

"Could they operate in pairs? Could the rooms you haven't examined yet contain the receiving circuits?"

"It's possible, sir, but I believe it unlikely. The rooms we've checked were picked at random throughout the entire vessel, and so far we have found virtually no variation. Each one contains a single transporter—transmitter—and a subspace receiver, the output of which appears to be channeled to the central computer."

"Have you been able to activate any of the transporters yet? Send a beacon through to determine where they go?"

"No, sir. Even though the panels give us direct access to a great deal of the circuitry, including control circuitry that could normally be manipulated directly, we can't do anything with it. There are just too many safeguards, all far more complex and more difficult to analyze or work around than those in the access panels. Until we find a way to neutralize those safeguards, it's impossible to activate any of the equipment in those rooms."

"How soon do you anticipate success, Mr. Argyle?"

"There's simply no way to predict, sir."

"But you must have *some* idea, a feeling, at least."

"I do, sir, but you won't like it."

Picard scowled. "Tell me, Mr. Argyle! Obviously, the longer you stand there avoiding my questions, the longer it will be until—. Just tell me, Mr. Argyle."

Argyle swallowed audibly. "I don't think we *can* activate the transporters, sir."

"But you've already told me that at least one of them has already *been* activated, Mr. Argyle. That is why, according to your earlier reports, Commander Data and Lieutenant La Forge are missing!"

"I know, sir, but in that case, the vessel's own computer did the work."

"And what's to stop you from getting it to do it again?"

"The safeguards, Captain. As I said, they are much more complex than those that protect the access panels. The central computer—and each and every transporter so far—appears to be, in effect, tamperproof. Without the necessary code, any attempt to do *anything* with them, either directly or through the computer, results in total destruction of all key circuits."

"But certainly the *Enterprise* computer could be linked to this computer and—"

"Feed in a million codes a second, until it hits the right one? Yes, it could, but it wouldn't help, unless it hit the right one the very first time. Once a wrong code is entered, you don't get a second chance. The circuits are on their way toward a meltdown within milliseconds. We already lost one that way, and there's nothing to indicate that any of the others are different."

"Then remove the self-destruct circuits. You apparently were able to do so with the doors."

"Impossible, sir. Everything is so completely integrated that no individual circuit can be removed without either destroying a thousand other circuits or triggering a meltdown. Argyle shook his head. "It would be like attempting to do a heart transplant if the heart and brain—and lungs and liver and every other organ—were a single, inseparable unit—the walls of the heart doubling as brain tissue, for instance."

Picard grimaced at the image and was silent a moment. Finally he said, "Very well, Mr. Argyle. You and your team will continue until every room on that vessel has been opened and the contents analyzed. Meanwhile, the *Enterprise* will continue to expand its search pattern until we've covered every millimeter within whatever the range of these one-way transporters turns out to be. Keep me—"

"That's another problem, sir," Argyle broke in. "The range of the transporters could conceivably be greater than you might expect."

Picard frowned, thinking uneasily that his search had already progressed, unsuccessfully, thousands of kilometers beyond the maximum range of Federation transporters. "How much greater, Mr. Argyle?" he asked quietly.

"Conceivably thousands, even millions of times greater," Argyle said, swallowing audibly. "There is, I feel, a distinct possibility that they operate through subspace. And if that's true, Commander Data and Lieutenant La Forge could be hundreds of parsecs from here."

Geordi and Data watched as the door slid open, revealing an elevator with the same ubiquitous stylized face on the back wall. The side walls were contrasting colors, one the same vibrant yellow as Shar-Lon's uniform, the other a depressing slate gray, and Geordi wondered if the two colors were intended to carry the same theme as the two murals. Shar-Lon himself stood silently after punching a code into the keypad that controlled the elevator. He didn't look at either of his passengers, and his infrared image showed Geordi that every exposed particle of his skin had turned almost lifelessly cold, as if he had slipped into shock.

But as the elevator rose toward the weightlessness at the hub of the habitat's endcap, the old man's body straightened and his sagging features, despite their expressionlessness, lost at least a decade. From the elevator, he ushered them through a series of doors to a deserted hangar containing several small, primitive shuttlecraft. All had the stylized faces emblazoned on their sides, some no bigger than an identifying mark, like an insignia of rank, but some more than a meter across. Leading them to one with a transparent canopy over the combination passenger and pilot compartment—an observation bubble? Geordi wondered—Shar-Lon keyed open the door and gestured them inside. As he floated in after them, as his fingers touched the shuttle's controls, his infrared profile improved, as if some inner debate had been at least temporarily resolved.

Smoothly, he guided the shuttle through the hangar airlock and, once outside in the glaring sunlight, gave it a sharp burst of acceleration, then sent it through a ninety-degree turn and almost simultaneously brought it to rest. The blue and white planet from the viewscreen now suddenly spread out before them, less than thirty thousand kilometers distant.

For a long moment, Geordi simply looked at the planet. If there had been even the slightest lingering doubt that the alien transporter had sent them across parsecs rather than kilometers, the view before him now vanquished it. This planet was real, not an image or an illusion.

"Without your Gifts," Shar-Lon finally said, his voice now a hushed, reverential whisper, "this world of ours would be a burned-out cinder."

"Explain," Geordi said, keeping his voice uncomfortably stern.

For several seconds Shar-Lon was silent, and some of the emptiness seemed to return to his features. Then they took on a look of sadness, and Geordi couldn't help but think of an actor preparing to deliver a difficult soliloquy.

"Though it shames me to say it," Shar-Lon began, "my people were, decades ago, little more than savages. Savages who had gained the knowledge that would have made it possible for them to destroy themselves and every living thing on our world. When your Repository of Gifts was discovered orbiting our world, there were nearly a hundred separate nations. Real peace had not existed at any time in our history, and more than a quarter of our nations had their own private arsenals of nuclear destruction. Some had been placed in orbit, some hidden beneath the ground, others beneath the sea."

"It's a familiar pattern," Geordi said solemnly, when the old man paused, as if waiting uneasily for a response.

Shar-Lon's eyes widened a trace but he didn't turn his face from the planet. "Then you have bestowed your Gifts on others as well as ourselves?"

"Of course," Geordi improvised, earning a sideways glance from Data, "although not many have used them as wisely as you. Tell us, Shar-Lon, how did you first come to use our Gifts? Was it you, personally, who received them?"

"It was," he said promptly, and for a moment his eyes glazed over, as if lost in the memory. Finally, without prompting, he went on. "I was the Chosen One. During that time of my life I was, though it pains me to admit it, as savage as any of the others on our planet. Earlier, in my youth, I had worked long and hard for peace. I had been among the first to join the group that bore our name, but I had quickly grown disillusioned. I realized that, far from being true peacekeepers, we were little more than agitators, and ineffective ones at that. We had few members and no power, and our protests were barely noticed. Angered by the futility of our efforts, I deserted the organization and threw myself into what I saw then as the only alternative—a world in which my own nation was powerful enough to maintain a peace that could be guaranteed in no other way.

"It was foolish, I know, but that desertion was, I realized later, an integral part of my destiny. Without my disillusionment and desertion, my retreat into destructive nationalistic pride, how could I have been accepted into the military of my nation? And without that acceptance, how could I have gained the trusted position that allowed me to be in that precise place, at that precise moment, when the Signs were given and your Repository of Gifts was revealed?"

Once again Shar-Lon fell silent, the infrared patterns of his face blotchily uneven.

"Tell us about it," Geordi prompted again. What Shar-Lon had told them so far was virtually useless as far as concrete information went. "Tell us what happened."

"Yes," Data added, suddenly sounding pleased with himself, "our superiors will be most interested in a detailed account of precisely what you did. As my colleague has said, your use of the Gifts has been unusually successful, and the details of that use could be quite informative. They might even be of use to our superiors, allowing them to analyze what happened and then to improve the methods by which they provide such Gifts to others in the future."

Geordi suppressed a smile as Data finished. For someone who'd complained of being inexperienced in the techniques of deception, he was learning fast.

"My colleague is correct," Geordi confirmed. "There are countless other worlds like your own, and our superiors are always open to the possibility of improvement, so that someday all worlds will be able to make as good use of our Gifts as you."

And with that final application of shameless flattery, Shar-Lon seemed to once again resolve whatever conflict had been raging within him, and he began once again to talk. And as Shar-Lon talked—or recited—Data's faultless memory recorded all the words, and Geordi continuously sorted through them for anything that might provide a clue as to the true nature of the

"Repository" and its "Gifts" and how he and Data could make use of them to find their way back to the derelict and the *Enterprise.*

Fifty years ago, Shar-Lon said, he and his brother Shar-Tel had been pilots in their nation's space defense force. Specifically, they had been two of more than twenty pilots who took turns shuttling supplies and replacement personnel to the manned spy satellites and missile launching platforms that kept virtually every square meter of the planet's surface under constant surveillance—and equally constant threat of instant destruction. Every nation with a strong enough economy either had similar satellites or had even more nuclear missiles somewhere on or under the planet's surface, all targeted on other, similarly armed nations. None of the missiles had been used except in tests, but hardly a year went by that a dozen minor wars with conventional weapons weren't being conducted somewhere. So far, none of the conflicts had reached the point of no return, where there would be no choice but for someone to launch the first missile, but it had been touch and go more than once.

"The Sign appeared to me on my twenty-eighth birthday," Shar-Lon continued, his voice now almost a monotone despite the recurring infrared evidence of an inner conflict that refused to stay entirely submerged for more than a minute or two at a time. "My brother and I were piloting a supply shuttle with no other personnel on board. We had achieved our preliminary orbit and were preparing to inject into the transfer orbit that would take us to the orbit of our satellites. As we waited for the signal from the ground that would confirm our on-board computer's calculations, I found myself simply watching our world slide by below me. And a thought came to me, the same thought that had entered my mind again and again, literally hundreds of times, since long before my first flight, since the very first time I had seen the images of our world brought back from the earliest satellites decades before. It came to me that the obvious beauty of our world was horribly, blasphemously inconsistent with the deadly games its inhabitants —including, by then, my brother and myself— were continually playing. And then—"

Shar-Lon paused and his face, in Geordi's infra-red vision, showed a flush of seemingly genuine emotion, as if the moment he was recalling was powerful enough to force aside whatever inner conflicts currently plagued him.

Shar-Lon waved a hand at the planet. "And then, for just a moment, the entire planet from horizon to horizon shimmered and twisted before my very eyes, as if it were a reflection on the rippling surface of a lake.

"And then, literally in the blink of an eye, it turned blood red. Its oceans, it continents, its clouds, all were suddenly bathed in a rippling vision of blood.

103

"And in that instant, I recognized the vision as a Sign, and I knew what it portended. In that instant, I knew that my world was about to die. It was about to be turned into a charnel house, a globe of death. Somehow, the missiles were going to be launched, and every living thing on the planet's surface would die.

"The knowledge terrified me as nothing before had had the power to do. I had seen the missiles in their satellite cradles. I had seen their devastating power in demonstrations and tests, and I knew their numbers. And I knew the ease with which they could be launched.

"And then, more vivid than reality itself, I saw what was to come.

"I saw our cities turned to radioactive slag and rubble, the countryside transformed into poisoned, lifeless deserts.

"I saw our people dying, in a hundred different ways, at a hundred different paces.

"I saw my own brother's flesh seared from his bones.

"I saw myself, my body weakened and dying in slow agony with no one left to minister to me or to the millions like me who had had the misfortune to survive not just seconds or minutes but months.

"I saw our entire world shrivel and die, and I could only watch helplessly. For I knew there was nothing I could do to keep the vision from coming true. There were hundreds of actions I could take that would *begin* the destruction, but not one that would allow me to prevent it from happening or to stop it once it had started. Even the single action that was in my power at that very moment—to use the supply shuttle we were piloting to ram and destroy the missile satellite we would soon be approaching—would not only mean our own instant deaths but could possibly trigger the very holocaust I knew must be prevented.

"Finally, when I had recovered my senses enough to speak, I tore my eyes from the vision and looked to my brother, and I realized that he had not seen. His attention had been on our instruments, rechecking the alignment of our guidance system as he always did before the maneuver that would take us into the transfer orbit.

"And then, as I started to speak, the signal came from the ground station, telling us that, according to their instruments, our trajectory had been somehow disturbed and that a minor course correction would be needed before we could begin the injection into the transfer orbit. At virtually the same instant, before I could get my brother's attention away from his instruments, the Sign faded, revealing our world still untouched.

"For a moment, I was filled with relief. It had been a delusion, I told myself as my brother fed the new data into the computer, a delusion brought on by the guilt I felt for my part, however small, in the madness that was destroying our world.

"But then, only moments later, as the computer ordered the required split-second firing of the main engine, the Sign returned. Our world was again bathed in blood, and I knew then that it was no delusion.

"For my brother saw it, too.

"But he did not see it for the Sign that it was, and when I tried to explain, he only ridiculed me.

"But then, when our world was at its darkest and bloodiest, the Repository of your Gifts appeared. It completely blotted out the terrible image of our dying world, and he could no longer deny the reality of what we were seeing. And a moment later, the ground station told us that our own image on their radar screens had been obscured by a larger but indistinct image.

"And in that instant, as the physical reality of your Repository was confirmed, I realized that here was our salvation.

"And I knew also that it was my responsibility, mine and no other's, to bring about that salvation.

"I, whose impatience had driven me to desert the ranks of the Peacekeepers nearly a decade before, had now been chosen to keep our world from the bloody holocaust that would otherwise destroy it. And your Repository, not the feeble though well-intentioned efforts of my former companions, was the means I had been given to accomplish that task.

"But my brother did not understand. He saw not salvation but a terrible threat, a threat of which the world must be warned. And I could not stop him. Short of slaying him myself, which I obviously could not bring myself to do, I could not stop him from contacting our superiors, those very madmen who, with similar madmen in other nations, would be responsible for beginning the carnage that I now had the means to avoid.

"So I took the only action that I could—I journeyed to the Repository. Even as my brother spoke to our superiors, his mind so absorbed with the image of the Repository that he was unaware of my actions, I took both his space gear and my own and entered the airlock and sealed it. Then I donned my own space gear and left the shuttle, taking my brother's gear with me. When he realized I had gone, he begged me to return. Our superiors, he said, were going to send a missile to destroy the Repository—the Invader, they foolishly called it—and that if we did not move out of range, we would be destroyed as well.

"But I continued. I had no choice. I had been chosen, and I could not retreat.

"And as I approached the Repository—as my brother maneuvered the shuttle safely away—the final Sign was given to me. For a moment, my trajectory through space took me to a point from which I was able to glimpse our world beyond the Repository, and in that moment I saw that its image—that our world itself—was even more beautiful and clean than it had ever been. Not a trace of the blood remained, and the blues and greens and whites that marched across its surface were more vivid than ever I had seen them.

"It was then that I *knew* I would be successful in my mission.

"And when I reached the Repository, even as I first touched its unbroken surface, I was quickly judged worthy and taken in, as if by magic, through the very walls.

"And there I stayed, with only the supplies in mine and my brother's space gear to sustain me, until I mastered the use of your Gifts.

"At first, I was able only to destroy the missiles that were foolishly sent against me, first by my own country and then by other nations that blindly joined my own in their mad effort to destroy me. In the end, when the many uses of your Gifts were fully revealed to me, I was able to seek the missiles out in their hidden places and hurl them into space and destroy them there.

"And when they were all destroyed, when the bloody threat of planetary death was removed, I gathered my former companions around me to rejoice that our world, finally, was free to put away its mindless weapons and live in peace. Even my brother," he added, with the first genuine smile since they had left the habitat, "eventually came to understand what we had found that day and joined us in our work."

As he finished, Shar-Lon touched the shuttle's

controls and set it to turning. Slowly, the planet drifted away, until it was replaced by the habitat, and for the first time Geordi and Data were able to see the entire assembly.

The endcap they had emerged from, the perpetually sunward end, was gently rounded. The kilometer-long cylinder itself was a dull gray except for the mirrored strips that reflected the sunlight into the interior through the three transparent strips between the valley land areas. From the center of the opposite end, the tubular hub extended another two hundred meters, ending in a cluster of angular assemblies surrounded by a massive parabolic mirror nearly a kilometer in diameter. Obviously, that was the power station. The sunlight focused by the mirror would be more than enough to provide for all the habitat's power needs, whether they extracted that power by means of solar panels or by using the heat to drive old-fashioned steam turbine generators.

"In their gratitude, the people gave us this, the World of the Peacekeepers," Shar-Lon said, his voice once again flatly unemotional, as if speaking by rote, "from which we can continue to watch over them with your Gifts. Its construction would have been impossible without the peace and sanity brought about by your Gifts, but once the suicidal need for weapons and armies was eliminated, anything became possible."

For another long moment, Geordi absorbed the

sight. For a world of this limited technological level, he realized, the habitat was indeed remarkable, particularly since there was apparently no moon from which to draw raw materials. Unless they had found and towed an asteroid of convenient composition, everything that had gone into the kilometer-long cylinder had to have been hauled out of the planet's deep gravity well, apparently using nothing but chemical rockets. The project had to have been truly massive.

Then Shar-Lon was maneuvering the shuttle back toward the airlock at the sunward end of the cylinder. Pulling in his breath, Geordi forced such thoughts from his mind. No matter how these people had managed to build a habitat, no matter what hardships it might have put them through, it was none of his business. His only concern, his and Data's, was the "Repository" and the "Gifts" it contained and the possibility that, with an awful lot of luck, one of them might still hold the key that would return himself and Data to the *Enterprise*.

Chapter Eight

"SEARCH PATTERN COMPLETED to forty thousand kilometers, sir," Lieutenant Worf reported from the conn. "Results negative."

Picard suppressed a grimace. In the first pattern, they had covered every cubic millimeter within twenty thousand kilometers of the so-called derelict, which was already more than the maximum range of the *Enterprise* transporters. Yet they had found nothing larger or more complex than hydrogen atoms. No evidence of shields. No evidence of cloaking devices. No evidence of life forms or even the disintegrated remnants of life forms. No evidence of *anything*.

Now they had completed a search out to forty thousand kilometers, and still there was nothing. Chief Argyle's speculation that the derelict's transporters might somehow work through subspace rather than normal space was looking more likely with every passing hour. Either that or Data and La Forge had been transported to a vessel that possessed cloaking or shielding devices far more advanced than anything in Starfleet's technological repertoire. Even if the theoretical vessel had departed immediately under either impulse power or warp drive, the *Enterprise* sensors would have picked *something* up—again, unless the theoretical alien vessel had a cloaking device that gave it much greater freedom of action than anything the Federation had.

"Ensign Carpelli," Picard said abruptly. "prepare to beam Chief Argyle and Commander Riker back to the *Enterprise*. Lieutenant Worf, take us to within transporter range of the derelict. As soon as Chief Argyle and Commander Riker are aboard, expand the pattern to eighty thousand kilometers and resume the search."

Picard stood and strode up the ramp toward the door to the Ready Room. Behind him, Worf had already executed the automatic maneuver that would take them to within transporter range.

In the Ready Room, Picard stood silently for a moment as the door whispered shut behind him. Closing his eyes, he breathed deeply, forcing his muscles to let go of the continuing tension that had dogged him from the moment the two men had vanished. When his eyes opened, they fell on the tiger fish, swimming lazily in their aquarium tank, and for another moment he enviously imagined himself doing the same, lazing in comfortable waters that both supported and soothed him.

A trace of a smile pulled at his lips. Like the fish, he was constantly on display. Unlike them, he was constantly aware of a shipload of watchers and of the necessity to present the proper image, to keep his weaknesses and insecurities hidden behind the façade of command—except for those rare moments when he retreated here, the one spot on the entire *Enterprise* that could be completely his, completely private.

But he could not indulge himself, not now, not for more than the few seconds he had already stolen. Not ten minutes ago, Chief Argyle had reported that the last of the compartments on the derelict had been opened, and that its contents were no different from that of all the others: a one-way transporter and some subspace receiving circuitry, neither of which could be activated without the virtually instant destruction of every vital circuit.

But this time, Riker had been with Argyle. And the two of them, Riker had said, had come up with a plan that they had to discuss with him.

A plan that might, Riker had admitted, destroy the derelict completely, killing anyone taking part in the plan.

But it was also a plan that had at least a chance of locating Commander Data and Lieutenant La Forge, even a chance of getting them back, if they were not already dead.

When Riker and Argyle entered the Ready Room barely a minute after Picard had retreated there, the captain motioned them to seats. They sat, Argyle still with a touch of uneasiness, Riker himself with unaccustomed formality.

"As I understand your reports, Mr. Argyle," Picard said bluntly, "your team has had no success in determining how to disarm any of the transporters and allow them to be activated."

"That's correct, Captain."

"And that without activating them, there is no way to determine their destinations?"

"That is also correct, sir."

"Then what in blazes is this plan the two of you have devised?"

Argyle darted a glance toward Riker, obviously deferring to the first officer the honor of making the presentation.

Riker leaned forward slightly in his chair. "We know that both the short-range transporter in the 'control room' and at least one of the other transporters has already been activated once, Captain, when they 'relayed' Commander Data and Lieutenant La Forge to whatever their final destination was. We also know the approximate conditions under which that activation occurred. And finally, we have a theory as to *why* the activation occurred."

Picard frowned when Riker paused. "Well, Number One?"

114

Riker exchanged a glance with Argyle and then continued. "Using the coordinates our own transporters locked onto, we were able to pinpoint the location of Data and Lieutenant La Forge at the moment the first transporter picked them up. They were *not* on the transporter platform. They were at least five meters from it, in the door to the corridor. With that information as a starting point, we looked at the design of the transporter platform again. It appears capable of locking onto any object—any living object, we suspect—within either that room or the adjoining control room—and transmitting it to any one of the other transporters."

"But why did it choose to lock onto Data and La Forge at that precise moment? Did they accidentally trigger it themselves? Or did the *Enterprise* transporter beams somehow activate it?"

"No, sir. What we *think* happened is that it was activated as a result of the radiation leaking from the antimatter core. We think the radiation leakage triggered an automatic evacuation system, a system designed to get anyone in that room—in or out of the hibernation chambers—out of there, hopefully to someplace safer. Just what the interaction between that transporter and the ones in the other rooms was, we don't know, may never know completely. But we feel sure that the program in charge somehow sorted through all the possible destinations, picked one, and, in effect, forwarded Data and La Forge there."

"But you don't know which of the hundreds of other transporters did the relaying? Or, even if you do, you can't determine its destination without turning it on, which you can't do without making it destroy itself." Picard shook his head. "I don't see where this gets us, gentlemen."

Riker pulled in a breath. "What we propose, sir, is that we reproduce the original conditions—the radiation levels, primarily—to see if we can trick the evacuation program into sending someone else to the same place. Someone better prepared and better equipped to get word back to the *Enterprise.*"

Picard's scowl deepened. "I don't like it, Number One!"

"I don't like it either, sir," Riker said, "but from what Mr. Argyle tells us, it could be the only chance we have!"

"But how *good* a chance?"

"That's not the point, Captain. The point is, it's the *only* chance. I'm more than willing to take it."

"I could order you not to."

"I know you could, Captain."

Picard was silent a long moment, his eyes holding Riker's, looking for any trace of doubt, any indication of misgiving.

But there was none. There was only what he had always seen in his first officer's eyes when lives depended on his actions: determination.

He looked at Argyle. "And your evaluation, Chief?"

"The same as Commander Riker's, sir. It has a chance of succeeding, but I have no idea how good that chance is. There's simply no reliable way to calculate the odds."

"It goes without saying that you understand the risks, Number One."

"Of course, sir. And I will be certain that anyone who volunteers to accompany me will understand them as well."

Finally, Picard nodded. "Very well, Number One. Inform me when you've made the necessary preparations."

"Of course, sir," Riker acknowledged, turning sharply and striding toward the door to the bridge. Argyle, with a final glance at Picard, followed, leaving the captain alone with his decision.

"Would you do us the honor of speaking to the Council of Peacekeepers and allowing us to properly thank you for our salvation?"

Shar-Lon, his inner emotional state (as far as Geordi could read it) fluctuating wildly from minute to minute, turned to face Geordi and Data as his private elevator began its slow descent from the weightlessness of the hub.

"The knowledge that the Gifts have been used wisely is thanks enough," Geordi said, almost blushing with the pompous cliché. It was even worse than the other things he had found himself saying in response to Shar-Lon's high-flown rhetoric.

Shar-Lon himself, his features beginning to once again sag from the increased centrifugal force as the elevator continued toward the outer rim of the endcap, nodded sagely, if uneasily. "That is of course true," he said, "but I know my fellow Peacekeepers would be gravely disappointed, particularly those of the Council of Elders, those who served on the first Council. They have waited more than fifty years to express their gratitude. Surely, you would not deny them that opportunity."

"Of course not," Geordi said, but added firmly, "however, until we can be more certain of the reception we would receive, we feel it would be best—and safest—if knowledge of our presence were limited to as few of your people as possible."

For a moment, it seemed that the old man was going to continue to protest, but then he lowered his eyes in submission. "It will be as you wish. Your mistrust is understandable in light of the attack you have already suffered."

"Yes," Geordi said evenly, "it is. Therefore, it will undoubtedly also be understandable to you that we wish to return to the Repository as soon as possible to make a report. Our superiors can be quite impatient."

"Surely you are not leaving! Not this soon, before we have the chance to—"

"Of course not. The report is merely a preliminary one," Geordi said, and then added, ominously, "However, if it is not received on schedule, other representatives—other less understanding representatives—may well be sent to determine the reason for the delay."

Shar-Lon almost shivered at what he took to be a rebuke. "I would do nothing to keep you from your tasks," he said apologetically. "I will assign my most trusted men to escort you back to the Repository."

Geordi nodded. "Thank you, Shar-Lon. Your understanding is appreciated. However, if it's possible, there is one person with whom we would like to speak before we make even this preliminary report."

"Anyone at all! But who—"

"Your brother. I believe you said his name is Shar-Tel."

Shar-Lon's face stiffened for a moment. "I wish it were possible," he said finally, "but it is not. Shar-Tel was killed more than a decade ago."

"Killed? How?"

"He was the victim of someone suffering from the same delusions as the one who attacked you."

"Oh? These delusions, then, must be more common than you've suggested."

"No! Most assuredly not! It is only that those few who suffer from them are prone to wildly irrational acts such as these. Their effect is therefore grossly out of proportion to their number."

"I see. And just what are these delusions? Why would they make anyone want to kill us?"

Once again, Shar-Lon's infrared image indicated renewed inner conflict. "I hope you will not be offended if I speak plainly," he said, forcing his eyes up to Geordi's face and the enigmatic Visor.

"Of course not. The plainer the better."

"There are those few—and I repeat, *very* few—who have, from the very beginning, resented your Gifts and the use to which the Peacekeepers have put them. I realize it seems insane, but those demented few would rather their nations were free to destroy each other—and the rest of the world—than submit to those few limitations that are necessary for us all to live in peace. They have never been able to adapt to the civilized ways that have prevailed since your Gifts allowed us to rid the world of the terror of nuclear destruction."

"Then they're not so much deluded as misguided?"

"Either term, I fear, is exceedingly generous." A new, more genuine intensity crept into Shar-Lon's words. "To my own mind, these people are the very essence of the evil that your Gifts allowed us to overcome. It is difficult to understand how anyone, anywhere, could be as deluded as they, but for those delusions to exist here, on the Peacekeepers' world itself, is virtually inconceivable.

Geordi nodded, trying to look understanding. Shar-Lon's rhetoric and shifting inner moods were making him more and more nervous. He was also becoming more and more convinced that his spur-of-the-moment decision to invent the fictional "superiors" who could drop in at any moment to exact vengeance had been right. With someone as seemingly unstable as Shar-Lon, the truth—that he and Data were helplessly alone and knew nothing whatsoever about the so-called Builders—could very well have gotten them killed.

"There are people like that on every world," Geordi said. "However, we can discuss such matters later. Right now, it's imperative that we return to the Repository and report to our superiors. Unless," he added, making it sound like an afterthought, "there are others, like your brother, who were witness to your discovery and first use of our Gifts."

"There were none," Shar-Lon said quickly. "And my brother was not truly a witness to anything but the Sign itself. Only once, shortly before his death, did he even enter the Repository."

"Very well," Geordi said, resisting an impulse to ask why there had been only the one visit. "Then we have only to wait until you have located some-

one you can trust to return us safely to the Repository. And remember, our time is limited."

Despite the increasing gravity, now almost Earth
normal, Shar-Lon pulled himself erect, as if coming
to a decision. "I will take you myself," he said,
reaching for the keypad to reverse the elevator and
send it back toward the hub and the shuttle hangar.

But before his fingers had entered the code, the
elevator door opened on the same odd room they
had been in before.

But this time a half dozen men, all at least as old
as Shar-Lon, sat in the semicircle of chairs, waiting.
A seventh, only slightly younger, stood by the
elevator, his hand reaching out to block the door
from reclosing. All wore the familiar belted uniform, but in a sedate gray and without the stylized
face. Geordi and Data both tensed, their hands
starting toward their phasers, but they stopped the
motion when they saw that none of the men was
armed.

"So, Shar-Lon," the one by the door said, momentarily lowering his head in a motion that was
less a bow than a simple acknowledgment, "it is
true. The Builders have returned."

"Yes, Ki-Tor, it is true," Shar-Lon said stiffly.
"But I did not call for a meeting of the Council of
Elders."

"Nonetheless, you have one." The others tenta-
tively nodded their agreement.

"Not at this time!" Shar-Lon snapped. "The Builders wish to be returned to the Repository, and—"

"You will not keep them from us *this* time, Shar-Lon!"

"That is not my intention, Ki-Tor, I assure you. They have come to judge what use we have made of their Gifts, and now that they have seen, they must make their report. To do that, they must return to the Repository. Surely you would not interfere with their wishes."

Ki-Tor turned to Geordi and Data. "Are those your wishes?"

Geordi hesitated. These were obviously contemporaries of Shar-Lon, and possibly, no matter what Shar-Lon had said, they might know something useful about the alien vessel, the "Repository."

"We do need to make a preliminary report to our superiors shortly," Geordi said, "but if any of you were ever directly involved in the use of our Gifts, we would like to speak with you."

Ki-Tor frowned. "Shar-Lon has not *allowed* anyone but himself to be directly involved. He has shared the Gifts with no one. Even now, as we all reach the ends of our lives, he has refused to pass those secrets on, or even to share the least of them."

So, Geordi thought disappointedly, Shar-Lon is the only game in town. "Then yes, our wishes are to return to the Repository," he said. "However, we

123

will be most interested in meeting with all of you as soon as we have completed our report and received new instructions from our superiors."

Geordi's words seemed to be all the reassurance Shar-Lon needed. Abruptly, he touched a spot on the buckle of his uniform belt. Within seconds, the door in the far corner of the room opened, and a blue-uniformed, hawk-faced man stepped inside sharply. His eyes virtually glinted as he looked about the room at the Elders.

"You know my deputy, Kel-Nar," Shar-Lon said. "He will escort you out. This uncalled gathering of the Elders is now concluded. You will be notified when—and if—the Builders wish to speak further with you."

As the last of the Elders moved reluctantly out of the room, someone in a blue uniform—neither Kel-Nar nor one of the original three, Geordi noted quickly—appeared in the door, glanced toward Geordi and Data, and motioned for Shar-Lon to come toward him. Frowning, the old man complied.

As they came together near the door, the younger man began to speak rapidly, his lips only inches from Shar-Lon's ear, the words too soft for the Translator to pick up. Shar-Lon shook his head and turned away, but the man gripped his arm and continued to speak urgently. Finally, with a grimace, Shar-Lon turned to Geordi and Data.

"I am sorry, but I must delay our return to the Repository for a few moments."

"Is something wrong?" Geordi asked as he and Data stepped out of the elevator.

"That is what I have to find out. I will return as soon as possible."

And then he was gone, the door closing soundlessly behind him.

Apprehensively, Geordi looked back at the elevator, its door still standing open. A moment later, he switched off his Translator, and motioned for Data to do the same.

"We are not pretending to have malfunctions anymore?" the android asked as he complied.

Geordi shook his head. "Considering the act we've been putting on, it would be 'out of character.'"

Data considered a moment and then nodded. "I see. If we continued to have 'malfunctions,' it would detract from the 'front' you have been putting up."

Geordi smiled nervously. "Right, Data. I just hope this 'front' is doing us some good, not just getting us deeper in trouble. And to tell the truth, I'm beginning to wonder." He looked again at the door through which Shar-Lon and the others had left. "In fact, I think we had better have our phasers ready, just in case."

"What is it you suspect?"

"I wish I knew. Something's just not right, Shar-Lon being called away like that." Geordi shook his head, frowning at himself. "That's the trouble with playing it by ear. You never know you've done something wrong until it's too late."

"'Playing it by ear?'"

"Another old expression, Data. It just means I—I've been making things up as I go along. Reacting to whatever happens in whatever way 'feels right' at the moment. No logic or common sense involved, but right now, things definitely do not 'feel right.'"

Data looked at Geordi silently for more than a second. Then he nodded thoughtfully, and his voice once again had a faintly wistful quality when he spoke. "It is another form of human intuition—similar to that which prompted you to make the reference to Kansas."

"Something like that. Or maybe it's a sign of a disorderly mind." Geordi shook his head again, feeling discouraged. "We could *really* use Counselor Troi here. She could at least tell when we were being lied to. And maybe whether this Shar-Lon character and his friends are just strange or outright crazy. I can get readings of sorts by checking them out in the infrared portion of the spectrum, but that's not much more reliable than my 'hunches.' There are only a couple of things I *am* sure of—or almost sure of, anyway. For one, I don't trust anyone who orates instead of talks, the way Shar-Lon does most of the time. And we're not going to find any real answers here in the habitat. Our only chance of getting out of here is back at the so-called Repository. Agreed?"

"Agreed, Geordi," Data said, somewhat relieved to be back in an area where logic seemed to apply. "The Repository would appear to be another artifact abandoned by the same group that abandoned the derelict we found in deep space. Therefore, no matter what our initial survey of the artifact shows, it is the only place in which the equipment necessary to contact or return to the derelict can possibly be found."

"Right. The technology of whoever built those things had to be the equal of the Federation's—or ahead of it, at least in the field of transporters. There's no way a Federation transporter could've tossed us *this* far. And what Shar-Lon was describing—his 'Signs'—sound a lot like what could happen if a cloaking device of some kind was breaking down."

"Yes. It would not be surprising if a device of such age were to fail."

Geordi sighed faintly. "The question is, what *else* has failed? How much of what we couldn't find back there wasn't really missing, just malfunctioning? The transmitting half of the transporter, in particular. And how much is *really* missing? If we could just figure out what the 'Repository' was doing here in the first place, why it was in orbit around this planet at all, not to mention why it was abandoned—or why the original derelict was abandoned, and what *it* was doing out there in the middle of nowhere—"

Geordi broke off, smiling ruefully. "But the only thing that's important is getting back inside the Repository and getting some kind of control over whatever *is* in there. And if Shar-Lon could learn to control it, apparently fairly quickly, there's no reason we can't do the same."

"If the controls are associated with the helmet," Data said, "it will have to be you who learns their operation, Geordi. It was decidedly inhospitable when I attempted it."

"I know. That must have been another 'booby trap.' The helmet must analyze brain-wave patterns or metabolic parameters or who knows what, and then only accepts those that match the specifications put in there by whoever built these things. And it tries to kill anyone who doesn't meet those specifications."

Geordi paused, shaking his head. "I'd be willing to bet that the Builders never thought that anybody but themselves could meet those specs, whatever they are. They wanted to make sure nobody but themselves would ever be able to get inside and take things over. That sort of thinking would fit right in with the kind of paranoid mind it would take to equip a place with an antimatter bomb that could be triggered just by having someone beam aboard."

"Yes," Data said when Geordi fell silent, "I have been considering that and other aspects of both this object Shar-Lon calls a Repository and the derelict from which we were transported. As a result, I have been able to establish some tentative correlations with certain information from other sources. If—"

"You have a theory about these things?" Geordi interrupted, suddenly excited. "Something that can get us out of here?"

"No, Geordi, I do not see anything in the correlations that could help us in any way. However, perhaps they would be useful to your intuition."

"Then let's hear them!"

"As you wish. As you know, the sector of space through which the *Enterprise* was traveling is largely unexplored by the Federation. However, the Ferengi have in the past bartered information with the Federation, and some small part of the information the Federation received may concern this sector."

"I'd heard about the bartering," Geordi said, his enthusiasm of a moment before already fading. "But I also heard that we got shortchanged. I don't know what the Federation gave the Ferengi, but I heard that what we received was virtually all second- and thirdhand, some little more than rumors or legends, just stories they'd collected from the various races they've traded with over the centuries. Fairy tales, even, about as reliable as—as *The Wizard of Oz.*"

"That is true, Geordi. However, there are elements that are common to many of the stories, and one of those common elements concerns a vessel that could be said to resemble the Repository quite closely."

"Oh? And when are these vessels supposed to have existed? And who did they belong to?"

"All the summaries say is that, at some indeterminate time in the past, in a number of widely scattered star systems, vessels similar to the Repository are said to have been found orbiting a number of class-M planets. None was said to be functional, however, nor did any contain a living being."

"Anything in the summaries about the purpose of the vessels?"

"Nothing. However, there are stories involving other class-M planets whose inhabitants are said to have been on the verge of achieving space travel but were kept from it, some by an undefined 'catastrophic event,' others by 'alien invaders.' Whether there is any real correlation—"

"So *that's* what they are!" Geordi said, shaking his head. "Guard posts!"

"Guard posts?"

"Yes! Don't you see? It all fits! The derelict

was—well, I don't know *exactly* what it was, but it was some kind of central hub or headquarters or something for those guard posts. I'll bet each one of those transporters in the derelict connected to a different guard post, around a different planet. That's why the transporters only operate in one direction, so if one of the planets *did* manage to get a team into space and get into the guard post, they'd never be able to get any farther. They'd never be able to get at the headquarters or whatever."

"But why would they have guard posts orbiting these planets? If they were prison planets—"

"I don't know, not for sure, but I'll bet their paranoia had a lot to do with it. I'll bet—" Geordi broke off, grimacing. "Unfortunately, *none* of this helps us figure out how to get in touch with the *Enterprise.* If anything, it means our chances are worse than before. It means the transporters were *designed* to be one-way, designed to keep intruders —like us, like Shar-Lon—from gaining access to the derelict."

"Are you saying, Geordi, that your intuition indicates that we will never return to the *Enterprise?*"

Geordi shook his head. "No, that's what *logic* tells me. Intuition tells me that no matter what we find out about the Repository, we've still got a pretty good chance of getting back, one way or another. Captain Picard isn't going to give up until he finds out how those transporters in the derelict work, and when he does, he's going to figure out a way to find us. The captain doesn't—"

"Someone is coming," Data broke in, and Geordi tensed, the fingers of one hand almost touching his phaser while with his other hand he turned his Translator back on.

But it was Shar-Lon, his frown now a scowl.

"Trouble?" Geordi asked.

"Only foolishness," the old man snapped, but then, as if he had suddenly realized whom he was talking to, his voice softened. "Come," he said, gesturing toward the elevator, "I will transport you to the Repository at once. I can only apologize for the delays. And for the unforgivable behavior of the Elders."

Geordi said nothing, and then he and Data were stepping into the elevator.

The doors closed behind them, and the elevator started upward, Shar-Lon maintaining an apologetic silence. When the elevator stopped and the doors opened, they were virtually weightless again.

Shar-Lon led them through the same series of doors as before, and within a minute, he was once again keying open the same shuttle door.

Abruptly, a second door to the shuttle hangar swung open, and three men, wearing purely utilitarian shirts and trousers rather than uniforms, burst through.

All three wore masks concealing the bottom

132

halves of their faces—and all three were holding guns, already aimed at the vicinity of the shuttle, as if the intruders had known approximately where their targets would be before the door had been opened.

Before even Data could react, three triggers were squeezed.

Chapter Nine

WHEN PICARD HAD first told Counselor Deanna Troi what Commander Riker was planning, she had reacted little more strongly than she had to any of the hundreds of other missions he had successfully carried out over the years on this and other ships. For a time, she remained on the bridge, watching the viewer with Picard as the search continued, waiting for Riker to report that he had completed his preparations. Like Picard and everyone else on the bridge, she hoped that some hint of another derelict, cloaked and hidden, would emerge from the hundreds, the thousands of readings being taken every second. She hoped that Geordi La Forge and Data would be found, safely, before it came time for Riker to carry out his possibly deadly experiment.

But the hope, while heartfelt and genuine, was rational and controlled, and, as always during crisis situations, she kept her mental net open, listening for signs of extreme or inappropriate emotions, for signs of incipient panic anywhere on the ship.

And, so far, she had detected none. As always, even under the most difficult circumstances, the crew was functioning effectively and efficiently.

But then, unexpectedly, a ripple of uneasiness tingled icily through her, and she looked about sharply, searching for its source. Lieutenant Worf was still at the conn, monitoring the instruments stoically as the *Enterprise* followed its complex but ultimately repetitive search pattern. The captain alternately occupied the command chair next to her own and paced from the conn to the science stations, impatiently reading the instruments over the operators' shoulders. Lieutenant Brindle, who had replaced Lieutenant Yar when she had insisted on volunteering to accompany Riker, monitored the tactical station.

All those on the bridge, Troi could sense, were uneasy, but it was a controlled uneasiness, a controlled tension typical of the state they were in during any time of danger, a controlled tension that made them more efficient, not less. But even if one of them were more nervous than usual, she told herself, there was ample reason. Rarely had there been so many unknowns as were involved in this mission of Riker's. There were unknowns at every step: unknown destination, possibly parsecs distant. Unknown—and alien—transporters that operated not through normal space but subspace. And certainly unknown perils were waiting for them, not only at their destination but in the transporting itself.

So to be uneasy was normal under the circumstances.

But then, for no discernible reason, within the space of a heartbeat, the tension notched upward.

And during that same heartbeat, she realized— or perhaps simply admitted to herself—that this time it was different. The uneasiness that she had been sensing was not that of Picard and the others.

It was her own. The phantom image of her own growing uneasiness was simply being echoed back from those around her.

And as the realization came, that echo of uneasiness was suddenly imbued with a startling sense of urgency. And, to her own dismay, the uneasiness began to rapidly escalate toward fear.

For another minute, she continued to sit still, gripping the cushioned arms of her chair, her eyes looking at but not seeing the star patterns as they shifted in the viewer, and all she could see in her mind's eye was Riker as he stepped onto the transporter platform.

Angrily, she tried to force the image away. It was always difficult when Riker led an away team to an unknown world, into unknown dangers, but it had never been like this.

This was more than simple apprehension for his safety. This—

Abruptly, she stood up and strode to the forward turbolift. She had never been able to fully understand or control the odd mixture of Betazoid mental powers and human intuition, but now and then they seemed to combine and virtually scream for her attention.

As, she had suddenly realized, they were screaming now.

The seconds in the turbolift seemed to stretch endlessly, and as the doors opened on the corridor only yards from the transporter room, she virtually leapt out, raced down the corridor and had to slow to give the transporter room door time to slide open to admit her.

Inside, she lurched to a complete stop, the urgency that still held her in its grip reaching a crescendo.

On the platform stood Yar and Riker. Both wore heavy-duty radiation suits and each carried, in addition to the standard away-team paraphernalia, a compact subspace radio transceiver and a not-so-compact phaser rifle. The helmets of their radiation suits were in place, only their eyes showing through the transparent slits. Riker was already raising his arm in a gesture to Ensign Carpelli at the controls.

But then he stopped and turned his head slightly to face Troi.

Through the narrow slit in his helmet, his eyes

met hers, and he saw in them the urgency that had brought her racing here.

And she saw in his what she had seen there so many times before—that his duty to Starfleet and to his ship and its crew came above all else. That what he was doing now was carrying out his duty, nothing more.

As she had countless times before, she reached out to touch his mind with hers, even though she knew his human senses could not feel the full impact of that touch.

Imzadi, she whispered silently, though she knew there would be no response. *Imzadi. Beloved.*

But this time there was a response. Or was it, like the uneasiness and fear, merely an echo of her own thoughts?

Imzadi, it said, *I will always be with you.*

And even through the narrow slit of the radiation-suit helmet, she saw from his eyes that the words were real, that their minds were, in that moment, making a contact that they had never fully achieved before. Her own intensity, the urgency that had gripped her increasingly and had come to a jarring climax as she had entered the transporter room, had made it possible, however briefly.

And it terrified her all the more, this sudden, unprecedented touching of their minds.

There had to be a reason that it had, of all times, come now.

At this particular parting.

They had parted a hundred times before, under far more intimate circumstances, and it had not come.

But now, in the midst of a thousand distracting tensions, it had come.

But then the touch was gone, leaving only its memory.

And the terror its brief coming had inspired.

She could only watch, helpless, as Riker completed the gesture to Carpelli that he had begun immeasurable seconds before. A second later, he and Yar were gone, swallowed up by the energies of the transporter.

As the triggers were squeezed, there was not the series of deafening bangs that, in that instant, Data had been expecting. Though he had never personally encountered projectile weapons of the kind Geordi had said their earlier attacker had carried, his memory banks contained the information that such weapons propelled their projectiles by means of chemical explosions, and he had naturally assumed the resultant sounds would have been painfully loud, particularly in a location such as the hangar, where the acoustic properties of the metal walls would cause the sound to be reflected rather than absorbed. But there were no explosions. Instead, there was only a series of "poofs," little louder than sharp exhalations of breath.

And he felt, not the thudding impact of the

deadly projectile he had also been expecting, but only a sharp pricking sensation in his shoulder.

Automatically, his hand darted to the affected area and came away an instant later with a tiny dart, the half-inch point of which had easily penetrated his uniform and the flesh beneath.

Turning sharply, he saw that similar darts had struck both Geordi and Shar-Lon, but they were not plucking them out as he had done. Without hesitation, he snatched the darts from their bodies.

And as he did, he realized both were rapidly verging toward unconsciousness.

An instant later, two things happened virtually simultaneously.

A shimmering, similar to that of a transporter but less intense, flowed briefly around Shar-Lon.

And there was another poofing sound, and he felt a second pricking, this time in his arm. Snatching it out, he turned back toward the three attackers, noting out of the corner of his eye that Shar-Lon had vanished. The result of one of the "Gifts," he assumed. The disappearance, however, didn't seem to startle the attackers any more than it had Data. All now had their eyes and weapons centered on Data, not the spot where Shar-Lon had been standing, and varying degrees of apprehension were beginning to appear on their faces.

For a moment he thought of simply drawing his phaser and stunning the three of them in rapid succession, but he did not. While the darts—

obviously drugged—had little effect on himself, there was no way of knowing their effect on Geordi, particularly if he were struck by more of them. And no matter how quickly Data drew and fired, at least one of the three attackers would be able to get off an indeterminate number of shots, some of which might hit Geordi. And he didn't want to stun them all anyway, not until he could question at least one of them about not only the drug but their motives.

Data's eyes went to Geordi once again, seeing that he was fully unconscious now but seemingly suffering no other ill effects. His breathing was still regular and deep, his muscles relaxed, not tense or spasming.

I will follow your lead again, Geordi, he thought, and purposely let his own muscles go slack, releasing the darts from his hand and letting his body sway very slightly in the zero gravity, just as Geordi's was doing.

His golden eyes open only a slit, he watched the three approach. They moved slowly, warily, their eyes and weapons still trained on Data.

At two meters, they stopped, eyeing Data apprehensively.

"The first dart must not have penetrated the clothes," one of them said uneasily. His words were slightly muffled by the makeshift mask, and his eyes darted to the Translator as it delivered the English version of his words.

"Or his metabolism is different," another said.

"They look like they're from totally different worlds. Take a closer look. We don't have a lot of time before they start waking up."

Still holding his weapon, the one that had spoken first eased himself forward, peering into Data's eyes, apparently looking for some indication of consciousness.

Data waited, continuing to sway limply but letting his arms float upward with seeming aimlessness but in the general direction of the one who now hovered less than a meter away. The other two, apparently less suspicious than impatient, seemed to be slightly relaxing their grips on their weapons as they began to edge forward.

Suddenly, Data's right hand whipped out, grasping the weapon while his left caught the man's arm in an unbreakable grip. Before either of the other two could realign his weapon and fire, Data jerked the first man around until he shielded Data from the other two. The man's magnetic boots came free of the floor, as did Data's, but even as they began to spin through the air, Data found the trigger of the weapon and squeezed it twice in rapid succession.

The darts struck home, and one of the two targets had just enough time to mutter something untranslatable, probably a curse, and then both were as limp as Geordi.

The third, still in Data's iron grip as they tumbled through the air, suddenly regained his voice.

142

"We mean you no harm!" he almost shouted. "The darts just knock you out for a few minutes!"

"I see," Data said, pausing as he maneuvered his body so as to bring his boots in contact with the top of one of the shuttles as it seemed to pass beneath him. "Why did you wish to render us unconscious?"

"Someone wants to talk to you, that's all!" the man said, apparently too frightened to struggle.

"We can neither talk nor listen if we are unconscious," Data pointed out as his boots touched and anchored to the shuttle. Quickly, he started down the side and back toward Geordi and the others. "Can you explain further?"

The man blinked, the fear in his face beginning to be replaced by puzzlement. "We have to—to take you to this someone," he said.

Reaching the others, Data set the man down, his boots attaching themselves to the metal floor. Stepping back and keeping the dart gun trained on the man, Data reached out with his other hand and took the weapons from the limp fingers of his companions. "Why did you feel it necessary that we be unconscious while you transported us?" Data asked.

"We had to get you away from Shar-Lon," the man said.

"Would Shar-Lon object to our talking with this individual?"

"We didn't want—" the man began, but then cut himself off sharply. "I can't say any more," he said.

Data looked at him curiously. "Do you mean that you cannot? Or merely that you will not?"

But the man only shook his head, saying nothing.

"Very well," Data said, "we will wait until my colleague awakens."

"No!" Suddenly, the man was agitated, as if he had only then remembered something. "As soon as Shar-Lon awakens, he will send his men for us!"

"I see," Data said. "Shar-Lon *would* object to our talking to this person."

For a long moment, the man was silent, his eyes going from Data to the door to Shar-Lon's elevator, as if he expected someone to come bursting through at any moment. "Yes," he said, "Shar-Lon would object."

Data glanced at Geordi, trying to imagine what the other would do. He would, of course, "play it by ear," but what would his ear tell him to do? Hurriedly, Data ran through his memories of everything Geordi had said since Shar-Lon had first appeared.

And as he did, one statement emerged: "I don't trust anyone who orates instead of talks, the way Shar-Lon does most of the time."

Therefore, if these three represented a group that opposed Shar-Lon—and armed themselves not with deadly projectile weapons but with the mechanical equivalents of phasers set on stun—it was

144

to his and Geordi's advantage to speak with that group's leader, who was, logically, the only one who could have sent these people.

For another moment, Data inspected his reasoning and decided that, though his decision had been reached by logic rather than intuition, it would be acceptable to Geordi when he awakened.

"Very well," Data said, "take us to this person who wishes to speak to us. We will not need these," he added, taking the dart guns one at a time and deliberately bending the barrels before tossing them aside. The man's eyes widened as he watched, and Data realized that, whether he had intended to or not, he had just continued "putting up the front" that Geordi had begun with Shar-Lon.

Taking his phaser in hand, Data picked up Geordi and tucked him under his arm. "If you will transport your colleagues," he said, gesturing with the phaser, "we can go to meet your leader."

His eyes widening even further, the man gripped his companions' arms and, glancing apprehensively over his shoulder at Data, pulled their magnetic boots from the metal floor and began to tow them toward the door the three had lunged through a few minutes before.

After passing through half a dozen doors and deserted, barren open spaces, they entered what was apparently the habitat's hub, a circular tube running the length of the satellite. By that time,

Geordi was beginning to come around. The other two took another couple hundred meters, by which time Geordi was awake enough to ask what had happened. By the time Data had finished explaining, they were at the far end of the habitat and the other two were fully conscious as well. Somewhere along the route, the three had, a bit sheepishly, removed their masks.

"I couldn't have done better myself," Geordi said with a faint grin when Data had finished.

Then they were beyond the main cylinder of the habitat, working their way through the maze of pipes and steam turbines in the power station. Finally, they emerged from the far end of the power station and approached the airlock that marked the end of the hub. It looked not unlike the dummy airlock in the Repository, and Geordi discreetly scanned the area for evidence of transporter circuits.

But there were none, and when the door swung open with only a faint scraping sound, Geordi saw that the outer door of the airlock was fully functional. Gesturing the other three inside, Geordi and Data followed. As the door closed behind them, faint reddish lights mounted above the door came on. Attached to the walls were a dozen bulky, old-fashioned spacesuits.

"These aren't the best," one of the three said in nervous apology, as he and his companions each began taking down a suit and putting it on, "but it's only forty or fifty meters to where we're going."

Geordi smiled slightly. "Thank you, but it won't be necessary," he said, fully activating his field-effect suit. The men's eyes widened slightly but they said nothing.

Then, after each had had his suit checked by one of the others, the air was evacuated and the outer door unsealed. Outside, a cluster of objects of varying sizes and shapes hung suspended from the framework that anchored the giant parabolic mirror. On several, Geordi could see open airlock doors, including one stubby cylinder that reminded him of one of Earth's first long-term space "houses," Skylab. Others looked like abandoned fuel tanks with airlocks grafted onto them, and yet others were larger, more complex structures, some with holes where massive airlocks had apparently been removed. Finally, he realized that this collection must be some of the "construction shacks" that had been used by the early workers on the habitat.

By then the leader of the group was directing Geordi and Data to a cable fastened at a point just outside the habitat airlock. It led directly into the heart of the cluster of long-abandoned construction shacks, and two of the men were already moving slowly along it, pulling themselves hand over hand through space.

147

Geordi, suddenly uncomfortable, motioned for the third man to start. When the man was three or four meters out, Geordi put his phaser away, uneasily gripped the cable and pulled himself free of the habitat. Weightlessness inside the habitat or even inside a shuttle had not bothered him, but here, he belatedly realized, if he lost his grip, he wouldn't simply float away and bounce off the nearest wall. Unless he was lucky enough to be floating in the direction of the habitat or one of these construction shacks, he would simply keep on floating. There were no *Enterprise* transporters here to snatch him back in, not even a tractor beam. He might even, he realized with a twinge, drift into the focus of the parabolic mirror, which would put his field-effect suit to a test its designers had probably never envisioned.

Looking back, he saw Data just behind him, his pale features reflecting only their usual interested curiosity.

Swallowing, Geordi turned and began moving forward, far more slowly and carefully than either of the men on the cable ahead of him. They moved with a casual ease that suggested they had made these same moves many times before, their only uneasiness apparently caused by the presence of Geordi and Data.

Finally, after the longest fifty meters of his life, Geordi came to the far end of the cable. It was attached to one of the Skylab-like objects, this one with an airlock even more primitive-looking than those on the habitat. The first man to reach it already had it open, and Geordi waited as all three entered.

Slowly, cautiously, Geordi worked his way from the cable into the airlock. Data followed at a more rapid pace, and then the outer door was being closed and air being pumped in.

And the inner door opened.

Inside, in Spartan surroundings that matched the Skylab-like exterior, an old man was waiting. Wearing purely utilitarian shirt and trousers not unlike those worn by the men who had accompanied them, he was roughly the same age as Shar-Lon but considerably more slender, with no more hair than Captain Picard. His eyes widened only slightly as he noted, first, the lack of standard suits on Geordi and Data, and then the fact that Geordi and Data both held their phasers while his own men were unarmed. He watched interestedly as the faint glow of the field-effect suits faded into nothingness when Geordi and Data deactivated them, once again leaving the magnetic field around the boots.

"You are the one who wished to speak with us?" Geordi asked as the three removed their helmets.

The old man nodded. "I am. And since you have come even though my men appear to have lost their weapons, can I assume you wish to speak with me as well?"

"It looks that way, doesn't it?" Geordi said, still

holding his phaser. "But we might be a little more positive if we knew what you wanted—and who you are."

"Quite right, of course." The man smiled faintly. "What I want is to simply find out who you really are—and what your purpose is in coming here. As for who I am—If I know my brother as well as I think I do, you may have already heard about me. My name is Shar-Tel."

Chapter Ten

"READY, LIEUTENANT YAR?"

"Ready, Commander Riker."

For another second, Riker and Yar, unrecognizable in their radiation suits, stood silently, their magnetized boots planted on the derelict's floor as close as possible to where Data and La Forge had been standing when the derelict's transporters had snatched them away.

"Ready, Captain," Riker said finally.

"Very well, Number One. Mr. Argyle, begin removal of core shielding."

Argyle, in Engineering, acknowledged. He sent the initiating signal to the remote units that, only hours before, had struggled to put the shielding in place.

"Lieutenant Worf," Picard said, "keep Ensign Carpelli and the away team informed of the radiation level at all times. Ensign Carpelli, be ready to pull them off the derelict the instant there's any indication of trouble."

"Ready, sir."

At the science station, Worf began intoning the radiation-level readings.

"Any activity, Number One?"

"Nothing yet, sir."

"First shield removed, Captain," Argyle reported.

"Begin removing the next, Chief."

For nearly a minute, there was only silence except for Worf's continued announcements of the radiation level.

"A light in the control panel just began flashing, sir," Riker's voice came. And, a moment later: "And now there's a map on the screen. It looks like a map of the derelict itself. Yes, I'm sure it is. And right in the center, where the antimatter must be, there's a green circle, also flashing. It's obviously an alarm system of some kind, meant to alert whoever's running things, probably whenever something too big for the computer to handle on its own comes up."

"And a message just appeared across the bottom of the screen," Yar put in. "No language I recognize. Recording for future analysis."

"Excellent, Lieutenant," Picard said. "Anything else?"

"Tricorder shows activity in the hibernation units, but nothing else."

"Radiation level approaching the intensity that

triggered transporter operation before," Worf reported.

"You heard that, Number One, Lieutenant Yar," Picard put in. "Watch yourselves."

"Yes, sir, we plan to."

"Beginning to remove third shield, sir," Argyle reported.

"Slowly, Mr. Argyle, slowly," Picard cautioned. "The radiation level is almost where we want—"

"Antimatter core output increasing rapidly, sir," Worf broke in abruptly. "Radiation level also increasing, already higher than estimated transporter trigger intensity. Either the derelict's power controls have failed again, or something has—"

"Mr. Carpelli!" Picard snapped. "Bring them back!"

"Energizing, sir," Carpelli came back instantly.

"Another transporter already in operation, sir," Worf said, "on the derelict."

"Carpelli!"

"I heard, sir! I'm trying, but interference from that other transporter is—"

"New coordinates, Mr. Carpelli!" Worf rumbled, punching a key that sent them to the transporter room instantly. "Riker and Yar are now at these coordinates. The first transporter—"

"Locking onto communicators at new coordinates now," Carpelli said tersely.

"Yar! Number One!" Picard called. "Hold on! We're bringing you back!"

But there was no response.

"Energizing!" Carpelli said again.

"Antimatter core in terminal overload sequence, sir!" Worf said. "At this distance—"

"I know, Lieutenant! Mr. Brindle! Ready to raise shields the instant Carpelli confirms the away party is back!"

"Ready, sir," Brindle responded from the tactical station.

"I've lost them!" Carpelli's agonized voice came over the intercom. "Interference from—"

"Don't explain! Just get them back!"

"I'm trying, but—"

"No time, sir," Worf broke in. "Terminal overload in five seconds!"

"I can't get them!" Carpelli shouted. "The interference—"

"Three," Worf said implacably. "Two—"

"Shields, Mr. Brindle!"

"Shields up, sir!" Brindle responded, his words overlapped by a blinding flare that filled the viewer. An instant later, the entire ship shuddered as the shields struggled to absorb the raw power of the annihilated antimatter.

And Counselor Deanna Troi, her eyes wide in pain, her knuckles white as she gripped the arms of her chair, screamed silently in her mind.

Picard's intense "Bring them back!" were the last words Riker heard before he felt the energies of the transporter grip him. An instant later, the walls of the alien vessel vanished from around him, and he waited for the main transporter room of the *Enterprise* to reappear.

But it didn't.

Instead, when he felt the transporter release its grip, indicating he had arrived at his destination, there was only utter blackness and a harsh metallic odor. But the darkness and the odor barely had time to register on his senses before the grip of the transporter reasserted itself.

And this time, shockingly, a kaleidoscope of colors erupted all around and within him, twisting and shifting in mind-wrenching patterns that he knew instinctively could not exist.

In normal space.

In that instant, Riker knew that it was not the *Enterprise* transporters that had snatched him from the disintegrating, radiation-drenched derelict.

It was the same transporter that had taken Data and La Forge—and, as Argyle had suspected, it operated, not through normal space, but through subspace.

Suddenly, even as the thoughts raced through his mind, the colors vanished.

Everything vanished, as if all five senses had been instantaneously wiped out.

Terrifyingly, even his memories began to fade, giving him only time enough to think: The derelict's transporter was destroyed while we were still in transit, and the energies that were Tasha and I are being scattered through subspace itself.

And then even that thought faded, and he existed only in the single instant that was the immediate present. He had no past and no future. He simply existed.

But then, after a time he had no way of measuring or even of comprehending, he felt something.

A tug, faint and distant, dragging him away from the nothingness that was all he could, at that moment, conceive of.

Suddenly colors flared around him again, and, an instant later, his memories flared within him, and for a moment his own returning thoughts and memories were as chaotic, as frightening as his impossible surroundings.

But then, as if he had been thrown a lifeline, a thought rose out of the chaos, and he clung to it.

And his mind cleared.

The chaos of swirling, impossible colors faded.

And as the world solidified around him, he heard a sound, and realized with a start that it was his own voice whispering a single word, over and over: *Imzadi, Imzadi, Imzadi . . .*

But the lifeline, the link that had kept his mind from being scattered irretrievably during those endless moments before the subspace transporter energies had been gathered and reintegrated into

156

the mental and physical whole that was William Riker—that lifeline was gone.

Geordi kept the surprise from his face. He wasn't sure what he had been expecting . . . but Shar-Lon's dead brother Shar-Tel was definitely not it.

"As a matter of fact, your brother did say you were dead," Geordi said. "Right after I asked him if I could talk to you. I take it he has a reason for not wanting that to happen?"

"He would have," the man said, his smile turning grim, "if he knew I was still alive."

"He doesn't know?"

"I'm reasonably certain he doesn't. But that's a very long story, and before we get into it, I'd like you to answer a question."

"If I can, and if you'll answer a few of ours."

"Gladly," Shar-Tel said, "Now, my question: *Are* you the people who left that thing orbiting our planet? And if so, what is it, and *why* did you leave it?"

"Your brother believed we were the ones," Geordi said, still cautious.

"My brother, unfortunately, believes a great many things these days, not the least of which is that he was deliberately chosen to save our world, using that thing we stumbled across."

"And you don't?"

"Do I look like a fool?"

Suddenly, for reasons he couldn't explain to

157

himself, let alone to Data if he should ask, Geordi laughed. Maybe it was nothing more than the fact that the man's slender build and almost hairless scalp, not to mention his suddenly sharp tone, reminded him of Captain Picard—or, rather, Captain Picard as he might be in another thirty years— and that reminder made him feel good.

"No, we're not the ones who left it here," Geordi admitted. "As for what it is, that's something we'd very much like to know ourselves. We have a few wild guesses, but that's about all. Anything you can tell us would be greatly appreciated."

Shar-Tel frowned for a second, but then he grinned and turned to the others. "You'd better get back, before my brother misses you and starts making some guesses as to what you've been up to," he said. "He didn't recognize you, did he?"

"No, he didn't see our faces. But Vol-Mir may have some explaining to do. He had to improvise something to keep Shar-Lon occupied long enough for us to get in position, and he said Shar-Lon was more than a little suspicious when the 'emergency' turned out to be a false alarm."

Shar-Tel grimaced. "Don't compound the problem. Get back there, now. I'll be all right."

The men nodded and, with varying degrees of relief, replaced their helmets and reentered the airlock. As it hissed shut behind them, Shar-Tel said: "I suspect your story is as long as mine, so we had better get down to business."

158

"Before we get too involved," Geordi said, "I have a question myself. Can you or your people take us back to the Repository when we're finished here?"

Shar-Tel's frown returned and his eyes darted toward the closed airlock. "Why?"

"So we can try to find our way back to where we belong."

"Oh? Does that mean you didn't come here intentionally?"

"Geordi," Data interrupted, clicking off his Translator.

Geordi hesitated, noting the suspicious look that was growing more pronounced on Shar-Tel's face. Then, leaving his Translator on, he said, "What is it, Data?"

The android, in almost a parody of a significant glance, aimed his golden eyes momentarily at Geordi's Translator.

"It's all right, Data. I think we can trust Shar-Tel."

Data considered the situation. "Ah," he said, "I believe I understand. Does this mean we are no longer 'putting up a front'?"

Geordi shook his head, smiling ruefully. "That's right," he said. "I'm still playing it by ear, and right now, my ear tells me to drop the front."

Data considered another moment, then switched his Translator back on. "That is good. 'Putting up a front' is not easy."

"From that little exchange," Shar-Tel said, "can I assume you have not been entirely truthful with my brother?"

"Not entirely. But you haven't answered my question. *Can* you take us to the Repository when we're through?"

"I think some of my people can get you there, yes."

"But you're not sure?"

"Let's see how my brother reacts to being knocked out and having the two of you disappear. I think it would be best if, when we are through talking and you understand the situation, you return to my brother and let him take you to the Repository. It would be less dangerous for all of us."

"Dangerous? You mean like when someone tried to shoot us in the Repository airlock when we were being taken to see your brother?"

Shar-Tel's face darkened into a scowl, directed not at them but at himself. "I'm sorry," he said. "I can see what you must have thought when my men fired those knockout darts at you. If I'd known— Considering the apparent ease with which you disarmed them, can I assume they're lucky to be alive?"

Geordi started to shrug, intending to let Shar-Tel draw his own conclusions, but then he stopped. "No," he said. "Our phasers were set on stun— that is to say, they would have had about the same

160

effect that your dart guns did. We don't use lethal force unless absolutely necessary."

"Phasers? Those are your weapons? Could you—" Shar-Tel broke off sharply, shaking his head. "I'm wasting time on details," he said. "Tell me, since you let my brother believe you were his mystical 'Builders,' did he ask you to speak to his Council? Did he say that he wanted everyone to see and hear you, so they could thank you for having delivered our world from certain destruction?"

"Something like that, yes."

"And I assume he also told you how he was given the 'Signs' and was found worthy of being admitted to the Repository? And then was granted the privilege of saving the world? With the 'Gifts' he found there?"

"Pretty much. Are you saying it isn't true?"

Shar-Tel sighed. "Unfortunately, what he said is true, in a distorted sort of way."

"And you plan to tell us the undistorted version?"

"I suppose I had better, if all you've heard is my brother's version."

Taking in a deep breath, Shar-Tel began. "As he told you, it was fifty years ago when he and I stumbled onto that abandoned alien vessel orbiting our planet. Who put it there or why, or why they abandoned it, or what caused the 'visions of blood' or whatever they were, I have no idea. I'd hoped you might know, since you are said to have ap-

161

peared out of nowhere inside the vessel, but you say you don't, and I can only take you at your word."

"We think the 'visions of blood,' as you call them, were caused by the failure of whatever kind of cloaking device the vessel was equipped with," Geordi volunteered. "When a cloaking device is working properly, it makes a ship invisible, but when one begins to fail, almost anything can happen. All wavelengths can be red-shifted, which is probably what happened here, or certain wavelengths could be blocked while others are passed."

"So it was just luck that the world turned red instead of blue or green?"

"Probably," Geordi said, nodding, and Shar-Tel laughed sharply.

"I wonder what kind of symbolism my brother would've read into a world turned yellow or purple!" the old man said, and then looked at them with a new intensity. "What else can you tell me?"

"Virtually nothing else," Geordi said, shrugging. "All we know for certain is that the vessel orbiting your planet appears to be linked by one-way transporters—matter transmitters—to another abandoned vessel somewhere in interstellar space, one that had been abandoned more than ten thousand years ago. We *think* that at one time there were several more of these 'Repositories,' as you call them, scattered all over this part of the galaxy, orbiting planets similar to yours."

"And the reason for these vessels being where they are?" Shar-Tel asked.

"All we have are wild guesses on that point," Geordi said, ignoring Data's briefly questioning look. "In any event, we were exploring that other ship when one of its transporters was accidentally activated, sending us here. And all the two of us want right now is to find a way to return to that other ship, or to find out where we are and figure out a way to get word back to our own ship to let them know where we are so we can be picked up."

Shar-Tel was silent a moment, the intensity in his eyes turning to a hunger, a curiosity that Geordi had seen in Captain Picard's eyes more than once when they were approaching an unknown world. The old man obviously wanted to ask a thousand questions, but, with an equally obvious effort, he forced his mind to concentrate on more practical matters.

"Ten thousand years," he said finally. "After that much time, is it safe to assume that whoever abandoned these vessels will not be coming back?"

"It's unlikely," Geordi said, "but I learned a long time ago that nothing is impossible."

Shar-Tel nodded with a faint smile. "Yes, I have little doubt of that anymore myself. But we digress. Again. After Shar-Lon and I found the alien vessel, there was no stopping him. A discovery like that was not the sort of thing that any

163

individual should go charging into blindly, and I insisted we notify our government, immediately, so they could send up some qualified scientists to investigate it properly—or make contact, if there were living beings in it. At that point, we didn't even know it *was* a derelict. It could have had a dozen aliens in it, ready to blast us at any second.

"But my brother wouldn't listen. I don't know what kind of embellishments he's added to his story recently to explain his actions, but as far as I've ever been able to tell, he was simply full of the same kind of wild impatience that had prompted him to join the Peacekeeper organization when he was in school and then to desert it two years later, when it didn't move fast enough or effectively enough for him. Whenever he became involved with something, he wanted to *do*, not plan. And then, when one of our one-time enemies intercepted my communications and learned that Shar-Lon was inside a newly discovered alien spacecraft, presumably getting his hands on all kinds of advanced alien technology, someone panicked and launched a missile at the Repository."

Shar-Tel paused, grimacing. "Or possibly I'm being unfair. After fifty years, my own memory may have become a bit biased and selective. But regardless of his motives, my brother managed to slip out of our shuttle, taking my spacesuit with him, and somehow get inside the alien ship." A sudden light came into Shar-Tel's eyes. "It must have been those things you call transporters—which must also be what he uses to make himself vanish whenever he gets in a tight situation, such as when my men used a dart gun on him just now."

Geordi nodded. "He must have some kind of remote-control linkage with the Repository. And you're right about how people get in and out of the Repository. There's apparently a short-range transporter that moves things in and out of the vessel itself. The 'airlock' is a dummy, built over the transporter circuitry. I assume your brother built it to keep the real method of entry a secret?"

"He did. Before he let anyone else even approach. I don't know how he was able to do it, any more than I know how he was able to find every nuclear missile everywhere on the planet and then detonate them nearly half a million kilometers out in space. All he's ever told anyone is that his 'powers come from the Gifts.' Like these 'transporters' you were talking about."

"I'm afraid it would take more than just transporters to do some of the things he seems to have done. Or at least more than the kind of transporters we're familiar with."

Shar-Tel frowned. "You're saying that whoever built these vessels is even more advanced than you?"

"In some ways, apparently yes."

Shar-Tel was silent a moment, as if absorbing the unwelcome information, but then, abruptly, he continued his interrupted story. "After the missiles were all destroyed, the world went crazy, almost literally. To a lot of people, my brother was a savior, almost a god, especially to a few hundred of the more fanatical members of the Peacekeepers. And to tell the truth, I can't really blame anyone for feeling that way. The world had been living with the threat of nuclear war for decades, and suddenly, all because of what he did, the threat was gone, virtually overnight."

"He said there were a few who were against it," Geordi said, "a few who bitterly resented not being able to kill each other by the millions anymore. He said it was people like that who tried to kill us. And *did* kill you."

Shar-Tel shook his head. "It's nowhere near that simple. As I said, a lot of people thought my brother saved the world, and I have to admit that it's conceivable that we might have wiped ourselves out if we'd been left alone, but I seriously doubt it. We'd managed to muddle through nearly seventy years without someone pushing the wrong button, and we *were* making progress. We'd hit the peak in the number of warheads a decade before, and we were actually on the way down. And more conventional wars were winding down each year than were breaking out, so it looked like we'd peaked there, too. There had even been talk of a World Council. Until my brother took charge."

Shar-Tel paused, shaking his head again. "There

166

were a lot of people—there are quite a few even now—who think that he was 'possessed' by an alien sprit when he got inside the Repository. It was a—a 'trap' left there by the aliens, the so-called Builders, and it caught my brother and took him over."

"But if all he did was destroy all the nuclear missiles on all sides, why would anyone think—"

"Because that *isn't* all he did!" Shar-Tel flared, his anger suddenly erupting. "He turned our world into a prison planet! And for the last fifty years, he's been justifying it by spouting that nonsense about being 'chosen'!"

With an effort, Shar-Tel paused and pulled in a calming breath. "Before he went into the Repository, he may have been wildly impatient and suicidally impulsive, but beyond that, he was as normal as anyone else. Like me, he knew it was simply an alien ship of some kind he was entering, not some mystical object put there for his personal use. But when he came out, after the missiles were all destroyed, and there was no way anyone could get at him, he was talking the way he's still talking today. Personally, I think it was just too much for him to take, mentally. Suddenly, he had all the power he had ever dreamed of having, and he couldn't accept responsibility for it, for what he was doing with it. So he invented a 'higher authority' to take the credit—or blame."

Data's golden eyes widened slightly. "You are

saying that your brother, who holds that his enemies suffer from delusions, has himself been the victim of a delusion?"

Shar-Tel shrugged. "Either that or he really *is* possessed. All I know is, he changed. Or *was* changed. And he turned what he had done into a religion, with himself as its prophet. He wouldn't allow scientists—or anyone else—into the vessel so they could try to find out how the 'Gifts' worked. He collected the hard core of the Peacekeepers and 'anointed' them, saying they were his 'messengers of peace.' But then one of them got himself killed, which wasn't all that surprising, considering how a lot of people felt about Shar-Lon by then. And when that happened, my brother forced everyone out of the space stations that a dozen nations had been occupying for decades, and he 'gave' those stations to any of that bunch that wanted them. Somehow—those transporters again, I assume— he pulled the regular crews out and put his inner circle of Peacekeepers in. He even pulled the stations out of their orbits and collected them all here, around his 'Repository.'"

So the 'Gifts' include tractor beams, Geordi thought. *And maybe phasers as well?*

"This is part of one of the earliest stations right here," Shar-Lon said, gesturing at the structure they were in. "And then, once he had the others all gathered around him, so to speak, he demanded that this so-called 'World of the Peacekeepers' be built. It was *supposed* to be just the first of several space colonies, 'stepping-stones to the stars,' he called them, so a lot of people who hadn't seen through my brother yet were in favor of the project, for a lot of reasons, at least when it started. The whole fleet of shuttles from all the nations was used, and, somehow, it got built. But then, just when it had been completed, someone put a bomb—a conventional bomb, not a nuclear one, which is apparently the only kind the 'Gifts' are able to detect—in one of the shuttles and tried to blow my brother and his entire world up.

"So *he* blew up the *shuttles,* every last one of them, and no one has been allowed off the planet's surface since. No one has even *tried* for the last twenty years. And he transferred all the Peacekeepers from the other space stations to his newly built world, and there they've stayed ever since. There's room for five or ten thousand, but there are fewer than a thousand of them, including second and third generations, all born and raised up here. For a while, he tried bringing other Peacekeepers up, but by that time there were very few left on the planet's surface that would admit to being one. And when some imposters were sent up, and they tried to sabotage things, he discontinued it.

"Since then, virtually everyone down there would gladly slit all our throats if only they could reach us. Nations have gone back to fighting each other, even more often than before. And if things continue this way in the future, our whole race will just stagnate here. No one will ever be allowed off the planet's surface. So you can see why I sometimes almost take the 'possession' idea seriously. If whoever left the Repository here simply wanted to keep us confined to our own planet, they couldn't find anything more effective than what my brother's been doing for the last fifty years. Unless they simply blasted us back to the stone age with their weapons."

"And you and your group?" Geordi asked when Shar-Tel fell silent. "Where do you fit in? Your brother said you had joined him willingly."

Shar-Tel sighed. "Halfway through the project, yes, but it was solely in hopes of being able to eventually talk some sense into him, or at least keep him from getting even further from reality than he already was. Needless to say, I failed miserably. As for my 'group,' it's a few dozen second- and third-generation Peacekeepers. With my help, more and more of them are beginning to ask questions and realize that, no matter what my brother did fifty years ago, things have been messed up pretty badly ever since. Now, we are all united—those of us up here, those on the planet below—in our desire to bring peace to the world. A peace that won't have been forced on us by an alien technology, and a possessed madman. A peace that, instead, will come from an elimination of rabid nationalism and militarism; an evolution beyond our minds' calamitous territorial impulses."

"From what you've said, there are good reasons for people to want to kill your brother, but why us?"

"As I said, there are fewer than a thousand people here, but even so there are almost as many different kinds as there are down on the planet. There are a few, for instance, who live in constant fear that the 'Builders' will someday return and 'punish' us for breaking into their property. It wouldn't surprise me if your would-be assassin is one of those. He may have decided to shoot first and ask questions later. And there's Kel-Nar, who's interested in only one thing—becoming my brother's heir, which means he has to talk my brother into teaching him how the 'Gifts' work. I can't imagine why he would want to kill you, but anything is possible. And there are the ones my brother calls 'deluded,' meaning they've made the mistake of letting him know that they see him for what he is, a paranoid dictator who's virtually killing the planet he insists he saved. I suppose one of them might've been afraid you would give him even *more* power than he already has."

"Then why haven't they killed *him?*"

"They *have* tried, more than once, but he's normally very careful, much more careful than he has been today. I was surprised to hear that he came out of his private quarters to take you on your tour, let alone that he planned to ferry you back to the Repository. Normally, except on the view-screens he gives his speeches on, he's pretty much invisible. I suspect that your coming has rattled him considerably—especially if you convinced him you were really the Builders. He's been desperate to meet you—them—for forty years, but he's also almost certainly terrified of it. Despite what he says in public, I've always been convinced that there's one little corner of his mind that knows what he did after he destroyed the missiles was terribly wrong. If I hadn't thought that—and thought that I had a chance to reach him and somehow convince him of it—I never would have joined him in the first place. I think that a part of him has been deathly afraid all along that if the 'Builders' returned, they would see how wrong he was, too. So, now that you have showed up and impersonated the 'Builders'—"

"Except that we told him what a great job he'd been doing," Geordi said. "Although, come to think of it, we didn't guarantee that our 'superiors' would approve. And we told him we'd come specifically to check up on his use of the Gifts. But you're probably right about his own doubts. That would at least partially explain why he seems to have been in a complete emotional turmoil since the moment he first spoke to us." Geordi recounted what his infrared observations of Shar-Lon had shown him.

Shar-Tel nodded. "It sounds as if he's closer to a

breakdown than ever, which makes my reason for talking to you all the more urgent. Although, since you're not the 'Builders' after all, you may not be able to help."

"What *do* you want from us?" Geordi asked. In infrared, Shar-Tel was starting to look pretty tense himself.

Shar-Tel grimaced. "I'd better just come out with it," he said, pausing again to pull in a deep breath. Can you—*will* you—destroy the Repository?"

Chapter Eleven

"CARPELLI! DID YOU get them?" Picard's voice sliced through the chaos as the *Enterprise* continued to shudder in the aftermath of the massive antimatter explosion.

For a long moment, as the flare of the almost-overloaded shields faded and the ship regained its stability, there was no answer, only the insistent alarms and the ship's own responses, more rapid and more effective than any human's could ever be.

And then, instead of Ensign Carpelli replying from the main transporter room, Counselor Troi, unclenching her fingers from where they had bitten into the arms of her chair, said: "They are gone."

Picard spun toward her. "What's that, Counselor?"

"They are gone," she repeated. "I felt them go, an instant before the explosion."

"Go? They were killed, you mean?"

She shook her head. "I do not know, but I do not think so. There was something else, a moment *after* the explosion. I cannot be certain—the emotions of the crew were almost blinding me—but I believe I sensed Commander Riker."

"But surely you would recognize—"

"I *would,* and I *did,* but there was something different, something distorted." She shook her head. "I cannot describe it any better, Captain."

"But you feel they *were* alive after the explosion?"

"I do."

"Ensign Carpelli!" Picard snapped, turning from the Counselor. "Respond!"

"I'm sorry, sir," Carpelli's subdued voice came back finally. "I couldn't get them back after they were transported to those new coordinates. There simply wasn't time. The interference—"

Picard cut him off. "Lieutenant Worf, you had them on the sensors. What happened? Were they relayed out of there before the explosion?"

"Reviewing the readings now, sir," Worf said, leaning over the science stations. "It's impossible to be certain, sir. Their life-form readings appear to have vanished almost a half second before the explosion, but if they were still in transit when the transporter was destroyed—"

"I know, Lieutenant. They may have been transmitted, but not received." Picard was unable to totally suppress a shiver.

"Yes, sir," Worf rumbled. "That is a possibility."

"But it is also a possibility that they were successfully transported to the same place as Lieutenant LaForge and Commander Data. Is there *anything* within sensor range?"

"Nothing that wasn't there before, sir, except for the energy and particles of the exploded derelict."

"Very well." Abruptly Picard turned toward the tactical station. "Lieutenant Brindle, try to raise them on their subspace transceivers."

"Already trying, sir. No response as yet."

"Keep trying. What range—"

"Impossible to predict precisely, sir. With the irregularities in subspace—"

"A guess, then, Mr. Brindle," Picard snapped.

"A hundred parsecs at the very least, sir, possibly many times that, depending on the local subspace configuration.

"Thank you, Mr. Brindle," Picard acknowledged, then turned abruptly to the conn. "Ensign Gawelski, lay in a course that will take us to every star system within five parsecs in as short a time as possible. We're beginning another search. It will continue until either we find them or we contact them via subspace."

"Aye, sir, plotting course now."

"Counselor Troi, if you sense anything further, anything at all, no matter how vague or uncertain or distorted, that could possibly be connected with Commander Riker—or Lieutenant Yar—let me know instantly. Is that understood?"

"Understood, Captain."

"Course plotted and laid in, sir," Gawelski reported.

"Then get under way, Mr. Gawelski. Maximum warp, now!"

And the search began.

"I am *not* your *'Imzadi,'* Commander Riker!" Lieutenant Tasha Yar's voice, muffled by the hood of the radiation suit, held a mixture of annoyance and embarrassment.

Blinking, Riker clamped his lips tightly together as he realized that his involuntary whispers must have been more audible than, in those first disoriented moments, he had thought.

Forcing the remaining traces of nausea and dizziness away, he took a second to steady himself and let his surroundings—still weightless, he realized —come into focus. He and Yar were in—what? Another derelict? There was virtually nothing in the room except a massive airlock, something that looked like a hibernation chamber on a waist-high pedestal, a viewscreen that took up the upper half of one wall, and an uncomfortable-looking chair bolted to what was apparently meant to be the floor.

Yar, he saw, had removed her hood and was scanning the room intently, her tricorder in one hand, her phaser rifle in the other.

"Sorry," he began, removing his own hood, but she abruptly gestured for silence with the tricorder.

Wordlessly, she pointed at the hibernation chamber, and Riker glanced at his own tricorder. There was a humanoid life form directly behind the pedestal.

Nodding, he raised his own phaser rifle, and the two moved slowly apart, toward positions that would give them a view of the far side of the pedestal from opposite directions.

But before they had gone more than a meter, an old man in a garishly bright yellow uniform stood up abruptly and stepped into full view, his hands held out from his sides, palms open and empty.

And he began to talk, nervously but deliberately. Within a minute, the Translators had picked up enough from the words and mind of the old man to begin to do their job.

"Where are the two who were here earlier?" Yar broke in sharply, ignoring the partial translations of the old man's words.

The old man, already nervous, looked as if he were going to faint at her words. "I do not know, I swear!" the man said. "At their request, I was returning them here, to your Repository, so they could make their preliminary report to you, when we were attacked!"

"Attacked?" Yar waved the phaser rifle menacingly. "What happened to them?"

The man cringed. "I can only assume they were captured, but—"

"Captured? By whom? Why?"

"By my enemies—by *your* enemies!"

"We *have* no enemies here!" Yar snapped, giving the phaser rifle another menacing twitch. "Or we *didn't*—until our friends were attacked and kidnapped! Explain!"

Trembling, the old man, who said his name was Shar-Lon, did his best, using the viewscreen to show them the planet and the habitat. Impatiently, Yar prodded him along whenever he began to lapse into oratory, and within a few minutes she and Riker had a rough idea of the situation. For the moment, they said nothing to contradict the story that Data and La Forge had improvised. Yar's aggressive, no-nonsense approach in fact only seemed to reinforce the story, particularly the part about the "impatient superiors" waiting in the wings.

"Before the darts rendered me totally unconscious," Shar-Lon finished, "I was able to mentally activate that aspect of your Gifts that is capable of returning me instantly to your Repository. I regained my senses only moments before you yourselves appeared. I only regret I was unable to bring your colleagues safely with me."

"Lieutenant Yar," Riker said, gesturing at her Translator as he snapped off his own.

Briskly, she followed suit. "I can probably locate their communicators with the tricorder if they're within range," she said.

"Get on it then, Lieutenant," he said as he

unsnapped the cover of the radiation suit's utility pouch and extracted the subspace transceiver. "While you do, I'll contact the *Enterprise* and hope that they can home in on our signal."

"Aye, sir," Yar acknowledged briskly, making the necessary adjustments to her tricorder. As she did, Riker snapped on the transceiver, preset to the frequency the *Enterprise* would be listening for.

"Enterprise, this is Commander Riker."

But there was no response.

"Lieutenant," he said after his fourth unsuccessful attempt, "try your transceiver."

Wordlessly, she stowed the tricorder and took out her transceiver and flicked it on.

But she had no better luck than Riker.

As she frowned and tried a second, then a third time, Riker brought out his tricorder, adjusted a series of control settings, and played it first over his own transceiver and then Yar's.

Yar looked up at him sharply. "What is it?"

Turning the tricorder so she could see the screen, he shook his head. "They're both dead," he said. "Every subspace circuit is burned out. We're as cut off from the *Enterprise* as Data and La Forge."

"Destroy the Repository?" Geordi frowned as he looked at Shar-Tel.

"You've seen my brother. You know what he's done," Shar-Tel said. "What the effects of the

180

Builders' technology have been." Shar-Tel looked pleadingly at Geordi. "Help us save our world!" he pleaded.

Geordi shook his head. His instincts—and his infrared observations of the man—led him to think that Shar-Tel was telling the truth, but how complete a truth was it? Shar-Lon, too, had told the truth, as he saw it, but it had been woefully incomplete and badly misleading.

Geordi frowned. "I can see your point. But are you sure you want to destroy the Repository? There's a lot of information there, if you can just get control of it away from your brother and get some scientists in there."

Shar-Tel shook his head. "If it were possible to get control away from my brother, his deputy Kel-Nar would have done it long ago, and that would have made the situation even worse."

"I take it you are not an admirer of this Kel-Nar."

"My brother at least has a conscience. I'm almost positive it was Kel-Nar who tried to kill me ten years ago, when he thought I might be getting too influential with my brother. He planted an explosive device in the shuttle he knew I would use when I finally decided to take up my brother's invitation to see the inside of the Repository. But it misfired, and I found it. I also finally realized just how ruthless—and persuasive—Kel-Nar really is, and that I didn't have a chance of convincing my brother of the truth. I'm virtually certain Kel-Nar had already killed a half dozen people, including anyone on the staff that got in his way."

"So you decided to let Kel-Nar think he had succeeded in getting rid of you?"

I knew my brother wouldn't believe me if I told him about Kel-Nar—and I knew Kel-Nar would just try for me again. Letting him think he had succeeded the first time seemed the only way to save my life. And I had enough friends by then who saw things my way and were willing to hide me out."

"Aren't you afraid we'll tell your brother all this when we're returned?"

He shrugged. "If you tell him, you tell him. After hearing him and hearing me, I have to assume you'll—"

"Geordi," Data broke in abruptly, "someone is coming." He was carefully monitoring his tricorder. "A single life form, and it appears to be following the same route that we followed to reach this place."

"Were you expecting someone, Shar-Tel?" Geordi asked.

"No one," the old man said, beginning to frown worriedly. "Did my brother give you something to carry? Something he could use to follow you?"

"Not that I know of," Geordi said, but a second later Data made a series of rapid adjustments to the tricorder and turned it first on himself, then Geordi.

His golden eyes narrowed slightly. He leaned forward and plucked a tiny wafer, barely half a centimeter across, from the back of Geordi's uniform. "This has been emitting an extremely low-power, modulated electromagnetic signal," he said. "From the pattern of the modulation, I suspect it is transmitting our words to whoever has the—"

Cursing harshly, Shar-Tel snatched the tiny disk from Data, placed it on the floor, and, holding his body in place by gripping a pair of handholds next to the door, crushed it with a solid blow of his heel.

And as the device was smashed, Geordi remembered. When they had entered the Repository airlock with the three, in the darkness just before the one had pulled a gun, one of the others had brushed against Geordi. He had thought at the time it was simply the result of dizziness or disorientation caused by the total darkness and weightlessness, but now it was clear that it had been more than that.

"The outer airlock—" Geordi began, but even as the words emerged, he heard the hiss of the airlock being evacuated.

Shar-Tel, launching himself swiftly and expertly through the zero G despite his age, reached the airlock before either Geordi or Data, but he was too late to reverse the evacuation. Once it was started, it proceeded to completion automatically. Whoever was out there would be inside the airlock in a minute or less.

"Who is it?" Geordi asked.

Shar-Tel scowled. "Someone working for Kel-Nar, of course. Or possibly Kel-Nar himself. Now that he knows he botched it last time, he's going to finish the job."

Geordi and Data drew their phasers and moved backward, anchoring their boots to the metal deck. Data, still holding the tricorder in his other hand, watched the display screen as they waited.

But the hiss of air reentering the airlock did not come.

"An electronic device is being placed on the far side of the inner door," Data said, looking up from his tricorder. "It appears to be a timer of some kind."

A pause, and then: "The life form is leaving."

But the outer door did not close. The clank that would have been transmitted through the metal of the airlock itself did not come. And when Shar-Tel tried to refill the airlock, the controls would not respond. The outer door was still open.

"Explosives!" Shar-Tel said. "That's what the timer is for. Kel-Nar is going to blow us up, just like he tried to blow me up ten years ago!"

"Burned out?" Yar frowned angrily at the offending transceivers. "They were in perfect working order on the *Enterprise.* I checked them both personally, sir."

"I don't doubt you did, Lieutenant," Riker said, "but they're dead now. They were probably burned out when we transported. Chief Argyle warned us the transporter might operate through subspace, not normal space."

And unfortunately he was right, Yar thought grimly. The distance they had obviously traveled proved that. And the energies involved in a transporter would have to be massively greater than those a transceiver normally handles. The very presence of those energies must have overloaded the transceiver circuits, the same way a nearby lightning strike could overload and burn out an old-fashioned electronic circuit.

They were cut off from the *Enterprise.*

She shook her head. The thought that it wasn't possible flashed through her mind, the thought that something like this simply couldn't happen to the crew of a Federation starship.

But the uselessness of such a thought struck her almost instantly. No matter how much she sometimes wished that the Federation and its officers were infallible, she knew that it simply wasn't possible. No organization and no person could be prepared for *every* eventuality. Mistakes and oversights were made, or, as now, something totally unforeseen—totally out of the experience of anyone in the Federation—shot down an otherwise faultless plan.

And even as the thought was being discarded, she was resuming her search with the tricorder. And this time, almost instantly, she located the communicators. Deftly manipulating the controls, she found that Commander Data and Lieutenant La Forge—or whoever was now carrying their communicators—were with a third humanoid life form. Hundreds of other similar life forms clustered in a cylindrical pattern nearby—the habitat Shar-Lon had showed them on the screen, she assumed.

"I've got them, Commander," she said, studying the tricorder screen.

"Excellent, Lieutenant." Clicking on his Translator, he scanned the screen of her tricorder and noted the control settings.

"Shar-Lon," he began, turning to the old man, who had been standing virtually motionless since the Translators had been turned off. Shar-Lon twitched at the sound of his name but said nothing, only looked penitently toward Riker.

"Show us the habitat—the World of the Peacekeepers—again," Riker said, gesturing at the viewscreen.

Ducking his head in a move that was less a bow than a twitch, Shar-Lon turned and hastily replaced the control helmet on his head. Within seconds, the habitat reappeared.

"There," Yar said, pointing at the area around the power station at the focus of the kilometer-wide mirror. "Can you show us that area in greater detail?"

Wordlessly, Shar-Lon complied, and the power station and a cluster of what looked like discarded parts of satellites and even full-fledged space stations expanded to fill the screen.

"They're somewhere in there, Commander, together with a third humanoid life form, presumably one of the kidnappers. At this distance, and without knowing the exact locations of the hundreds of others within the habitat, it's impossible to pinpoint their exact location."

"Shar-Lon," Riker said, "does that location mean anything to you? Do you know why the kidnappers would take our men to that particular place?"

The old man shook his head violently. "I understand none of this!"

"Can this machine," Yar asked, gesturing at the viewscreen, "show us inside those structures?"

"No, as you surely must know—"

Suddenly, soundlessly, an explosion blossomed on the screen.

A sudden wave of unbelieving fear, not for herself but for her two fellow crewmen, wrenched at Yar's stomach.

Chapter Twelve

"Do you have a spacesuit in here?" Geordi asked abruptly as he adjusted his phaser for maximum intensity and minimum dispersion.

Shar-Tel shook his head. "The only one is in the airlock. If they left it."

"Damn! Our field-effect suits will protect *us* when we cut through the door, but you—"

"You can cut through solid steel? That quickly?"

"Probably, yes," Geordi said, "but the vacuum—"

"Save yourselves, then," Shar-Tel said unhesitatingly. "There is no point in all of us dying—if you two can live."

Geordi looked at the old man, a lump suddenly forming in his throat. Once again, Shar-Tel reminded him uncannily of Captain Picard, and the thought of letting him die—

"Geordi," Data said quickly, "I think I have a solution." As he spoke, he took the field-effect unit from his own belt and held it out to Shar-Tel. "I can survive and function in a vacuum for considerably longer than a human, certainly long enough to reach the habitat airlock."

The old man looked questioningly at Geordi. "Is this true?"

Geordi nodded, angry for not having thought of it himself. "It is. Take it."

Flicking on his own suit, Geordi turned to the airlock. With the tricorder, he located the electronic timing device, very near the center of the door. Behind him, Data showed Shar-Tel how to activate the field-effect suit.

"But you—" the old man began to object again.

"I will almost certainly survive without sustaining serious damage," Data reaffirmed. "My body is not fully organic, as are yours and Geordi's. It can therefore withstand greater stresses for greater lengths of time."

"But if the suit is still in the airlock when we get there, Data," Geordi said, "get into it. There's no point in taking any more risks than absolutely necessary."

"Of course, Geordi," Data agreed, and then stood back as Shar-Tel was suddenly enveloped in the auralike glow of the field-effect suit.

"You say this will protect me as well as my own suit?" the old man asked, his voice slightly muffled by the envelope of energy, his tone still slightly skeptical.

"Perhaps better, at least for the short term,"

Data confirmed, and then turned to join Geordi at the airlock door.

Using his Visored senses to locate the bolts that barred the door, Geordi pointed one out to Data and raised his own phaser to the other. Holding their phasers less than thirty centimeters from the door's surface, they pressed the firing studs.

For a half minute, then a full minute, there was only the fizzing crackle of the phaser beams as they ate into the metal. Then, suddenly, the air began to hiss out as the seal was broken.

But the phasers burned on, and by the time the bolts were fully cut through, the vacuum inside was nearly as complete as that on the outside.

Data, seemingly unaffected except for a slight puffiness of his features, gripped the door and swung it inward in eerie silence.

Tapping Data on the arm, Geordi gestured forcefully at the spacesuit still hanging in the open airlock. As Data floated through the door, Geordi turned his attention to the timer and the explosives. Ignoring the incomprehensible blue-green symbols flickering in a tiny window on the timer, he quickly located the wires that would, when time ran out, carry the detonation current to the circular cake of explosive, but before he could tear them loose, Shar-Tel was next to him, gripping his arm.

"What is it?" Geordi asked puzzledly, the sound of his voice carrying thinly through the temporary link between the field-effect suits.

Pointing at the flickering symbols, Shar-Tel said, "There are nearly ten minutes left. That will be more than enough time to reach the airlock and—"

"You want to let it explode?"

"It might be safer if whoever did this thinks he succeeded."

Geordi glanced at the cluttered interior. "What about your supplies? Everything you have here will be destroyed."

"I have nothing here. This is a meeting place, not a dwelling."

"Then where—"

"I will take you there. If we do not continue debating until we *are* blown up."

Taking his hand from Geordi's arm, Shar-Tel broke the connection and moved past him toward Data, who had just donned the spacesuit. With a last apprehensive look at the flickering green symbols and the explosive, Geordi followed.

On this return trip, Geordi moved more rapidly along the cable than he had on the way out, and the three of them were inside the airlock with minutes to spare. Data quickly removed his spacesuit and hung it with the others that lined the lock. Geordi's infrared vision showed that one of the suits had been recently used, but there was no way of telling who had been wearing it. Inside the hub, then, Data brought out his tricorder.

"Humanoid life form at the far end of the hub," he said, "almost to the sunward endcap."

"That's him," Geordi said. "Almost back to where he can be seen by witnesses when the explosion goes off. Let's go."

The three were making their way through the pipes and turbines of the power station when it came, a brief, muffled shock, like a soundless earthquake. There was silence as the three looked back in the direction of the airlock.

Suddenly, both Geordi's and Data's communicators came to life. "Commander Data, Lieutenant La Forge," Riker's crisp baritone came through sharply, urgently. "Respond immediately."

"I *knew* the captain wouldn't give up!" Geordi almost shouted, and then he slapped at his communicator insignia. "This is Lieutenant La Forge, sir. Data and I—"

"Are you all right, Geordi? Data? We saw the explosion."

"Where are you?" Lieutenant Yar's voice broke in.

"Data and I are back inside the habitat, in the power station," Geordi said, "and we're fine—now that *you're* here. But before you beam us up—"

"I'm sorry, Lieutenant," Riker broke in, "but we can't beam anyone up. The *Enterprise* isn't here, just Lieutenant Yar and myself."

"Not here? Then how—" Abruptly, Geordi stopped. "The derelict," he said, his exuberance of a moment before replaced by a new apprehension. "It got *you*, too?"

"It did," Riker said, then went on to explain what they had been attempting and what they had overheard from the *Enterprise* during those last seconds before they had been caught by the derelict's transporters. "We can't be positive," Riker concluded, "but the odds are that the derelict was destroyed."

A leaden feeling gripped Geordi's stomach. "Then even if we *were* able to reverse the transporter, we still couldn't get back."

"Probably not, but that's no reason not to try. With Shar-Lon's help, we may—"

"You've met Shar-Lon? He was with us when—"

"When you were attacked," Riker broke in. "He told us what happened. He's here in the—the 'Repository' with us. He was here when we arrived. But who attacked you? And are they the ones who set off that explosion?"

"No, that was someone else. We can't be positive, but—" Geordi's words came to an abrupt but momentary halt. "It might not be a bad idea to turn your Translators off," he said, quickly checking his communicator to make sure it would pick up only his own voice and nothing from his own Translator or from Shar-Tel. Data, noting Geordi's action, followed suit.

"They've been off since we contacted you, Lieutenant," Riker said. "From what Shar-Lon told us, it was obvious that you two had been playing along with his assumption that you were the so-called

Builders. It seemed best to let him continue thinking that way, at least until we had a chance to confer with you so we could keep our stories straight. Now, you were about to tell me who attacked you. And why."

"It wasn't an attack, just a—a kidnapping of sorts. Shar-Lon's brother, Shar-Tel, wanted to talk to us, but Shar-Lon doesn't know Shar-Tel is still alive. He thinks—"

"It is time he knew," Shar-Tel broke in. "Events are moving rapidly, and I have decided it is time we talked, particularly now that you have arrived. He never listened to me when he thought I was alive, nor to my people after my 'death,' but perhaps he will listen to *you,* at least as long as he continues to believe you are the Builders."

"He could be right, Commander," Geordi said after passing Shar-Tel's words on, "but there are still a few things Data and I had better explain before we let Shar-Lon back into the loop."

"The two of you obviously are more familiar with the situation here than Lieutenant Yar or myself. We'll defer to your judgment."

Hurriedly, Geordi, with only an occasional correction of detail from Data, told Riker and Yar what they had learned from Shar-Tel. "He and his group feel the only way they'll see their dream of a world government fulfilled is to destroy the Repository," Geordi concluded. "And they want our help to do it."

Riker grimaced. "I can see why he feels that way. And if there truly is no other solution, I could even see some justification under certain interpretations of the Prime Directive for helping him. After all, the Prime Directive is meant to allow new civilizations to develop without interference or exploitation from more-advanced civilizations, and for the last fifty years this civilization has been the subject of extreme interference, particularly if there's any truth to the suspicion that Shar-Lon was influenced by something or someone on the alien vessel. And if Shar-Tel's version of events is the true one. But *we* are also more technologically advanced than Shar-Tel's civilization, and the Prime Directive certainly applies to our own influence here as well. So perhaps our main responsibility here is to neutralize whatever problems our presence has caused."

"Any debate on the subject may be academic in any case, sir," Data volunteered. "Without the help of the *Enterprise,* I doubt that the vessel can be destroyed. Any attempt to use one's phaser within the vessel or in its immediate vicinity would almost certainly result in one's being rendered instantly unconscious by one of the vessel's defense mechanisms. Geordi and I have already undergone the experience, and it is quite effective."

"And if Shar-Tel himself were able to destroy it," Geordi added, "there's the danger that the antimatter core could go out of control and detonate. The habitat is too close for that. It would be destroyed, or at least damaged badly enough to kill everyone on board."

"In any event," Riker said, "our primary concern at this point is to find our way back to the *Enterprise*. And unless there's more that you haven't told me, it seems to me that we would have the best chance of coming up with a solution if we all work together, back here in the Repository."

"There are a couple of things we'll have to be careful of, sir," Geordi said. "First, Shar-Lon has been in control of the Repository for fifty years, so he knows more about its capabilities and how to utilize them than any of us are likely to be able to learn very quickly on our own."

"But if he thinks we're the Builders," Yar put in, "he'll get suspicious if we have to ask him how to operate it."

"Exactly," Geordie said. "All we know is that it's operated through that helmet somehow."

"We saw Shar-Lon use it," Yar said. "Certainly if *he* can do it—"

"There may be some tricks we're not expecting," Geordi said, remembering what the helmet had almost done to Data. "Having him explain it to us would make it a lot safer. But you're right. If we ask too many questions, he'll probably get suspicious. And if he decides we're *not* the Builders, I have no idea how he'll react. His brother thinks he's unstable, and from what I've seen of him, I'd agree. He tries to put up a brave front, but he was in pretty ragged condition most of the time Data and I were with him. Also, he obviously has at least some control over the Repository, even when he *isn't* wearing that helmet. Otherwise he wouldn't have been able to get it to transport him back there when he was hit by that knockout dart."

"So you're saying we have to be careful in dealing with him," Riker said.

"Very careful, sir."

Riker was silent a moment. "Very well, Lieutenant," he said. "Can you three reach the Repository?"

Geordi paused, looking down the hub toward the sunward endcap. They had been moving as they talked, and now they were beyond the power station, nearing the habitat proper. "Shar-Tel, can you operate one of those shuttles and take us to the Repository?" he asked.

"I am sure there are shuttles I could gain access to."

"Then let's get moving," Geordi said, and then, to Riker, "We're on our way, sir."

From that point on, the hub, though now barely three meters in diameter, was clear of obstacles— an empty, weightless cylinder with a ring of handholds every few meters. At Shar-Tel's suggestion, the three launched themselves along it.

"It will be much quicker than 'walking,' " Shar-Tel pointed out as they floated along, he and Geordi touching the wall and relaunching themselves every third or fourth handhold while Data floated in a geometrically straight line, using the handholds only to keep his velocity constant in the face of losses due to air resistance, "and I fear we have no time to spare. My brother will be growing impatient or worse, especially since he was not allowed to understand what you and your colleagues were discussing these last several minutes."

For a minute, then two, the three continued, Geordi picking up speed as he gained confidence and proficiency.

But halfway toward the sunward end of the hub, they came to the longest of a dozen or more transparent sections, through which they could look "down" in all directions at the three valleys that ran the length of the habitat. The earlier ones had been only a meter or so in length, and they had slipped past almost before the distant images could register, but this one was nearly ten meters long, and the images—

"Data! Shar-Tel!"

Twisting in the air, Geordi managed to grab the ring of handholds in the center of the transparent section.

"What is it, Geordi?" Data called, gripping the ring of handholds at the sunward end of the transparent section. Beyond him, Shar-Tel caught the next ring and looked back worriedly.

"Something's going on down there," Geordi

said, focusing his attention on one of the habitat valleys.

Twenty or more of Shar-Lon's blue-uniformed "staff" were fanning out from a large, yellow-painted door in the endcap, he saw. Here and there, some of the valley inhabitants—a man and woman working in one of the garden-sized farms a hundred meters from the endcap, a half dozen teenagers playing something that could have been some form of volleyball, an older man coming out of a large, plain building halfway down the valley in what was apparently a manufacturing or food processing area—were stopping whatever they were doing and looking toward the endcap.

Frowning, Geordi switched to telescopic vision. As the floor of the valley seemed to swoop upward toward him, he saw that every one of the uniforms included one of the same primitive but deadly projectile weapons that the three who had come to the Repository had carried.

And standing back near one of the endcap doors, grimly watching the progress of the group directly before him and occasionally glancing upward toward the other two valleys, was Shar-Lon's deputy, Kel-Nar. Geordi had only seen him once, when he had escorted the Elders from the room, but his hawklike face was not one that was easily forgotten.

"Shar-Tel," Geordi called, "it looks like Kel-Nar has most of your brother's 'staff' out in force, conducting some kind of sweep. I assume this removes any doubt that he's the one behind the bombing. And the eavesdropping."

Grimacing, Shar-Tel launched himself back toward the transparent section and, within seconds, was peering down at the valleys. He paled as he looked, and in infrared, his reaction was even more pronounced.

"It does," Shar-Tel said, almost shuddering as he turned away from the scene below and aimed himself toward the endcap again. "It also means he's acting even more rapidly than I'd feared. Now that he knows I'm alive—*was* alive—and that I not only wanted to destroy the Repository but had fairly widespread support, he's searching for the place where I've been staying and the people who've been hiding me for the past ten years. God knows what he'll do if—when—he finds them."

"Would he actually harm them?" Data asked innocently as he and Geordi launched themselves down the hub after Shar-Tel.

"I very much hope I'm wrong," Shar-Tel said over his shoulder, "but I fear he would do virtually anything."

"But your brother—certainly *he* can control him," Geordi said. "I can contact the Repository now, while we're still on our way, and I can tell Shar-Lon what Kel-Nar is doing."

Shar-Tel grimaced again. "But that would mean telling him about me, about the opposition to the way he has been handling the Repository. Even if I'm face to face with him when he's told—" He shook his head. "In his current state, there is no way of knowing how he will react, even if he believes us. And with the power he commands through the Repository, he could be far more dangerous than Kel-Nar."

Geordi, giving himself another push with a passing handhold, couldn't disagree. He remembered the continual emotional turmoil Shar-Lon had appeared to be in virtually the entire time he and Data had been with him.

And then they were at the sunward end of the hub, exiting through the door that led to the shuttle hangar. With no convenient handholds, they resumed "walking" as Shar-Tel glanced about at the shuttles.

"That one," he said, pointing to one next to the one Shar-Lon had used. Unlike most of the others, this one was equipped with a mechanism that would allow it to dock with another vessel. "If the code has not been changed—"

Suddenly, another door to the hangar burst open, and a pair of blue uniforms appeared.

Chapter Thirteen

"SYSTEMWIDE SENSOR SCAN complete, sir," Worf rumbled. "Humanoid life forms on fourth planet, but no evidence of advanced technology. All satellites appear to be natural."

"No response on the subspace transceiver frequency, sir, nor on any hailing frequency, subspace or standard," Lieutenant Brindle at the tactical station reported.

"Counselor?" Picard looked toward Troi, but she only shook her head.

"I detect nothing," she said softly.

Picard nodded, letting his eyes flicker shut for just a moment. "Very well. Mr. Gawelski, next system, maximum warp."

For an instant, everyone froze. Then, almost simultaneously, the two uniforms reached for their projectile weapons.

But before they could finish the move, Data was thumbing his phaser. One of the projectile weapons wasn't touched, while the other, being raised by its owner when Data's second phaser burst struck, went spinning through the air. Geordi, stretching as high as he could, caught it as it sailed over his head. Data hurried forward and took the other, straining as he bent the barrel. Shar-Tel's eyes widened slightly at the sight, but then he smiled faintly.

"No wonder my brother believed you were the Builders," he said, watching as Geordi tossed the other projectile weapon to Data for the same treatment.

Then, with a last glance at the unconscious uniforms, they were in the shuttle.

Once through the habitat airlock and into space, it was only minutes before they were approaching the Repository. Though it was totally featureless except for the dummy airlock, Geordi's spectro-graphic vision revealed spots that might have been disguised phaser and tractor beam ports.

"Whatever the material in those spots is," he said, "it appears to be stressed in some way that makes it transparent to most forms of energy— except for certain portions of the electromagnetic spectrum, including everything from mid-infrared to mid-ultraviolet, which takes in the visible-light range of most life forms native to class-M planets."

To Data, it looked like nothing more than a quarter-size version of the original derelict. From the exterior dimensions, it was obvious that the room he and Geordi had been in before took up less than a tenth of the space. Other than the antimatter in its core and a faint indication of the transporter circuitry in the vicinity of the dummy airlock, the tricorders showed little. Some kind of shielding was obviously still operating. The *Enterprise* sensors might be able to penetrate it, but not tricorders.

"We're right outside," Geordi said, tapping his communicator insignia, "about to dock with the outer airlock."

"We're ready," Riker's voice came back. "We've been trying to prepare Shar-Lon as much as we could—without getting too specific and tripping ourselves up."

Geordi thought briefly of asking if Shar-Lon could get the Repository to transport them all inside without their having to go through the preliminary charade of docking and entering the outer airlock, but he discarded the idea. Not knowing how Shar-Lon was going to react to what he was about to be told, Geordi felt safer having the shuttle firmly attached. If worse came to worse and Shar-Lon reacted by simply shutting down the Repository, trapping them all, there would be at least a chance that their phasers could cut through the Repository bulkhead between the two halves of the dummy airlock, thereby turning it into a real one. Although, he thought with a mental grimace, just getting back into the shuttle, even back into the habitat, might not do them that much good, considering the way the situation was developing.

But at least it was an option that they wouldn't have otherwise.

Finally, the docking was complete, and they were in the darkness of the outer airlock.

Once again, Geordi felt the grip of the short-range transporter and saw the dull flare of its energies.

In the inner airlock, as Data began unsealing the door, Geordi took Shar-Tel's arm and positioned him in the corner at one side of the door, so that he would not be immediately visible when the door opened.

With a grating sound, the inner door swung open.

Shar-Lon stood meekly at one side, swaying slightly in the zero gravity, his face reflecting his obvious relief at their return. Riker and Yar, still clad in their radiation suits, the hoods pushed back off their heads, stood waiting a couple of meters from the door, in front of the empty hibernation chamber and its pedestal.

Restraining an unprofessional impulse to hug them both in greeting, Geordi turned to face Shar-Lon, paying particular attention to the old man's infrared profile. At the moment, it seemed almost normal.

"Shar-Lon," he began cautiously, "it's good to see that you were no more harmed than we. I assume it was your use of one of the Gifts that delivered you here so promptly."

205

"It was," the old man said quickly, almost eagerly. "I deeply regret that I was unable to bring you here in the same manner."

"It may have been just as well that you couldn't," Geordi said. "As it turned out, the people who attacked us—well, they weren't *really* attacking us. They just wanted to talk to us."

Shar-Lon's eyes widened slightly. "But the explosion! I saw it, and your superiors told me you were almost—"

"We escaped without harm," Geordi cut him off, "but the explosion was set off by a different group, not the ones who wanted to talk to us."

Shar-Lon stiffened. "Then you know who was responsible? Tell me, and I will deal with them as harshly as you desire."

"You may have to do just that," Geordi said, earning a questioning glance from Riker and a puzzled frown from Yar. "But there is something else we have to tell you first. Those who wished to talk to us—" Geordi paused, pulling in a breath. "They—their leader—wished to speak with us about your use of the Gifts."

Abruptly, Shar-Lon paled, and the reaction in infrared was even greater. But then, just as abruptly, almost before the first, frightened reaction could register, the old man's features tightened in defiance.

"Who is this so-called 'leader'?" he asked. "And what nonsense did he wish to tell you?"

"You know of this group, then, Shar-Lon?"

"I told you there are a few deluded individuals who have opposed me—the very ones who tried to harm you yourselves upon your arrival, and who killed my own brother."

Suddenly, before Geordi could stop him, Shar-Tel stepped into view in the door of the airlock. "We are *not* deluded," Shar-Tel said, "and we did *not* try to kill anyone, now or ever, least of all myself! It was your own deputy, Kel-Nar, who tried—and failed!"

Stunned, Shar-Lon looked as if he were going to faint. Had there been any gravity, his knees would surely have buckled.

"Shar-Tel? This is impossible. You—" Abruptly, Shar-Lon, now pasty pale, swung on Riker and Yar. "This is a test! I know your Gifts can produce illusions, and this is one! But why? You have already told me I have made proper use of your Gifts—"

"I am no illusion," Shar-Tel said, moving forward until he could grip Shar-Lon's arms and force his brother to face him. "I am as real as you."

"No!" Shar-Lon jerked away, bumping into Riker. "They are able to use their Gifts with more proficiency than I, to give their illusions solidity, that is all!"

Shar-Tel shook his head and looked toward Geordi and Data. "Tell him! Tell him I am real! Tell him the *truth* of what he has been doing!"

"Truth?" Shar-Lon almost shouted. "What truth? The truth is, I have used the Gifts to save our world from inevitable destruction! *That* is the truth!"

"That is *your* truth, not ours! And no matter *what* you did a lifetime ago, what you have done since that time has been disastrous! You have betrayed—"

"No! I will not listen to this lying phantom!" Shar-Lon's eyes fastened pleadingly on Geordi's face. "If you wish to test me, I am willing to undergo anything you wish, but not this cruel trickery! I have shown you the use to which I have put your Gifts! If you wish to see more—"

"It is not trickery, Shar-Lon," Geordi said, feeling the old man's pain in his own heart. "I'm sorry, but your brother is real. He wasn't killed ten years ago. He escaped the explosion, just as we all three escaped another a few minutes ago. And there is at least some truth in what he says. No matter how well you may have used the Gifts at first—"

"But you *told* me—"

"We did not know how you had been using the Gifts since that first time," Geordi said, realizing he was handling it badly but unable to devise anything better, now that Shar-Tel had barged in with his emotionally loaded accusations, "but now that—"

"Then I have failed! I was Chosen, but I have

failed! I can do nothing now but return the Gifts and leave the Repository to you!"

Abruptly, Shar-Lon fell silent, his eyes clamping tightly shut. His brow wrinkled in concentration.

A moment later, an envelope of transporter energies flickered around the old man, and then he was gone.

His heart pounding, his entire mind and body a massive lump of shame, Shar-Lon activated the Gift—the last Gift he would ever use. He felt the Gift enfold him, saw the faint glitter as it surrounded and took him. For what he knew would be the last time, the Repository faded from his sight.

Suddenly, the world's spinning imitation of gravity gripped him, and his off-balance body, already weakened and trembling from the shock of the Builders' words, was sent reeling, tumbling onto the still-rumpled bed in his living quarters.

He made no effort to sit up, no effort to move at all.

Slowly, the stomach-churning shame faded, leaving an emptiness that was even more painful.

He had failed.

He had been Chosen, and he had failed.

As he lay on the tangled covers of his bed, trying to cope with the overwhelming disaster that his life had suddenly become, fragments of memories, apparently suppressed and nearly forgotten—or simply distorted beyond recognition—for fifty years, began to force their way painfully into his consciousness.

They were memories of his first encounter with the Repository, but memories of feelings, not of events. The central events themselves had never faded, only the feelings that had accompanied them, the motives he had attributed to himself, the details with which he had ever more elaborately embellished the encounter over the decades.

Despite what he had always claimed, despite what he himself had virtually come to believe over the years, he now remembered—allowed himself to remember—that he had been frightened from the very moment the Repository wavered into view. But his impatience, his eagerness to see what the mysterious object really was, had overwhelmed the fear, and he had acted. But as he had drifted slowly from the shuttle to the Repository, as his mind had the time to consider rationally what he was doing, the fear had escalated into terror, overwhelming his impatience and curiosity.

But he had not turned and retreated. No matter that his emotions were by then virtually paralyzing him, he had not turned back, and it had begun to enter his mind that he was not *able* to turn back. Something was forcing him to go on, something in the Repository itself, he had told himself at the time, although he had ever since insisted that the only reason he had gone to the Repository was the sure foreknowledge of what was to come, a fore-knowledge inspired by the revelations of the Signs.

And when, impossibly, he had been snatched through the solid wall of the Repository into its barren interior, he had almost fainted from sheer terror.

Only when he had found himself, inexplicably, removing the helmet of his spacesuit and slipping the skeletal, pulsing Repository helmet onto his head in its place, did any semblance of calmness return. His entire body had been tingling, inside and out, but somehow, as the tingling faded, so did the fear.

But then, impossibly, he had begun to remember things he had never known, and the terror returned.

Slowly, bit by painful bit, he had "remembered" how to use the Gifts. And as he remembered, it was as if the Gifts became an extension of his own body, as if new sensory organs and new limbs had sprouted from that body.

And when it was over, when that first immersion in the Gifts had shuddered to an end and a semblance of calmness had once again been forced upon him, he had known that he had been given not only the ability but the responsibility—the *duty*—to use those Gifts to destroy the weapons that threatened his planet with annihilation.

It was *then* that he had realized what the Signs

had portended, not when, minutes or hours earlier, his world had turned blood red before his eyes. No matter what he had told others over the years, no matter what he had even told the Builders themselves a few short hours ago, no matter what he himself had come to believe over the years, it was then, not when the Repository first appeared, that he had realized he had been Chosen, that the fate of his world had been placed in his hands.

But he had had no time to think, no time to consider what his actions were to be. No sooner had he emerged from that first immersion than the first missile came swooping toward him from one of the enemy satellites. It was as if the Gifts themselves had detected its approach and awakened him to deal with it.

And deal with it he did. He had reached out with that strange, impossible sense he had never before possessed or even imagined, and located the nuclear heart of the missile.

And destroyed it.

And destroyed the next.

He had destroyed every missile that, in those first hours, was sent against him.

In the end, when he was once again able to immerse himself in the Gifts, he had remembered how to use the Gifts not only to destroy attacking missiles but to seek out and destroy every nuclear missile on the planet or in orbit around it.

When it was over, when he knew that the last

nuclear device had been destroyed, he couldn't remember whether the destruction had been his own idea or an idea imposed upon him by the Builders.

But it hadn't mattered.

With those Gifts, he had saved the world from itself.

And for fifty years he had *kept* it safe!

No matter what his brother said, no matter what the Builders themselves said, he *had* saved the world!

Abruptly, he sat up, his shame struggling to become defiance.

But as he pulled himself erect, he saw the room he was in.

For the first time in decades, he actually *saw* the room—the plush carpet, the shamelessly luxurious furniture, the one-of-a-kind paintings and holographs, and he was appalled at the glaring self-indulgence it revealed.

And looking down, he winced at the yellow of his uniform. For the first time, he could see how garish it was, how foolishly, humiliatingly vain.

And, though there was none here in this room, his mind's eye was assaulted by the hundreds, perhaps thousands, of representations of his own face, pompously benign, staring out from doors and walls and windows everywhere in the Peacekeepers' World, even from the uniforms of his staff.

He remembered how these had begun, in those euphoric early days: the "unifying symbolism" of the color of peace, the "inspiring symbolism" of his own image, the image of the man—the Peacekeeper—who had, in a matter of days, brought an end to the threat of planetary self-destruction.

And he had, he remembered with a new wave of shame, enjoyed every moment of it: the adulation and envy of the other Peacekeepers, the power, the knowledge that he among all men had been Chosen.

And, in the decades that followed, he had simply perpetuated the situation, accepting it without thought, until he was no longer even aware of what he was doing, let alone how and why it had all begun.

Not aware—until now—that, no matter what his accomplishments, he had been making an utter fool of himself.

And if he had been that blind to things as obvious as the endless, vain display of his own features, he asked himself bitterly, how good could his judgment have been in other, more important matters?

Had his destruction of the fleet of shuttles been justified? Or simply an angry whim?

Had his refusal to allow scientists to study the Repository been a fear that, in their studies, they would damage the Gifts beyond repair? Or that they would learn how the Gifts work and learn how to duplicate them, thereby diluting and eventually destroying his own power?

Altruism? Or vengeance and paranoia?

It was no wonder that the Builders had condemned him.

But he should at least have stood his ground, facing them, accepting whatever punishment they deemed fit. It had been the only honorable action left to him.

But he had failed even that test.

He had retreated, an act of utter cowardice, and now he could only wait, helplessly, for the Builders to exact their punishment. He had no illusions that, by this childish retreat, he could avoid it.

But then, suddenly, he realized there was still something he must do.

Because he was responsible for his own failure, he was also responsible for letting the World—the Peacekeepers' World that he had caused to be created—know of that failure. He was responsible for letting the Peacekeepers know that it was not *their* failure, but his and his alone.

Rising from the bed, Shar-Lon felt his age—the stiffness and weakness of his body—closing in on him for the first time in his life. He keyed open the elevator, averting his eyes from the now-grotesque-appearing stylized face that stared out from the back wall. Moments later, he entered the chamber where the Council of Elders met. Empty now, it was also where the Builders had been taken, where he had first greeted them after the murderous "greeting" already given them at the Repository by Ko-Ti. And from here he had hoped to have them speak to the World, to the Peacekeepers who had once been his colleagues.

But now . . .

With an effort that set his hand to trembling, he pressed the button that would put him in contact with his deputy Kel-Nar.

He waited, composing in his mind the painful confession he would have to make.

Then Kel-Nar's voice, filled with urgency, crackled from the speakers.

"Shar-Lon!" his deputy said, and then rushed on before the old man could speak. "Where have you been? We must talk, now! Those creatures calling themselves 'Builders'—*they are imposters!*"

For several seconds, Shar-Lon was stunned, his thoughts whirling madly, but then, suddenly, a massive feeling of relief swept over him as his mind flashed back across the last half dozen hours and he realized that what Kel-Nar had said was obviously true.

They *were* imposters!

Would the true Builders have allowed themselves to be rendered unconscious by their own Gifts?

Would not the true Builders have been able to come and go from the Repository without requiring help from the Peacekeepers' primitive shuttles?

Would the true Builders have allowed themselves to be captured so easily there in the shuttle hangar?

Would the true Builders not have simply returned themselves instantly to the Repository, just as Shar-Lon himself had done?

"Did you hear me, Shar-Lon?" Kel-Nar shouted as Shar-Lon's mind reconnected to the world around him. "Imposters!"

"I heard," Shar-Lon said grimly, all thoughts of shame and failure flushed from his mind by Kel-Nar's revelation.

"We must make plans, immediately," Kel-Nar said urgently. "Surely you understand that. We must be ready if more of them arrive."

"There is nothing to be concerned about," Shar-Lon said grimly. "I can deal with them."

"Even so, I must speak with you before you return to the Repository. Even though they are imposters, they do have powers beyond our own. There are things I have learned that must be considered."

"What things, Kel-Nar?"

"Things that can be discussed only face to face, in secrecy!" Kel-Nar said, desperation in his voice.

Shar-Lon grimaced. "As you wish. I am in the chamber of the Council of Elders."

Breaking the link to Kel-Nar, Shar-Lon turned

and swept back the drapes. The view of the Peacekeepers' World, always inspiring to him, now helped to wash away the aftermath of the emotional upheavals he had been subjected to. Slowly, he brought his thoughts fully under his conscious control once again.

Then, with a grim satisfaction and a concentration that drowned out the sound of footsteps pounding down the corridor toward the chamber, he revived the link to the Gifts and began the series of mental commands that would rid him of these imposters and their blasphemous condemnations once and for all.

Chapter Fourteen

"SHAR-LON! No!" Geordi shouted as the transporter field glittered around the old man. "We need your help!"

But it was too late. Shar-Lon was gone.

"Where is he?" Riker asked sharply. "Shar-Tel, can you get in touch with him? Can you get him back?"

Shar-Tel shook his head, but for a moment he said nothing, only pulled in a deep breath, as if bracing himself.

"I hope he is in his private quarters, where he will be safe at least for the time being," he said finally. "I doubt that he can be reached, but I would not bring him back, even if I could."

"But he's the only one who knows how to control—" Riker began, but he cut himself off abruptly, his already deep frown turning suspicious. "Unless *you* know how!"

Even before the words were out, Yar's phaser rifle

was trained on the old man. "Keep your distance from that helmet," she snapped.

Shar-Tel, perhaps remembering Geordi's and Data's phasers as they burned through the metal of the airlock door, cringed but recovered almost instantly. "Wait! Any use of your weapon—. You could kill me, but you would all be rendered unconscious an instant later. By the time you awakened—"

"He's right, Lieutenant," Geordi said, breaking in and speaking rapidly as he gave a brief account of the first attempt on his and Data's lives. "I was able to fire my phaser once, on stun, but I went under—even Data went under—before I could fire a second time. I assume it's some kind of automated defensive system."

"I suppose you're lucky the entire vessel wasn't vaporized," Riker snapped, then turned his scowl on Shar-Tel. *"Do* you know how to operate the equipment here?"

"No! Only my brother—. Please, let me explain, quickly! There is something I must do before it is too late!"

"What? What must you do?"

"There are a dozen ships on the planet's surface, held in constant readiness for launch," Shar-Tel said. "Now that my brother is at least temporarily not in control of the Repository, it is safe for them to launch."

"What ships are these?" Riker snapped. "Do

they have anything to do with your wish to destroy the Repository?"

Shar-Tel nodded vigorously. "They do, but that is not the immediate reason for summoning them."

"Then what is?"

"To stop Kel-Nar and his forces while we still have a chance," Shar-Tel said, and then went on to hastily outline what he and Geordi and Data had seen in the habitat. "He's starting his takeover, I'm sure. He must have heard virtually everything your men and I said before we found and destroyed the listening device. Most importantly, he undoubtedly now thinks that all he has to do to control the Gifts is to enter the Repository and put on the helmet. Until now, the only reason he hasn't simply killed my brother is that he was convinced he had to get Shar-Lon to willingly turn the control of the Repository over to him."

"Then you've thrown your brother directly into their hands!"

"Only if we delay! The ships are kept in constant readiness, and they can rendezvous with the Peacekeepers' World within two hours! In the state Shar-Lon was in, I doubt that he will venture out of his quarters within that time. Kel-Nar will not even be aware of his presence. He will assume Shar-Lon is still here, in the Repository, and he will concentrate on rounding up all of *my* followers. By the time he has completed that, the ships will be here."

"But if you hadn't driven your brother out,"

Riker protested, "if he had remained here, we could certainly have convinced him—"

"To allow the ships to be launched and to approach us unharmed?" Shar-Tel shook his head. "It is a possibility, but a remote one. In his paranoid state of mind, it's more likely that he would have decided you were not truly the Builders but part of a plot to steal the Gifts from him. In fact, it's possible he may come to that conclusion anyway, once he has time to think and brood about what happened. He may even try to return, which gives us all the more reason to move quickly.

"Remember, he can control at least some of the Gifts without having the helmet. You would be forced to stun him the moment he appeared, but that would result in *all* of us being stunned, by the Repository itself. And that would leave it defenseless to Kel-Nar, who is one of the few whom the Repository will admit without specific confirmation from my brother. By the time we awakened— if Kel-Nar allowed us to awaken at all—he could be well on his way to having as much control of the Gifts as my brother does. And in his hands—"

Shar-Tel shook his head. "Unlike my brother, Kel-Nar is interested in only one thing: power. Until now, except to two or three of his closest allies, he has maintained a fiction of his loyalty to my brother. He has been limited in what he could do, but once he gains control of the Gifts, he could not—"

"You seem to have it all pretty well figured out," Riker broke in. "But why has your brother even allowed these ships to be built?"

"He doesn't know about them."

"But if he was able to search out and destroy all the missiles fifty years ago, even those on the ground—"

"Those were nuclear missiles. Unless Shar-Lon has been deceiving everyone for the past eight years and really *does* know about the ships, the Gifts have limitations. As long as a missile—or anything else—remains on the planet's surface—or under it, or underwater—it can be detected only if it contains a nuclear warhead or an atomic drive. Once a missile has been launched, however, once it leaves the atmosphere and approaches orbit, it can be detected regardless of its makeup."

Riker studied the old man a moment, then turned to Geordi. "Lieutenant La Forge, what's your opinion? Is he telling the truth?"

"I've seen nothing to indicate that he isn't, sir. But, then, I didn't realize what he was up to with Shar-Lon just now, either—until it was too late."

"Even if we assume he's telling the truth," Yar spoke up, "what about the people who would be coming up in the ships?" Her blue eyes narrowed as she turned them on Shar-Lon. "Who are they? And why do you trust them?"

Shar-Tel looked taken aback by Yar's blunt questions. "They are people our group established

223

contact with more than twenty years ago. They feel as we do, that—"

"How can you be sure?"

"We have worked with them for years," the old man said. "Our goals are the same—to disable the Repository if at all possible, or, failing that, to keep its Gifts from ever again being used."

"And the people in the habitat—in your so-called Peacekeepers' World? What will your allies do with *them?*"

"Except for Kel-Nar and the two or three directly around him, nothing."

Yar shook her head angrily. "You make this sound like a *game,* Shar-Tel! Where everyone plays by the rules—*your* rules! Your brother has been a dictator—and a heavy-handed dictator at that. He's been running this entire planet for the last fifty years. To put it mildly, people down there don't like him—or *any* of you. What makes you think, once they get inside your world, they won't clean out *everyone?*"

For a long moment, there was only silence. Shar-Tel seemed suddenly tired, but then he straightened, and the resemblance to Picard struck Geordi once again.

"No," the old man said, "I am not naive enough to never have considered that possibility. However, when I think of the alternative—the continued wielding of this kind of power by my brother or, far worse, by Kel-Nar—I don't see that we have any choice. The chance has to be taken. And if we lose, if every Peacekeeper is killed in the process, it will be a small price to pay."

Yar continued to frown at Shar-Tel for another second, but then she nodded her agreement. "Quite right," she said, "if the dictatorship *does* end. If one of your friends from the surface doesn't pick it up where your brother left off."

Shar-Tel shook his head emphatically. "We have all—my people here, and those on the planet— seen enough of violence to last us a lifetime. Now we wish to build, not to destroy—without the help of this alien technology. We can and will have peace by learning to trust each other and delight in our differences, because, truly, there is no other way for us to survive." He glanced at the helmet. "I would destroy the Gifts this minute if I thought I could, but I cannot imagine it could be as simple as smashing that damnable thing to the floor."

"I doubt it as well," Yar said. "However," she added, patting her phaser rifle, "if things don't work out quite the way you hope, it's worth a shot as a last resort. These can do a lot of damage in a very short time."

Abruptly, she turned to Riker. "Sir, I recommend we allow Shar-Tel to send his message."

Riker nodded grimly. "All right."

The old man let his eyes flicker shut for just an instant. "Thank you. I will have to return to the shuttle, to use its radio."

"Very well. Lieutenant La Forge, stay with him."

"Yes, sir."

Then the two of them were stepping back into the airlock, Data closing it behind them. Inside, under Geordi's watchful Visor, Shar-Tel moved away from the inner door. A moment later, the transport energies gripped them both, and they were in the outer airlock.

Shar-Tel twisted at the latch, and then they were in the shuttle.

It took nearly five minutes for Shar-Tel to establish contact with one of his men.

"Shar-Tel!" a voice crackled over the shuttle radio. "What happened? Kel-Nar will have us all locked away if—"

"It was my fault, La-Dron," Shar-Tel broke in sharply. "I was careless, but I'll have to explain later. Right now, get word to the ships. Tell them to launch immediately."

"But the Repository—"

"Is under our control, at least for the moment. Hurry. This could be our only chance for peace, ever."

There was only an instant's silence, and then: "I will notify them immediately."

And the radio fell silent.

"And now, gentlemen," Yar's voice came from Geordi's communicator, "I suggest that we start learning what we can about these 'Gifts' ourselves. It would be nice if, before the hostilities start, we were able to find something that would get us back to the *Enterprise.*"

"Agreed," Riker said. "Lieutenant La Forge, I believe you said you had already tried the helmet once."

"I did, sir," Geordi said as he and Shar-Tel moved back into the outer airlock, "so I suppose I *am* the most logical candidate to try it again. When Data tried it, it almost killed him." Geordi went on to explain his theory that the helmet analyzed some aspects, physical or mental, of the wearer and, if those aspects didn't match the specifications put into the helmet by the so-called Builders, it tried to kill him.

"Shar-Lon and I are apparently close enough to those specs," he concluded as he and Shar-Tel emerged from the inner airlock, "since it seems to have accepted us both. However, I would appreciate one of you staying very close by and being very ready to get that thing off my head in case it suddenly changes its mind."

"Of course," Riker said. "We'll monitor you and it with the tricorders."

Geordi smiled faintly and picked the helmet from its spot on the wall. The last time he had seen or touched it was when he had snatched it from Data's head and hurled it across the room. Shar-Lon, he assumed, had replaced it. Or it had replaced itself.

Slowly, waiting for Riker and Yar to finish adjusting their tricorders, Geordi slipped the helmet on.

Abruptly, the planet once again filled the screen, and, inexplicably, a wave of apprehension, almost fear, swept over Geordi, and he couldn't help but think of what Shar-Tel had said about something "taking over" Shar-Lon when he had first put on the helmet.

"No preliminaries this time," Geordi said, suppressing the feelings as best he could. "The first time, I felt—well, it was a sort of tickling. I could feel something in my mind, and my body."

"I suspect that was the 'testing' about which you hypothesized, Geordi," Data said. "I experienced similar sensations, but only during the moments before the attempt to deactivate me was begun. But now that you have already been accepted, the equipment recognizes you and does not have to repeat the test."

"But can you *control* anything?" Yar asked pragmatically. "When Shar-Lon put the helmet on, he was able to control what we saw on this screen."

Even as she spoke, something happened within Geordi's mind.

Suddenly, it was as if he had eyes that he could open and close, that he could move from side to side. The sensations were similar to those he had experienced during those brief seconds when Commander Riker, given almost godlike powers by the entity that called itself Q, had restored his eyes, giving him normal, human vision.

And, like then, he knew without being told how to use those eyes. He simply "remembered" everything that was required, as if he had once known but had temporarily put it out of his mind.

But this time, his Visored vision remained intact, absorbing the chaos of wavelengths from which his mind normally and automatically extracted meaning and order. The other sense, the sense within his mind of having eyes that could be directed and controlled, was an addition, not a substitute.

And as he shifted those mental eyes, the view on the screen shifted.

As the habitat came into view, it was blurred into virtual unrecognizability by its relative closeness, but an instant later, Geordi "remembered" how to focus his mental eyes. And the image on the screen wavered, then became crystal clear.

Then the image expanded startlingly, and impulses that normally controlled his Visored senses, giving them telescopic and microscopic capabilities, seemed to merge with those that controlled his newly discovered mental eyes.

"Lieutenant," Yar said sharply, her voice edged with sudden apprehension as her eyes darted from her tricorder screen to Geordi and back, "be careful! New circuits are becoming active, similar to *Enterprise* sensor circuits but operating in the standard electromagnetic spectrum."

And Geordi "remembered" more.

On the screen, the image of the habitat expanded sharply once again, as if the Repository were rushing toward the habitat like an attacking starship.

Suddenly, seemingly only meters from the habitat's outer surface, the image flared into patternless chaos, but a split second later, an image returned.

But now it was an image of the inside of the habitat. The colors were dull and flat, the image itself slightly blurred, as if seen through a filmy filter.

"Sensor circuits extremely active, Lieutenant," Yar warned. "They must be providing the image you're getting on the screen."

"You seem to have tapped into something that Shar-Lon was never able to use," Riker said. "He didn't think it was possible to see inside structures with the Gifts."

"It could be related to the fact that I've used the Visor all my life, and I'm accustomed to making it do things that someone with normal eyes would never think of. It's—it's as if this viewer were physically a part of me, and I can control it the same way I control my own body." He paused, shaking his head and grinning involuntarily. "It's *fun!*"

"Can you find Shar-Lon?" Riker asked.

"I can try," Geordi said, sobering.

Collecting his thoughts, he focused on the viewer image, realizing as he did that there was a ghostly "double" quality to it, as if he were seeing the image both in the viewer and in his own mind, with the viewer image slightly less sharp. Turning his mental eyes slowly, he oriented himself. His "viewpoint" inside the habitat was halfway between the hub and one of the valleys, and as he absorbed the details, his momentary joy in the use of his newfound senses turned to anxiety. In the valley, Kel-Nar's men were still moving about. One, he saw, had his projectile weapon drawn and was shepherding a man and woman in the direction of the sunward endcap.

"That is La-Dron!" Shar-Tel's voice shattered the silence. "If he didn't have time to notify the ships—"

Shar-Tel fell silent as, suddenly, seemingly without a conscious command on Geordi's part, the viewpoint shot down toward the trio.

But as the figures expanded in the viewer, they also grew less distinct, as if a fog were growing up around them, as if the gauzy filter were growing thicker as Geordi approached. Until, at a half dozen meters, their features were no clearer than they had been at a hundred.

"Isn't there *something* you can do?" Shar-Tel asked, his voice filled with tension as he watched the shadowy figures continue toward the endcap.

"I don't know," Geordi said. "All I can do is—"

Suddenly, Geordi had a third hand.

It wasn't a physical thing, sprouting from his shoulder or chest, but, like his "eyes," a mental thing.

It existed in his mind.

And, like his eyes, he "remembered" how to use it.

He reached out, toward Kel-Nar's man.

"Lieutenant," Yar exclaimed, her eyes widening as she stared at the tricorder screen, "transporter circuits, quite powerful ones, have just become activated."

"I think I know why," Geordi said, taking the man in his invisible hand.

In a dull flare of transporter energies, the man vanished. La-Dron darted a look over his shoulder. His eyes widened. His mouth opened in the beginning of a gasp, but he clamped it shut. His eyes darting in all directions, he grasped his companion's arm, and both ran back the way they had come.

Geordi moved his invisible hand.

He followed the motion with his mental eyes, and the view on the screen swooped toward the sunward endcap.

He opened his hand.

In another flare of transporter energies, the man reappeared a meter above the surface of a path leading from the yellow door in the endcap. Arms and legs flailing, projectile weapon flying, he fell.

There was a low whistle, and Geordi realized it came from Yar. *"You did that?"*

"I *think* I did."

Abruptly, Geordi pulled back, until the entire endcap was visible on the screen. "Where is your brother likely to be, Shar-Tel?"

As if coming out of a trance, Shar-Tel jerked erect, almost detaching his magnetic boots from the Repository deck.

"There," he said, pointing, "is the window to the room you were first taken to. His living quarters are directly above, approximately there."

Swiftly, the area Shar-Tel had pointed to expanded on the screen, growing foggier and more indistinct as rapidly as it expanded, but a moment before the view was entirely obscured, the drapes that covered the wall-sized window in the chamber of the Council of Elders swept open.

Abruptly, Geordi pulled back and moved down, until the window was in the center of the screen.

Behind the window, blurred but recognizable, was Shar-Lon. He seemed to be concentrating fiercely, his eyes half closed.

Suddenly, the door to the room burst open and Kel-Nar, breathing heavily, lurched in, his projectile weapon drawn.

"It is Kel-Nar!" Shar-Tel almost shouted. "He found out my brother is there! He will kill him!"

Without thinking, Geordi reached out once

again, his invisible hand closing with startling abruptness around Kel-Nar.

But it was too late. Even as the transporter energies flared about Kel-Nar, he squeezed the trigger of the projectile weapon.

And Shar-Lon, already half turned, his eyes widening as he saw Kel-Nar and the gun, lurched backward as a hole, chest high on his left side, appeared in the yellow of his uniform.

Cursing silently, Geordi jerked his hand back, through the window and into the main body of the habitat, but before he could go farther, he felt a tingling all over his body, and he felt his grip loosening.

And Yar's voice was shouting in his ear: "Lieutenant, what are you doing? A *second* transporter, one involving several subspace circuits, is starting up. And it's focusing on *us, here!*"

"*I'm* not doing it!" Geordi said, but even as he spoke, he realized who *was* doing it.

"It's Shar-Lon!" he almost shouted, his mind racing as he released Kel-Nar to fall thudding to the habitat floor three meters below.

Shar-Lon was the only one who *could* be doing it, the only one who could be operating a "Gift" by remote control. Before Kel-Nar had shot him, Shar-Lon must have set one of the Gifts in motion.

Desperately, Geordi reached back inside the room and tried to grasp Shar-Lon, now sprawled on

234

the carpet in front of the window, red spreading rapidly across the front of his uniform.

But he couldn't. Something was blocking him.

And he felt the grip of the transporter grow tighter on himself.

"Whatever he's done," Geordi grated, reaching for his field-effect unit, "I can't stop it. Either he's still awake and blocking me, or he's got it set on automatic somehow. Either way, it looks like we're all on our way to *somewhere.*"

Almost simultaneously, Riker and Yar snapped the helmets of their radiation suits back in place, and Data reached out and snatched Shar-Tel to him, activating his own field-effect suit and forcing it into the old man's hand.

It was as Data was turning back toward Riker and Yar that the transporter took full hold.

The energies built around them.

And the Repository vanished.

Chapter Fifteen

SHAR-LON FELT NO pain as the bullet struck him, only surprise and a sudden numbness that made him wonder if his left side still existed.

And then he was falling, the image of Kel-Nar's contorted face still filling his fading vision. And as he fell, as he felt the thickness of the carpet thudding against his back, he realized the magnitude of the ghastly mistake he had made.

Desperately, he tried to remedy it, to reverse the action he had initiated with the Gifts, tried to call the Builders back from where he had banished them.

But he was too late.

The process was under way, and he did not have the mental strength, could not produce the mental clarity necessary to cancel or reverse it.

He could only curse himself for being a naive fool.

For years, Kel-Nar had been his deputy, and during every one of those years Kel-Nar had tried to pry from Shar-Lon the secrets of the Repository, saying again and again that it was wise and necessary for Shar-Lon to pass the secrets on. "If you die, there will be no one to carry on," he had said again and again.

And Shar-Lon had believed—had made himself believe—that Kel-Nar had been telling the truth when he said his only interest was to carry on the work of the Peacekeepers once Shar-Lon was gone. Even when his own brother had come to him and told him that Kel-Nar was dangerous, that he could never be trusted with the power of the Gifts, Shar-Lon's ego had not allowed him to believe any of it.

But now, too late, he realized that Shar-Tel and the others had been right. Kel-Nar's only interest was, and always had been, the power the Gifts would give him, not the good he could do for the world.

And in these last few moments, he had played directly into Kel-Nar's hands. He had believed—had *wanted* to believe—Kel-Nar's accusation that the Builders were imposters. But whoever or whatever they were, he now knew that they could hardly be worse than Kel-Nar himself. By using the Gifts to force them out of the Repository, he had removed the only obstacle in Kel-Nar's path. The Repository was now empty, and its Gifts would freely admit Kel-Nar.

And the work of the Peacekeepers would be destroyed.

With his last shred of consciousness, Shar-Lon struggled to activate the Gift that would bring an end to the Repository itself. Even that was preferable to allowing it to fall into the hands of one like Kel-Nar.

But it was too late even for that.

Before he could bring to bear even the brief concentration it would require, his consciousness flickered out.

Even as he snapped down the hood of his radiation suit, Riker couldn't help hoping that, despite La Forge's warning, the transporter energies he felt gathering around him would prove to belong to the *Enterprise.* But as they tightened their grip, the same mind-wrenching patterns that had enveloped him when he and Yar had been snatched from the derelict enveloped him once again, and he knew that, like then, the transporter was operating through subspace.

He had time to wonder if, somehow, the original transporters had been reversed, and they were being returned to the derelict—to the radiation-drenched spot where the derelict had been.

And in that moment, as the warped, kaleidoscopic energies raged about him and an image of the derelict and then the distant *Enterprise* itself flickered through his mind, he felt the same faint mental tug that he had felt during that first transmission, when, for a moment, it had seemed he was lost in the limbo between transmitter and receiver.

There was no image, no message, only a feeling, brief and tentative amid the chaos.

And then it was gone.

And the chaos of subspace energies was gone.

The real world of his radiation suit re-formed around him.

And echoing in the hood of that suit was the same whispered word that had emerged with him from that earlier transmission: *Imzadi* . . .

The third star system fell behind, as barren as the last. Picard stood motionless before the viewer, watching the next star in their search pattern already beginning to expand. Behind him, seated, Counselor Troi watched the viewer with him, her liquid eyes seeming to reach out and grasp at the images.

Since the moment the search had begun, she had remained before the viewer, motionless except for the steady rise and fall of her chest as her breath moved in and out with metronomic regularity. But what, she wondered bleakly, was she hoping for? No matter how long she remained seated here, the results were the same.

Instead of the one contact she longed for, she was instead continually overwhelmed by the emotions of those aboard the *Enterprise*. The captain's tightly controlled mixture of determination and anxiety, as sharp and tense as his own physical being, hammered at her with unprecedented strength. And Worf's dark, turbulent pattern, though deeply submerged beneath its Federation-imposed veneer, was clearer to her than it had ever been.

How could she even *hope* to detect anything from parsecs beyond this smothering mass of locally generated emotion? It didn't matter how powerfully transmitted it might be, nor how deep her own emotional link with the sender. Such a contact was, she feared, simply impossible.

And yet she could not forget that one moment . . .

The *Enterprise* had still been shuddering from the aftereffects of the derelict's violent demise. The tensions of everyone on the bridge, the flaring emotions of the hundreds of others throughout the ship, had been flowing through her, a vast, chaotic flood where only the closest or strongest emotions stood out individually.

And for one fleeting instant, Will Riker's mind had touched hers.

Wherever he had been, wherever the transporter had sent him before its circuits had been vaporized, he had existed long enough for their two minds to touch for that fleeting instant.

She could not bring herself to believe, no matter what the evidence, that that mind did not *still* exist somewhere.

"Arrival in vicinity of next star in ten minutes," Ensign Gawelski announced.

"Sensors indicate planetary system," Worf said, still scanning the science station instruments. "No details possible at this distance."

Picard acknowledged the reports brusquely, his eyes still on the viewer, where, under maximum magnification, the target star was beginning to show a disk.

Abruptly, he turned and lowered himself into the captain's chair, his spine not bending or slumping even the tiniest fraction.

Next to him, Troi forced her eyes from the viewer as, for a moment, the steely shell that held Picard's emotions in check seemed almost as much a physical reality as the man himself.

"Jean-Luc," she began softly, her slender fingers reaching out and touching the rigid back of his hand where it lay on the arm of the chair between them, "you are doing all that—"

Suddenly, she fell silent, her lips and fingers as motionless as stone as she felt a faint breath of contact.

Only in her mind did she involuntarily form the word, the thought, *Imzadi*.

Somehow, despite the literally painful waves of emotion with which the *Enterprise* crew still bombarded her, she was positive that, for a brief moment, she had felt Will Riker's mind once again touch hers.

And, in that same instant, in a flash of insight, she realized why the contacts had been possible. She realized what the conditions were that had allowed that first contact and this new, even fainter one.

In the first contact, though the mind had been unmistakably that of Will Riker, there had been a difference, as if that mind were being seen through a distorting lens. And it had come only moments after he had been sent—somewhere—by the derelict's transporter, a transporter that Chief Argyle had believed operated not through normal space but through subspace.

Riker's mind, in those moments, had itself been in subspace, where matter and energy were distorted in ways that could never be visualized, only described by the abstractions of mathematics, and where distances were meaningless in terms of normal space.

And now, during this second, vanishingly brief contact, she had once again sensed that same element of distortion.

He had once again been in subspace, she realized, and the distance between their minds had been virtually abolished.

Abruptly, she stood up, turning toward the aft stations.

"Lieutenant Worf," she said, her normally soft contralto startlingly sharp and urgent, "scan for any subspace activity, any disturbance, anywhere your sensors can reach."

"Right away, Counselor," Worf responded without hesitation as he recognized the urgency in her tone. His fingers darted across the controls.

Picard, already on his feet, was watching Troi closely. "You felt something, Counselor," he said. A statement, not a question.

"Yes, but unless the sensors—"

"I have something, Counselor," Worf rumbled. "Bearing one-two-seven, mark five-eight."

"Lay in that heading, Mr. Gawelski, now!" Picard snapped. "Distance, Lieutenant Worf?"

"Almost beyond sensor range, sir. At least one-point-five parsecs."

"Take us there, Ensign Gawelski, maximum warp. Lieutenant Brindle, try again to raise Commander Riker and Lieutenant Yar on their subspace transceivers."

And then, with the great ship under way toward this new destination, Picard turned to Troi.

"I assume, Counselor," he said with traces of the first smile to appear on the bridge since Riker and Yar had vanished, "that there is a good reason for your sudden interest in subspace activity?"

Returning the smile with an even fainter one, she nodded and began to explain.

* * *

The first thing Geordi realized as the transporter energies built up around him was that, though they swept through the same mind-wrenching patterns as those that had sent him and the others through subspace, they were not nearly as brilliant, not nearly as energetic.

He was, he had time to decide, once again being transported through subspace, but probably not as far.

Then the universe re-formed around him, and he saw that he was right.

He was floating in the vacuum of space. The same Earthlike planet hung below him, but it appeared much smaller. In the Repository, they had been less than thirty thousand kilometers above the surface. Here, he was at least a hundred thousand kilometers, perhaps more. A distance far greater than a Federation transporter was capable of, but nothing compared to the parsecs he and the others had been hurled across the first time.

Where *were* the others? he wondered suddenly, a leaden feeling gripping his stomach. Especially Data? Geordi had seen Data literally force his own field-effect suit onto Shar-Tel. He had almost certainly been counting on Riker and Yar having their own field-effect units with them. They could turn them on, and one of them could give his radiation suit to Data.

But if they had been separated—

Slapping at his communicator insignia, safely

inside the air pocket contained within the glowing aura of the suit, he called: "Commander Riker! Lieutenant Yar!"

A moment later, Riker's voice responded, followed almost immediately by Yar's.

"Is Data with either of you?" Geordi asked.

"I'm alone," Yar said.

"So am I."

"Data gave his field-effect suit to Shar-Tel," Geordi said. "I know he can survive unprotected in space far longer than any of us, but—"

"I have everyone on my tricorder," Yar broke in. "We're all within two or three kilometers of each other."

Annoyed at himself for not having thought of it himself, Geordi activated his own tricorder. Careful not to make any sudden move that could start him spinning helplessly, he scanned the space around him.

He spotted Data almost instantly, his distinctive android readings standing out from the others. He was approximately a kilometer and a half almost directly between Geordi and the planet. Shar-Tel, his readings differing slightly from those of Yar and Riker, was closest to Data, less than five hundred meters distant.

But Yar and Riker, their readings indistinguishable from each other, each with a communicator, were nearly two kilometers farther out from the planet, beyond Geordi, and more than a kilometer from each other. The two with the suits that could save Data were the farthest from him.

And there was no way of communicating with Data. Without his field-effect suit, there would be no envelope of air to transmit the sound from the communicator to his ears. *With* communication, with continuous coordination, there would at least be a remote, one-in-a-thousand chance that, if they detuned their phasers to boost the otherwise almost nonexistent recoil, they could use that recoil to maneuver themselves toward a rendezvous.

But without communications—

Directing his Visored senses toward where the tricorder had located Data, he spotted the android, a tiny speck against the background of the planet a hundred thousand kilometers below. Bringing up his telescopic vision, he saw that Data looked much the same as he had in the evacuated airlock earlier. The lack of pressure in the vacuum made his features slightly puffy, but he seemed otherwise unchanged.

But even as Geordi watched, Data's golden eyes closed, and his normally expressionless features seemed to become even more blank.

As if, Geordi thought, his stomach lurching queasily, the android were shutting himself off.

Which, Geordi realized abruptly, was the logical thing to do. He didn't know how long Data could function actively in a vacuum, but he suspected that, deactivated, he could last a long time. Perhaps longer, even, than Shar-Tel and Geordi himself in their limited field-effect suits. The air could be recycled only so many times, and even if it could be recycled forever, there was the matter of water and food. Field-effect suits were designed only for short-term use, a few days at best. And even the radiation suits that Riker and Yar were wearing, unless they had included provisions—

"We have to get *out* of here!" Geordi heard himself say, and then, from his communicator, came a faint, grim laugh.

"You won't get any arguments from *me,* Lieutenant," Riker's voice said. "Do you have any ideas?"

"Do you have any control at *all* over the Repository at this distance?" Yar asked. "You and Shar-Tel said that Shar-Lon was able to control it from a distance of several kilometers."

"I couldn't stop him from doing *this* to us, even while I was wearing the helmet," Geordi said.

"But if he's no longer using it," Yar said, "if Kel-Nar's shot killed him or even knocked him unconscious—"

"You're right," Geordi said, cutting her off and attempting to bury the guilt that he couldn't help but feel as the old man's bloody image filled his mind.

Focusing his telescopic vision on the space immediately surrounding the planet, he scanned for the habitat. At the same time, he tried to recapture the sensations he had experienced while wearing the helmet. The Repository's orbit could of course have taken it to the opposite side of the planet, in which case—

But then he spotted the habitat. It *had* been hidden by the planet and was only now emerging from its eclipse, but he saw that the plane of its polar orbit was such that it would be hidden only a small percentage of the time. It would be in range of his sight for at least two hours before it slid behind the planet again.

Scanning nearby space, he located the Repository, little more than a dull gray speck at this distance.

"I can see the Repository," Geordi said, raising his telescopic vision to its highest power, and then lowering it as he realized that even the slight rotational motion his body had acquired would make it difficult to keep the Repository from continually dancing in and out of the narrow focus of his vision at that level.

"Have you made contact with it?" Riker asked. "With the helmet?"

"Not yet."

"I respectfully suggest, sir," Yar put in, a touch of sarcasm not totally suppressed, "that we leave him to it, without the distraction of having to give us a progress report every thirty seconds."

And then there was silence.

Not knowing how else to start, Geordi visualized the helmet, imagining himself placing it on his head, trying to remember the exact sensations he had experienced.

He began with the physical feel of the helmet as it touched his head, the pressure of the fingerlike prongs.

And then the eerie feeling of eyes that he did not have, of "remembering" things that he had never known.

And, unbidden, the faint shiver of apprehension at the thought of Shar-Lon's "possession."

But as the shiver vanished, he realized that the phantom eyes had once again begun to form.

But they saw nothing. He was aware of their existence, but that was all.

And then he could feel the invisible arm that was the mental embodiment of one of the Repository's transporters, but it was as insubstantial as the eyes. The slightest effort to move it caused it to disintegrate, like fog before a wind.

Wishing once again that he had the ability to simply close his eyes, he did his best to blind his mind to the chaos of energies that assaulted his Visored senses, but here in space, unshielded by an atmosphere or the protective shell of a ship, the spectrum upward from ultraviolet through X-rays and cosmic rays was intensified a hundredfold, clamoring for his attention every instant.

But even with that vibrant distraction, he was not totally unsuccessful.

Slowly, ever so slowly, he felt those imagined

extensions of himself increase in strength. And he felt no resistance, as he had when he had been trying to grasp Shar-Lon.

But still the phantom eyes remained blind.

Until—

Suddenly, there was sight, so faint as to be almost lost in the chaos supplied by the Visor.

In the distance, a wavering phantom of the habitat floated before him.

And beyond that, far beyond, was a speck of light, little bigger than a star but with a startling intensity. It was, he knew instinctively, himself.

With sudden hope, he reached out, but his imagined arm collapsed into a powerless swirl of mist.

Then, as his frustration reached new depths, he felt something else, something solider, more substantial. It was not "alive" the way the imagined arm had been, but it did exist. And he could control it, the way he could control a club that he held in his hands. He could feel its mass tugging at him, feel an inertial resistance to his efforts, but it was not a part of him.

But somehow he was able to force it to grow, to push it outward, toward the speck of light that instinct told him was himself.

And he touched it.

In that instant, his control grew tighter. For the first time he began to wonder if they might have a chance of surviving, after all.

He began to pull, lightly at first, afraid that too

much strain would cause the phenomenon, whatever it was, to suddenly become as mistily insubstantial as the other had become.

"Tricorder indicates presence of a tractor beam," Yar's voice came through the barriers he had built up around himself.

Hearing the words, realizing what they meant, Geordi was suddenly elated.

"It's me!" he responded. "I couldn't control the transporter, but I stumbled across something else that it looks like I *can* control. I *think* I'm pulling us all in toward the Repository. But even if it's only me, once I get there, I can put the helmet on and get full control and transport you all back."

And suddenly he could feel himself being pulled. He could feel the acceleration of the tractor beam.

"Can you feel it?" he called.

"I can," Yar came back, overlapping Riker's "Yes, Lieutenant."

For a minute, then two, there was silence as the pull of the tractor beam continued to be felt.

Slowly, cautiously, Geordi turned a part of his attention to the inputs from his Visor. Despite the splitting of his attention, the pull of the tractor beam stayed steady.

Focusing his telescopic vision for shorter range, he once again looked at Data. The android's eyes were still closed, as if he were still in whatever standby mode he had placed himself in minutes before. A half kilometer away, Shar-Tel had begun to tumble slowly end over end. Not wanting to end up in the same situation himself, Geordi resisted the impulse to try to turn to bring Riker and Yar into his field of vision.

Focusing again on the habitat and then the Repository, he wondered what would happen when the Repository dipped behind the planet in its orbit.

Would the tractor beam release them? Would his own contact with the Repository be broken? Would he have to reestablish contact when the satellite reemerged from the planet's shadow? And if the tractor beam did release them, he wondered with a shudder, if it released them at the wrong time, when they were only a few thousand kilometers above the planet's surface, would they fall into the atmosphere and burn up like meteors before the Repository reappeared over the opposite horizon?

Suddenly, Geordi felt something. For a long moment, he couldn't imagine what it was. Like a solitary memory remaining behind after an otherwise forgotten dream, it seemed to have no connection to the reality around him.

Then he realized it wasn't a memory. It was something that was happening at this very minute.

The "airlock" transporter was operating. Someone was entering the Repository.

Abruptly, not knowing what else to do, he

"willed" the transporter to stop. Whoever it was who was trying to enter, whether it was Shar-Lon or Kel-Nar or one of his men, it could only mean trouble, probably disaster, for Shar-Tel and the four from the *Enterprise*.

But Geordi's efforts had no apparent effect.

Then, of its own accord, the transporter stopped.

Once again trying to block out the inputs from his Visor, he concentrated on his "eyes." If he couldn't stop whoever had just entered the Repository airlock, at least he could find out who it was.

But the image he was receiving, faint and indistinct except for the glittering speck that apparently was himself in the distance, was of the habitat.

Concentrating as he had never concentrated before, Geordi turned his distant eyes until they were directed back at the featureless gray box that was the Repository. A shuttle was attached to the airlock, but not the shuttle in which he and Data and Shar-Tel had come. That one was floating nearby, drifting lazily away from the Repository.

Willing himself forward, Geordi's phantom eyes approached the Repository.

Abruptly, they were through the wall, and the interior, blurry and translucent, was spread out before him.

The locking mechanism on the inner airlock door, he realized instantly, was turning. In another minute, whoever was in the airlock would be inside the Repository! Within seconds after that, he could be placing the helmet on his head!

Turning away from the airlock, Geordi forced his phantom eyes to focus on the helmet, forced his mind to blot out everything else, not only here in the Repository but in his hundred-thousand-kilometer-distant body.

And as he did, hope flared within him.

The helmet, unlike everything else in the Repository, was no longer hazy and indistinct. Now—now that he was concentrating on it and it alone, he saw that it was gaining a solidity it had not possessed only seconds before. And even as he watched, fighting to hold the intensity of his concentration, it seemed to solidify further, like a holographic image being brought into sharper and sharper focus.

His distant heart pounding, Geordi moved forward. The helmet was now so real it seemed that he could touch it.

And he did.

His phantom eyes flowed between the prongs and upward toward the apex where they joined beneath the faintly glowing silver light.

Suddenly, the rest of the Repository slipped into focus, becoming almost as solid and real-seeming as the helmet.

And he had control.

But not yet *full* control.

Instinctively, he knew that he did not, at this

distance, have the strength to mentally grasp the man in the airlock and transport him elsewhere. But himself, his own distant body—

Reaching out along the invisible solidity of the tractor beam, he grasped blindly at whatever he found at its end.

In his body, his Visored senses came alive as transporter energies suddenly began to build around him, and the sense—the reality—of being in two places simultaneously twisted at his mind almost as strongly as the impossibly distorted subspace energies that whirled chaotically about him.

In an instant, more quickly than by any transport he had ever experienced, he was in the Repository, the helmet on his head. But in that same instant, he realized that he was too late.

The airlock door was open. Kel-Nar was stepping through, one hand holding a projectile weapon already swinging toward him.

Lunging to one side, the helmet flying from his head, Geordi drew his phaser and fired.

A fraction of a second later, he felt the Repository's defense mechanism descend on him once more.

Then he felt nothing.

And a hundred thousand kilometers out in space, the tractor beam ceased to exist, releasing Riker and Yar into what was now a meteoric trajectory toward the planet below.

Chapter Sixteen

APPROACHING THE SYSTEM from almost directly above its ecliptic plane, the *Enterprise* sensors reached out.

"One-point-zero-four solar masses, sir," Worf announced. "Six planets, second one out perfect class M. No natural satellites but one artificial satellite with mass several times that of the *Enterprise*. No others detectable at this range."

Picard, holding his breath while Worf read out the statistics from his science station instruments, let out the beginnings of an explosive sigh of relief before catching himself and quieting the remainder of the exhalation.

"Take us in on impulse power, Ensign Gawelski, shields up," Picard said. "Lieutenant Brindle, Lieutenant Worf, be alert for—for *anything* indicative of a technology near or above Federation level. This could be the planet of origin of the owners of that derelict. Or of the beings that caused the derelict to be abandoned."

But as they approached the planet, the odds in favor of either possibility diminished rapidly. There were no subspace communications of any kind, only the stew of standard electromagnetic frequencies typical of a civilization in the early stages of space travel.

At ten million kilometers, Worf glanced up from his instruments. "Second artificial satellite detected, sir," he rumbled. "It appears to be less than one percent the mass of the first, but it does contain an antimatter power source, essentially identical to that in the original derelict but more thoroughly shielded."

Picard frowned. "And the power source of the larger satellite?"

"Unknown, sir, but there is no indication of antimatter or of atomic reactions of any kind, either there or anywhere on the planet's surface."

"Other satellites?"

"None detected, sir."

"Are you saying those are the only two artificial spacegoing structures in the system?"

"The only ones of any mass in the vicinity of the one class-M planet. To search the neighborhoods of the nonhabitable planets—"

"No, stay with this one." Picard turned to the tactical station. "Still no subspace activity, Lieutenant Brindle?"

"Still none, sir."

"Get those satellites on the viewer, Ensign Gawelski, maximum magnification."

As Gawelski acknowledged, the image of the planet shifted, and the viewer centered on a point roughly two planetary diameters above its upper edge. Picard's eyes widened as the image grew rapidly and he recognized the distinctive shape of the larger satellite. The smaller was still little more than a speck.

"More subspace activity," Worf announced, "a transporter of some sort. It appears to originate on the smaller satellite."

Picard turned sharply toward Counselor Troi, but she shook her head, frowning. "I have felt nothing, Jean-Luc."

"Any other readings relating to the satellite, Mr. Worf?"

"A slight increase in the antimatter power source activity coincided with the subspace transporter activity, sir, but—"

"Captain!" Lieutenant Brindle at the tactical station broke in abruptly. "Three Starfleet communicators registering!"

"Where?" A mixture of relief and new apprehension stabbed at Picard as he spun to face Brindle. Three communicators, not four.

"A hundred thousand kilometers above the planet, sir. Approximately—there." At his words, the planetary image in the viewer shrank and a faint circle appeared several planetary diameters out.

"Get us within transporter range, Ensign Gawelski, full impulse power," Picard snapped, not waiting for an acknowledgment. "Lower shields only on my order, Lieutenant Brindle, and keep the transporter room continuously updated as you refine the coordinates of those communicators. Mr. Carpelli, prepare to lock on."

Pausing, Picard glanced at the screen and the palely glowing circle. The communicators were there, but there was no way of knowing, yet, what they were attached to.

"Security!" he snapped. "Full detail to transporter room, now! And Dr. Crusher, a medical team as well, including someone who can look after Commander Data!"

And they waited.

"Sensor readings consistent with presence of Commander Data and two humans, sir," Worf announced as they neared transporter range. "They appear to be scattered, roughly two kilometers away from each other. A fourth life form, definitely humanoid and possibly human, is in the same area."

"The fourth crew member?" Picard asked sharply.

"Doubtful, sir," Worf responded, and then added, with a frown that made his Klingon features seem even more than usually menacing, "In fact, this life form appears to be encased in a field-effect suit, while commander Data is apparently unprotected. The commander's life readings are stable but low, only slightly stronger than those of a human in hibernation."

"You heard, Dr. Crusher?"

"I heard, Captain. We'll be ready."

"Locking onto communicators, Captain," Carpelli's voice came from the main transporter room. "Ready to energize as soon as we're within range and shields are lowered."

"Stand by, Ensign."

"New shielding being erected around smaller satellite, sir," Worf rumbled as he scowled at the science station instruments. "It is now totally enclosed. The output of the antimatter power source registered the beginning of a massive increase before our sensors were blocked out."

"It's not about to self-destruct, like the derelict?"

"Possible, sir."

"If it did, could it injure Data and the others?"

"If the amount of antimatter is equal to or greater than that consumed in the derelict's explosion, radiation damage is possible."

"Transporter range, sir," Gawelski reported.

"Take us the rest of the way in, Mr. Gawelski, full impulse power, now!" Picard snapped. "Mr. Brindle, I want those four, whoever they are, *inside* the *Enterprise* deflector shields."

As Picard had known they would be, the final thousands of kilometers were covered in less time than it would have taken to lock the transporters onto the communicators.

"Life forms within *Enterprise* shields, Captain," Brindle reported almost instantly.

"Excellent, Mr. Brindle. Ensign Carpelli, bring the three aboard." Turning to one of the ubiquitous black panels, Picard said, "Computer, show me the main transporter room."

Obediently, an image of the transporter room, Ensign Carpelli in the foreground at the controls, appeared in the panel.

Tensely, Picard and Counselor Troi and the rest of the bridge crew waited to see who would appear on the transporter platform.

The tractor beam had still been tugging them inward toward the Repository when Riker's and Yar's tricorders registered a buildup of transporter energies. A moment later, both Geordi and the transporter energies had vanished from the tricorder screens.

Then the tractor beam was gone, and they were once again floating free.

"Lieutenant La Forge!" Riker said. "Geordi!"

But there was no response.

"Lieutenant Yar—" he began, but cut himself off as he felt a transporter grip him. "It could be Kel-Nar," he snapped, rushing to get the words out before he was frozen for the scanning process. "He may have taken control of the Repository."

"I'm ready!" Yar returned, gripping her phaser rifle tightly, her finger on the firing stud. "From what Geordi said, you only get one chance in there, and I'm going to make it count!"

And the energies closed in on them.

But as the transporter gripped them, Riker suddenly felt the same contact he had felt twice before, during the subspace transmissions, but this time the distortions were not present, and he felt Troi's mind, not remote and anguished but nearby and filled with an equally powerful sense of relief. And then, out of the corner of the narrow eye slit of his radiation suit, he saw the leading edge of the *Enterprise* saucer!

Tasha! he tried to shout in warning, but it was too late. The scanning had begun, and a moment later the outlines of the *Enterprise* main transporter room began to take shape around him.

And there, as if her presence could speed the materialization process, stood Counselor Troi, only meters in front of him, right where Yar's phaser rifle would be aimed

"Tasha!" The name, frozen in his throat during the moment of transmission, exploded the instant the transporter matrix released him. "Don't shoot! It's the *Enterprise!*"

In the same moment, the sudden return of gravity was like a hammer blow, and he lurched forward, throwing himself in front of Troi. For the tiniest fraction of a second, Yar's finger tensed reflexively on her phaser rifle firing stud, but she snatched it back as Riker's shouted words and the suddenly familiar surroundings penetrated.

Data, still "turned off," crumpled to the floor of the transporter platform in a heap.

As Riker threw back the hood of his radiation suit, his eyes met Troi's in a flash of understanding, but an instant later he was looking past her at Dr. Crusher and her medical team and the security detail.

"Doctor," he said urgently, "Data's been in a vacuum without protection for several minutes. Lieutenant Yar and I are fine."

"Where's Lieutenant La Forge?" Yar cut in, flipping her own hood back and centering her gaze on Lieutenant Brindle at the transporter controls. "Didn't you bring him in a few seconds ago?"

"You are the only three we've brought aboard so far, Lieutenant Yar," Picard's disembodied voice replied from the bridge. "Who is the fourth life form in what I assume is Mr. Data's field-effect suit? Despite sensor readings, I had hoped *that* might be Mr. La Forge."

"No, it isn't, but bring him aboard anyway,"

Riker said. "His name is Shar-Tel, and it's a long story."

"Bring him in, Mr. Carpelli," Picard confirmed.

"Which circle, Mr. Carpelli?" Riker asked quickly.

"Number two, Commander, but what—"

"Lieutenant Yar," Riker snapped, "help me catch him when he comes in. He's going to be expecting the gravity even less than we were, and at his age—"

"Energizing, Commander," Carpelli said, and Riker and Yar positioned themselves on either side of the number-two circle.

A moment later Shar-Tel, enclosed in the faint glow of the field-effect suit, materialized. Riker and Yar each caught an arm before he could fall.

"It's all right, Shar-Tel," Riker said quickly. "We're safe now. This is the ship the others were telling you about. Our ship."

Shar-Tel's eyes widened and darted about, but there was no fear in his expression, only relief and, an instant later, a look of sudden intense curiosity, a look that, for a moment, reminded Riker of Captain Picard.

"What happened?" the old man asked anxiously. "Is my brother dead? Has Kel-Nar taken over the Repository?"

"We don't know," Riker said, "but if—"

"I must speak with La-Dron. If my brother is still

alive, he must be found! There may be time to save him!"

"We can't do anything here," Riker said, stepping off the platform and removing his radiation suit. "Everyone to the bridge, and perhaps we can find out what the true situation is."

"Yes, Number One," Picard's voice came from the com panel, "do come to the bridge. There are quite a number of things *I* would like to find out."

"On our way, sir. In the meantime, check out the Repository—the smaller of the two satellites. Lieutenant La Forge is probably on it, and probably in trouble."

"You heard him, Lieutenant Worf," Picard said. "Do your best. Number One, what *is* that satellite? It appears to possess the only antimatter power source in this star system."

Talking as he walked, followed by Yar as she escorted the slower-moving Shar-Tel, Riker explained the situation to Picard as quickly as possible.

Back in the transporter room, Data opened his eyes and sat up abruptly, almost bumping Dr. Crusher and the medical tricorder she had been scanning him with. For a moment he was silent, as if a final circuit breaker were being thrown while he absorbed the scene around him.

"I see that Geordi was right," he said. "The captain did not give up."

"Very well. Lieutenant La Forge, stay with him."

"Yes, sir."

Then the two of them were stepping back into the

"Data—" Dr. Crusher began, but he was already rising smoothly to his feet.

"I have already performed a self-check, Doctor," he said, "and I am once again fully functional. Where are the others?"

"On their way to the bridge, but—"

"Then I will join them. There is information I must obtain from the computer."

Under Dr. Crusher's concerned (and slightly suspicious) gaze, Data exited quickly.

Shar-Tel, his utilitarian shirt and trousers conspicuous among the crew uniforms, stood next to Lieutenant Brindle at the bridge tactical station. Picard, on Riker and Yar's recommendation, had already approved Shar-Tel's request to contact La-Dron. Just behind the conn, Riker and Yar were resuming their hurried summary to Picard of what had happened since Geordi and Data had been snatched from the derelict.

"The Gifts allowed me to *see* Kel-Nar shoot my brother but they did not allow me to interfere!" Shar-Tel was almost shouting to La-Dron. "There is no time to explain further! There may still be time to save him if you hurry! If Kel-Nar *has* gained control of the Repository, my brother may be our only hope!"

Even in the face of Shar-Tel's urgent tone, La-

Dron hesitated, but finally he said, "Very well. At least we would be no *worse* off than we were before."

Shar-Tel let out a shuddering sigh of relief as contact was broken.

Data emerged from the forward bridge turbolift unnoticed and moved directly to the secondary science station. Meanwhile, Riker and Yar had completed at least a first, sketchy summary for an impatient Picard.

"Lieutenant Worf," Picard said abruptly, "status report."

"At this distance, the satellite's shields are impervious to our sensor probes. Its shields are at least as effective as those of the derelict."

Worf's bass rumble, coming from only two or three meters behind Shar-Tel, brought the old man around, giving him his first direct look at Worf, who had turned toward the captain as he delivered his report.

Shar-Tel's eyes widened, and he instinctively drew back from the Klingon's impressively menacing features.

But Shar-Tel's reaction was only momentary. Blinking, he brought his eyes back to Picard.

"Can your ship destroy the Repository?" Shar-Tel asked bluntly.

"We are hoping to keep it from destroying itself," Picard snapped, "at least until we find a way of getting Lieutenant La Forge safely out. If he is indeed on board. After that has been accomplished, we will discuss the matter! Mr. Gawelski, take us in to five thousand kilometers. Lieutenant Worf, continue the sensor probes."

"Captain," Brindle at the tactical station broke in, "six ships, chemically powered, have left the planet's atmosphere and are entering orbit."

"Monitor and record any and all transmissions those ships make," Picard said, giving Shar-Tel a glancing scowl as he turned back to Riker. "Who do *these* belong to, Number One?"

As quickly as he could, Riker explained. Shar-Tel stood by, obviously more nervously impatient than he had been before Brindle's announcement.

"You called them up, Shar-Tel," Picard said, turning toward the old man. "Can you talk them into keeping their distance? Convince them to stay in a low orbit, away from your 'Repository' until we have time to sort the situation out?"

"That is what I *want* to do, Captain," Shar-Tel said quickly. "If Kel-Nar is in control of the Repository—"

"Never mind the explanation, just tell them to stay away. Lieutenant Brindle, try to establish contact. Shar-Tel, don't let them know where you are. Let them think you're wherever you normally would be."

Nodding his agreement, Shar-Tel hurriedly gave Brindle the frequencies needed to contact the ships.

"Five thousand kilometers, sir," Gawelski reported.

"Lieutenant Worf?"

"At maximum power, the sensors are able to penetrate to a limited degree at this range, sir. However—"

"One thousand, Mr. Gawelski," Picard ordered.

"No answer from the ships, Captain," Brindle reported. "They're receiving us, but they aren't replying."

"Shar-Tel?" Picard frowned at the old man. "Why?"

"I don't know, Captain."

"Keep trying, Mr. Brindle. And Shar-Tel—even if the ships are not responding, transmit your message."

"Sensors performing better at this range, sir," Worf said seconds later, as the *Enterprise* settled in at one thousand kilometers. "There are definitely two life forms aboard, both humanoid, one definitely human, possibly with a communicator."

"It's La Forge," Riker said with relief.

"Yes, sir," Worf said noncommittally. "If so, he is unconscious, as is the other life form. Two other humanoid life forms in a smaller, attached vessel are also unconscious."

"Unconscious?" Picard scowled. "Everyone?"

"It's probably the Repository's defensive system," Riker said, quickly recounting what Geordi had told him about his and Data's first encounter with it. "La Forge must have fired his phaser."

"How long will they be unconscious?"

"We have no way of knowing," Riker said. "When La Forge and Data were removed from the vicinity of the vessel, they regained consciousness in less than half an hour. But if they remain inside—" Riker frowned as he shook his head. "A system designed to defend the vessel itself against anyone who fires a phaser in or near it wouldn't be very effective if it let the offender wake up and do it all over again."

Picard's scowl deepened. "You're telling me that it will *keep* them unconscious—or even kill them eventually—unless we can get them out of there?"

"It's a possibility, sir," Riker said, "and it might be for the best. The continued unconsciousness, I mean, not the killing. If Kel-Nar awakened first—"

"I take your meaning, Number One. We had best find a way to get Lieutenant La Forge out of there, and soon." Picard looked around the bridge. "I am open to suggestions, information, even comments."

Data, who had been silently absorbed at the secondary science station from the moment he had arrived on the bridge, turned toward Picard. "I have no suggestions as yet, sir, but I do have some information that Lieutenant La Forge felt could be significant."

"Let's hear it then, Mr. Data."

"Very well, sir. During the last few minutes, I have been acquainting myself with the full details of the Ferengi-supplied information concerning this sector of space, and—"

"Ferengi-supplied information?" Picard's scowl began to return.

"Yes, sir," Data said. "The information the Federation received in exchange for similarly unverified information collected from other sectors by Federation exploration vessels."

Picard nodded. "Ah, yes, the 'rumor swap.' I remember. As I recall, neither Ferengi nor Federation officials were overly pleased once they had a chance to analyze the so-called information they received. Everything was second- or thirdhand, and related to events that transpired—if they transpired at all—thousands of years ago."

"Yes, sir, that is the information to which I refer."

"And you've gotten something useful out of it?"

"I believe so, sir. The information I have just now reviewed does appear to shed a certain amount of light on the origin and function of the two vessels with which we have become involved."

"Go on," Picard said when the android paused questioningly.

"Yes, sir," Data said, and went on to outline what he had told Geordi concerning both the vessels similar to the Repository reported in orbit around a number of class-M worlds at some time in the past, and the stories regarding other class-M planets being held back from achieving space travel, either by "alien invaders" or undefined "catastrophic events."

"At that point," Data went on, "it occurred to Geordi that the satellites were what he called 'guard posts,' and that the derelict was a central hub or headquarters from which they had all been controlled or supplied at one time."

"That makes sense, sir," Riker agreed, "or it would to the paranoid minds who built these things. Look at the one-way transporters, the self-destruct devices, and all the other 'safeguards.' To a civilization that thought the way this one apparently did, the idea of meeting another equally advanced or superior civilization would have been terrifying."

Picard frowned grimly. "So when they began discovering worlds with potentially 'dangerous' populations, instead of helping them or even ignoring them, they set about to make sure those worlds would never have a chance to advance to the point at which they could achieve space travel. In effect, they made prisoners of entire populations with orbiters like this one. Hundreds, possibly thousands of them."

Riker nodded. "They placed these orbiters around every planet where they discovered a population capable of eventually moving out into space and challenging them. I suppose we should be grateful they didn't simply sterilize the worlds. They probably had the power."

"And the hibernation units?" Picard mused. "Computers would do the day-to-day, year-to-year monitoring and awaken someone only when they spotted something they had been programmed to see as threatening—the first artificial satellite, the first nuclear explosion, the first anything that would indicate the civilization was developing a technology that would take it into space."

"Yes," Data said. "Such activities would account for the stories of the 'alien invaders' who kept entire planets from achieving space travel. It is also possible that self-destruct devices could account for the 'catastrophic events' which, according to the Ferengi-supplied information, were often powerful explosions of previously unseen objects in orbit around the planets. In those and other instances, there is also mention of 'great sicknesses' that followed the events—the result of radiation from the explosions, in all likelihood."

Riker grimaced. "And then, sometime in the past, they encountered a civilization that *already* had space travel, a civilization that may even have been their technological superior. And rather than try to meet the newcomers and make friends, they simply panicked. They retreated, back to their home world, wherever that is, setting off the self-destruct devices as they left, doing their best to wipe out all traces of their existence. But in a few rare instances—like the orbiter and derelict we've found—something went wrong, and they weren't destroyed."

Picard nodded. "It sounds all too plausible, considering the evidence. And when we stumbled across the derelict, there was just enough of its evacuation system still functioning to transport the four of you here, to the so-called Repository, probably the only orbiter still functioning."

Picard paused, pulling in a breath. "None of which, unfortunately, is all that helpful in our present situation," he went on grimly. "Our current priority is to find a way of getting Lieutenant La Forge safely *out* of there and back—"

"Sir," Worf interrupted, "the orbiter's power output is increasing again."

Picard turned sharply back to the viewer. "Mr. Brindle," he snapped, "maintain maximum power to our own shields. Mr. Worf, what is it doing with the power?"

"Unknown, sir. There are indications much of it is being fed to its shields, but—. Another power increase, sir, to the shields again."

"To the shields? Are they being strengthened?"

"No, sir, that is what is puzzling. The power appears to be going to the shields, but it is as yet having no discernible effect."

"A malfunction?"

"Possible, sir. This vessel *is* approximately the same age as the derelict."

Picard started to turn toward the tactical station to question Shar-Tel, but before his eyes left the viewer, the smaller satellite, the so-called Repository, flickered and vanished.

"Mr. Worf! What happened?"

"Some of the energy is now being radiated by the vessel's shields, but that is the only change."

"Is the satellite still there? Does it register on the sensors?"

"Yes, sir. Everything is as before. The life-form readings remain unchanged."

"Then what the devil—"

Abruptly, Picard fell silent, his jaw dropping as, between one heartbeat and the next, the most massive starship he or anyone else on the bridge had ever seen appeared in place of the vanished vessel.

Chapter Seventeen

SLOWLY, INEXORABLY, SHAR-LON was dragged back toward consciousness.

At first, he resisted, his befogged mind resenting the intrusion, fearing the pain that grew more intense with each step toward wakefulness, unable to cope with the utter exhaustion that made the very thought of even the slightest physical motion a torture.

But then, as his mind began to clear, he realized: *The Gifts are doing this. The Gifts are awakening me.*

With dizzying suddenness, then, he was awake. Beyond the exhaustion and the pain that seemed to be all there was to the left half of his body, he felt a pressure against his back, a prickling pain in his other leg. The chamber of the Council of Elders came into focus around him.

And as it did, he realized that he lay, not on one of the couches he so often used for resting before a Council meeting, but on the floor, one leg painfully twisted under him.

Abruptly, the excruciating memory of those last seconds, of Kel-Nar's treachery, of his own failure, came flooding back.

And with that memory came the realization that, somehow, he was being given a second chance.

They all—his brother, those on the planet below and, most of all, the Peacekeepers—were being given a second chance. A chance to choose the right path—the path of *real* peace.

The Gifts were giving him—forcing upon him—that second chance.

If he had the strength—the *will*—to use it.

Not daring to close his eyes for fear he would not have the strength to open them again, he forced himself to concentrate, to think. There was no way he could take control of the Gifts away from Kel-Nar, who surely must be in the Repository by now.

There was only one action that remained even remotely within his capabilities. The same action he had already attempted—and failed—even as his consciousness had flickered and died.

But now, with the Gifts reaching across space to give him a second and final chance . . .

Summoning up the last drops of his Gift-imparted strength, Shar-Lon focused on the Gifts, and he felt the link strengthen. There was even the illusion, for that brief moment, that his own dying body was strengthening.

With a mixture of triumph and regret, he gave

277

the series of commands that would bring destruction to the Gifts.

As his consciousness faded for the last time, he felt the confirming response from the Gifts. Paradoxically, his last moments were the first moments of true and total peace he had experienced in five decades.

Everyone on the bridge, even Data and Worf, was momentarily frozen by the image that had appeared without warning, without even the spatial distortions that normally presaged a starship's emergence from warp drive.

A glinting, metallic blue, the alien ship dwarfed the *Enterprise*. Any one of its three, rounded, fortresslike segments could have contained the *Enterprise*. Stubby wings extended out on either side of the forward segment, tipped with what could have been drive units or weapons, each as large by itself as a medium-class starship. Like a spacegoing mountain, it exuded an impression of raw, massive power.

Data was the first to recover.

"Captain," he said quickly, "the appearance of a ship similar to this is another phenomenon that occurs frequently in the Ferengi-supplied information, particularly in stories that allegedly originated among star-traveling civilizations rather than among planet-bound. In all instances, this phenomenon was said to have been followed within an unspecified but not lengthy period of time by an explosion of the type we have already discussed."

"This is what wiped out the other guard posts?" Picard breathed. "Perhaps these Builders of yours were justified in their paranoia. For a ship this size to travel, as this one seems to have done, by means of transporter rather than warp drive—"

"It did not travel by means of transporter, sir," Worf announced. "It does not even exist."

Picard turned sharply toward the Klingon. "Explain!"

"Sensor probes show that the Repository's shields have expanded radically. Their dimensions, in fact, now match the dimensions of the ship you see on the viewer, and they are producing the electromagnetic radiation that makes up the image."

"An illusion?"

"In the same sense that the images our holodecks produce are illusions, sir. The shields, in fact, have altered their nature so that they now include a somewhat primitive version of the force fields that give solidity to holodeck images. That is apparently what the power is being used for."

Frowning, Picard turned to the tactical station. "Mr. Brindle?"

"An illusion, sir," he agreed, "but a solid one. To less sophisticated sensor probes than our own—probes using only the standard electromagnetic spectrum—it would appear completely real."

"Then the explosions that, according to Mr. Data, follow the appearance of a ship like this—"

"Must be caused by self-destruct devices!" Riker finished Picard's thought when the captain halted abruptly, his eyes darting back to the image in the viewer. "And both the illusion and the self-destruction could be triggered simply by the approach of a starship, just as the self-destruct device on the derelict was triggered by our beaming aboard. The illusion of the massive warship must be a last-ditch effort to frighten the would-be attacker away, and if it doesn't work, the self-destruct sequence is activated."

"Lieutenant Worf," Picard snapped, "how powerful are the alien's shields now? Could we punch through them with our transporters? And bring Lieutenant La Forge out?"

"No, sir. Phasers, however, would penetrate easily."

Picard shook his head. "Not with Lieutenant La Forge in there! What about physical objects? If their shields have been altered so they are similar to our holodeck force fields—"

"It *is* possible, sir."

"We could take the *Enterprise* itself *inside* the illusion?"

"Yes, sir, I believe we could. However, we would have to lower our own shields to do so. The interaction between the two types of shields—"

"And once inside, we could beam Lieutenant La Forge on board?"

"If the conditions that exist at present do not change, yes, sir."

Picard turned abruptly to the conn. "Mr. Gawelski, take us inside that image, whatever it is. Mr. Brindle, lower shields only long enough to accommodate our passage. And Mr. Carpelli, be ready to lock onto Lieutenant La Forge's communicator and bring him in. Bring the other three aboard as well, if time and circumstance permit. Lieutenant Yar, Dr. Crusher, security and medical details to the transporter room, immediately."

The fortresslike image grew sharply, until only a single dome filled the viewer.

"Ready to attempt entry, sir," Gawelski reported.

"Shields down, Mr. Brindle," Picard snapped.

The only indication on the viewer was a faint shimmering. "Moving through on impulse power," Gawelski reported.

The image expanded even more, beginning to lose detail in the last seconds. What had seemed at a distance to be geometrically straight horizontal lines across the front of the dome were suddenly blurry, their edges irregular, like a painting viewed under a microscope, where seemingly smooth brush strokes of paint became jagged furrows and ridges.

And then it was gone, and the Repository hung in space before them.

But at the same instant, everyone on the bridge lurched backward as a pressure, like a strong, steady wind, pushed briefly against them.

"Passing through the force fields, sir," Worf rumbled in explanation from the science station. "We are now inside. There is—"

Abruptly, the Klingon fell silent as his fingers darted across the science station controls, his eyes taking in a newly appeared reading.

"Repository shields reverting to previous configuration, sir, and shrinking."

"Ensign Carpelli—"

"Locking on now, sir."

"Mr. Brindle, lock phasers onto Repository power source. Ready to fire as soon as Lieutenant La Forge is on board."

"Energizing now, sir," Carpelli reported.

"All four, Mr. Carpelli?"

"All four, sir."

"Lieutenant Worf, all still unconscious?"

"Still unconscious, sir."

"I have them, Captain," Carpelli reported.

"Shields up, Mr. Brindle! Ready to fire phasers!"

"Shields up, sir. Ready to—"

"Repository shields once again in place, Captain, enclosing only the Repository but still drawing increased power. Phasers will not penetrate."

"Hold your fire, Mr. Brindle. Lieutenant Worf, what—"

"New sequence beginning in Repository antimatter power source, sir," Worf broke in, "probably self-destruct by simultaneous detonation of all antimatter."

"Get us out of here, Mr. Gawelski!"

"Wait, sir!" Riker cautioned sharply. "It's too close! The habitat will be destroyed! There are a thousand people—"

"Mr. Brindle, the tractor beam!" Picard snapped without missing a beat. "How much time do we have, Lieutenant Worf?"

"Less than a minute at the current rate, sir."

"More than enough, if the tractor beam holds. Mr. Gawelski, take us radially away from the planet the instant the tractor beam has the satellite. If Mr. Data's Ferengi stories are true, this could be dangerous to the planet as well as the habitat."

A tense silence, and then: "Tractor beam activated and locked onto satellite, sir."

"Mr. Gawelski, full impulse power."

In the viewer, now focusing on the planet below them, the image shrank rapidly. In the foreground, the speck that was the Repository stayed constant.

At the science station, Worf began his countdown at twenty seconds.

At ten, the *Enterprise* and its trailing load were nearly one hundred fifty thousand kilometers out.

"Release tractor beam," Picard ordered sharply.

"Mr. Gawelski, reverse course, back toward the habitat. Keep us directly between the habitat and the Repository. They may need the shielding."

The released Repository continued outward, slowed only the minutest fraction by the now-distant planet's gravity.

It was nearly three hundred thousand kilometers out when it annihilated itself.

For an instant, it rivaled the sun, even at that distance, and the *Enterprise* sensors picked up a sleet of deadly radiation. The habitat, in the protective shadow of the *Enterprise* and its shields, would receive almost none, and the planet, protected by its atmosphere, would be untouched.

The glare faded, the radiation quieted, and it was over.

"Dr. Crusher," Picard said, "status report on your patients, particularly Lieutenant La Forge."

"Preliminary examination shows him to be in his usual fine health, Captain. I'll be a little more confident, though, when he awakens and I can talk to him."

"As will I, Doctor, as will I. And the other three? Is there any reason they should not be beamed back to their shuttle?"

"No health-related reasons, sir. They check out as well as Lieutenant La Forge."

"Make it so, Mr. Carpelli. The fewer of these people that become aware of the existence of the

Enterprise, the less disturbed the Prime Directive will be."

"It will have to be the other shuttle, Captain," Brindle said. "The one they used was attached to the Repository."

"Then the other shuttle. Lieutenant Worf, is it still in operable condition?"

"According to sensor readings, yes, sir."

Relieved, Picard relayed the information to Carpelli and turned to Shar-Tel. "I trust you have no objections to being returned in the same manner? With the Repository gone, though through no effort of ours, and with your group's ships on their way, you appear to be—"

"Captain!" Lieutenant Yar, back at the tactical station, interrupted. "It's Shar-Tel's friend La-Dron, trying to contact him."

Picard waved Shar-Tel to the tactical station.

Shar-Tel, swallowing audibly before he spoke, said: "Yes, La-Dron, what did you find?"

"I'm sorry, Shar-Tel. We were too late."

Shar-Tel slumped but then straightened again. "My brother is dead?"

"He must have died only minutes before we arrived, but even if we had gotten there earlier, I'm sure there was nothing we could have done. The bullet—"

"You don't need to go into detail," Shar-Tel snapped. "What about Kel-Nar's men? Are they still trying to round everyone up?"

"Some are, but when they learn what he did to your brother—"

"Tell them Kel-Nar is my prisoner. Tell them he attempted to take control of the Repository but failed. Tell them the Repository has been destroyed."

For a long moment, there was only silence. "Then we have won," La-Dron said softly.

Shar-Tel closed his eyes briefly, then let his breath out in a faint sigh. "Yes, we seem to have won. I will be returning shortly, bringing Kel-Nar and those who accompanied him to the Repository."

Another brief silence, and then La-Dron said, "As you wish. Though no one would blame you if it was learned that Kel-Nar was not still among your prisoners when you arrive."

Shar-Tel shook his head. "I will bring him."

Before he could more than turn from the tactical station, Yar was holding up a hand to signal him. "One of the ships is finally responding to your message," she said.

Picard smiled. "Shar-Tel, would you care to explain the situation to your comrades before you leave? Without mentioning the *Enterprise,* of course."

Shar-Tel hesitated, suddenly uneasy as he recalled his earlier exchange with Yar about the possible motives of those in the approaching ships.

"They're trying again, sir," Yar said, her eyes meeting Shar-Tel's after a brief glance in Picard's direction.

"As you wish, Captain," Shar-Tel said, straightening his shoulders and turning back to the tactical station.

"This is Shar-Tel," the old man began. "Who is this?"

"This is Lyn-Pron," the voice, now projected for all the bridge to hear, said.

The tension melted out of Shar-Tel, and he slumped in relief.

Of all the people who could have been leading the ships on this mission, Lyn-Pron was the one whose presence most gave him hope. Lyn-Pron was the one whom Shar-Tel had dealt with most, the one with whom he had worked out a thousand plans and a thousand alternates. The one with whom, over nearly two decades, he had become friends— or as close to friends as faceless voices with shared dreams could become.

"Did you receive my message?" Shar-Tel asked.

"We did, old friend, but—"

"It can be ignored," Shar-Tel broke in. "Everything is under control again. Our goal has been accomplished. The Repository has been destroyed. The explosion you undoubtedly saw only moments ago marked its end."

"Is this a trick, old friend?" Suddenly there was

suspicion in Lyn-Pron's voice. "We did indeed see an explosion, but it was nowhere near the Repository."

"It's a long story, and I don't know nearly all of it. Kel-Nar tried to gain control of the Repository—he killed my brother—but something happened. Kel-Nar himself was rendered unconscious and expelled from the Repository"—the old man paused in his improvisation, glancing at Picard, who was watching him closely—"and the Repository somehow moved itself to where you saw the explosion. If it had not, we would all have been killed, and the planet itself could have been damaged by the radiation. As I said, I'm sure my brother—"

"But the Repository had no propulsion systems, or so you have told me often enough."

"If Shar-Lon could make it seek out every missile on the surface of the planet and hurl all of them hundreds of thousands of kilometers into space before exploding them," Shar-Tel said, letting some exasperation show in his voice, "I'm sure he could make it hurl *itself* into space the same way. He was the only one who knew and used the Gifts, but he—"

"I believe you, old friend," Lyn-Pron said, and suddenly his voice was filled not with suspicion but with sadness. "I almost wish I didn't."

Shar-Tel frowned. "You wish you *didn't?* What—"

288

"What I have to tell you would be easier if I didn't, if I thought you were trying to trick me, if I thought you had taken sides with Kel-Nar or had been seduced by the power of the Gifts yourself, but—"

Abruptly, Lyn-Pron's voice cut off, and for a moment there was only silence.

Finally he spoke again.

"The others don't know I've contacted you," Lyn-Pron said. "They forbade it, after your last message."

"But why? I tried to warn you—"

"I know, I know. But they didn't believe you. They feared it was a trick."

"A trick? To save you from Kel-Nar?"

"A trick to delay us, to give Kel-Nar *time*—the time he needed to master the Gifts so he could destroy our ships, the way your brother destroyed the missiles that were sent against him fifty years ago."

"That's insane! Why—"

"I know, old friend, I know! But I am only one of many. I tried to convince them there was no trickery. Believe me, I tried, but they wouldn't listen."

"But surely now that the Repository has been destroyed and Kel-Nar is my prisoner—"

"I'm sorry, Shar-Tel, but it will make no difference, not to the others. This has never been a mission to aid you against Kel-Nar or simply to try to destroy the Repository. It has been a mission against *all* of you."

Shar-Tel's eyes met Yar's for a fraction of a second, and he saw the sadness in them, the sadness that, in her cynicism, she had been right.

"What *are* your plans, then?" Shar-Tel asked, his voice now flat and resigned. "Are you going to invade and take over our World?"

Lyn-Pron sighed, almost shuddered. "I wish we were, but we are not."

"Then what?"

"Destruction. That is all they will settle for, the total destruction of the Peacekeepers and their World."

Chapter Eighteen

ANGER, SHOCK, DISBELIEF—all raced across Shar-Tel's suddenly ashen face.

"This is madness!" he said, his voice shaking. "There are nearly a thousand people here, men, women and children! If you want Kel-Nar, you can have him! If you want *me,* you can have me! But the others—"

"After fifty years of tyranny," Lyn-Pron's voice overrode Shar-Tel's, "people no longer make distinctions. Except to myself and a few others who have come to know you over the last few years, you are *all* Peacekeepers. You are the ones who destroyed the entire fleet of shuttles. You are the ones who, with your Gifts, force us to pay tribute, to allow you to steal whatever you need to keep your World going. You are the ones who destroyed every ship we tried to launch for more than two decades. You are the ones who have refused to share even the tiniest fraction of the alien science you have access to. You are the ones who have held our entire world *prisoner* for fifty years! You—"

Abruptly, Lyn-Pron broke off, and everyone on the bridge could hear his heavy breathing. Finally, quietly, he resumed.

"I'm sorry, old friend, but that is how virtually every one of us feels, even among those who have worked with you all these years. There is nothing I can do to change it, nothing."

"Then why are you telling me this?" Shar-Tel flared, the color returning to his face with the anger. "To torture us? So we will not only die but will *know* we are *going* to die?"

There was a bitter laugh from Lyn-Pron. "There are those who would like nothing better, unless it was to torture you each individually for the rest of your lives. But no, I am doing this— and I'm risking my *own* life *to* do it. If someone caught me talking to you, now, I think they would turn their weapons on my ship even before attacking you. I'm doing this because I couldn't live with myself if I weren't honest with you. And because I can't bring myself to give up hope, even now."

"But you just said you *had* given up!"

"I've used every argument a dozen times, but—. There's an hour until we arrive, an hour until we blast a thousand holes in your Peacekeepers' World. I'll keep on arguing every second, but I'll also leave the main channel in our ships open, for you, for anything you can say or show us, anything at all."

"But if we do that, the others will realize you've told us—"

"I know, but it doesn't matter. If this fails—as I'm very much afraid it will—I don't think I want to live any longer anyway, not with your death, with the death of your world, on my conscience. Good luck, old friend."

And the connection was broken.

Shar-Tel turned to Picard. "Return me to the shuttle, quickly. I would like to have at least a few minutes in the World before—"

"No!" Counselor Deanna Troi, who had been listening painfully to the exchange, almost shouted. "We cannot allow this to happen, Captain! We must do something!"

"I agree, Counselor," Picard said, "and I am open to suggestions." He looked around the bridge. "We do seem to bear some of the responsibility, if not for the basic situation, at least for precipitating the immediate crisis. I am open to suggestions, anything that does not shatter the Prime Directive beyond repair."

"Sir," Data said almost immediately, "I have discovered additional, possibly quite significant correlations in the Ferengi-supplied information. Extrapolating from those, and other correlations to determine if they have any relevance to the current situations—"

"Go on, Data," Picard prompted impatiently.

"I believe the correlations do possess a relevance, sir. In fact, they suggest a possible solution to this problem."

It was not weightlessness that caused Lyn-Pron's stomach to churn as the transfer orbit his ship had been following neared completion, and the Peacekeepers' World grew larger on the radar screen before him.

It was frustration.

And guilt.

Frustration at not being able to convince the others to even *delay* their assault, let alone cancel it. Finally, he had told them of his conversation with Shar-Tel, of Shar-Tel's claim that the Repository had been destroyed. Yet he had still been unable to move them, and for a moment he had been in real fear they actually *would* turn their weapons on him. Even when, minutes ago, it had become obvious from their radar screens that the Repository was no longer where it had been for the last five decades, they dismissed it out of hand. "It's just another trick," one of the pilots snarled. "With those damned 'Gifts' of his, Shar-Lon can do whatever he wants to."

But Lyn-Pron's guilt was even more powerful than the frustration. For nearly a decade he had lied to a man who, despite his continued efforts to resist, to remain "objective," had become his

294

friend. The ships themselves, instead of being able to carry scores of men apiece, each had room only for one man—and scores of missiles. Their purpose had never been anything but destruction, not only of the Repository but of the Peacekeepers' World itself. He could not convince his allies that his destruction would be a poor foundation to build on for the peaceful world they so desired.

And now, in less than a quarter of an hour, Lyn-Pron would have to watch that destruction, helpless to lift a finger against it.

Abruptly, the monitor screen above the bank of controls flared into chaotic life.

Startled, he looked up. He had left the audio link open, but this—

"Lyn-Pron!" a harsh, accusatory voice came over the audio link from the other ships. "Is this another scheme to save your friends?"

But before he could deny it, before he could more than wonder if, somehow, Shar-Tel was responsible —an image emerged from the chaos.

And it *was* Shar-Tel!

But he was not in any part of the Peacekeepers' World Lyn-Pron had ever suspected existed, nor in the Repository, not unless Shar-Tel's descriptions had been lies plain and simple. In the dim light, stark black and deep orange were the only colors visible, except for Shar-Tel himself and his clothes. The air was permeated with a smoky haze that dimmed visibility even more, giving Shar-Tel an ominous, even menacing look. Behind him were banks of panels, not with recognizable controls or displays but with bizarrely shaped patterns of lights.

"Shar-Tel!" Lyn-Pron gasped. "What *is* this?"

"I am sorry, Lyn-Pron," the old man returned, but the voice, stiff and expressionless, was virtually unrecognizable, "but you were—"

Abruptly, he was cut off as a massive hand, its gray-black fingers extending clawlike from a metal-studded half-glove at the end of a similarly studded, leatherlike sleeve, grasped his shoulder and thrust him roughly aside.

Lyn-Pron gasped as the creature suddenly filled the screen. At least a foot taller and almost that much broader than Shar-Tel, it was dressed in heavy leather with an almost metallic sheen to it, a barbaric battle garb of some kind. Suspended from a massive ornamental chain around its neck was what could have been a sculpture or, Lyn-Pron suspected, the preserved head of a small, viciously fanged animal.

But the creature's own face and head—

It was humanoid, but far from human. Though dark, the color of decayed flesh, its mouth and bearded chin were almost human in shape, but above the piercing eyes and heavy brow ridge, a massive bony crest stretched from the top of the nose over the forehead and back almost half across the crown, where it was met by a roll of jet-black hair that fell over its misshapen ears and onto its massive shoulders.

"You are the fools who dream of destroying me," it said, its voice a bass rumble, its lips twitching in a derisive smile.

From one of the other ships, someone managed to ask, "Who *are* you?"

The figure laughed, the sound as deep and rumbling as its voice, as threatening as its appearance. "Among my equals—and there are few—I am known as Worf. To you, I am the owner of what you creatures have seen fit to call the 'Repository.' Did you not think I might take offense at your feeble efforts to damage it?"

"I would hardly call them feeble," another of the pilots said, his voice wavering as he tried to sound defiant. "We saw the explosion that destroyed it."

"Destroyed it? Does this look as if it has been destroyed? No, I do not allow my possessions to be destroyed so easily."

"We didn't know it was yours!" a third voice said, this one high-pitched with fright. "It had been abandoned! We merely—"

"I do not abandon my possessions, creature!"

"Then take it! We don't care if it is destroyed, just so we are rid of it!"

Again there was the laugh. "You do not understand, creatures. I have *many* possessions here, and I have no wish to give *any* of you up."

"Any of *us?*" Lyn-Pron burst out. "What insanity is this? *We* are not your possessions!"

"You think not?" The figure waved his left hand imperiously.

And suddenly Lyn-Pron felt his entire body tingle. The air around him filled with vertical streaks of light, and from the other ships came gasps and at least one scream.

For an instant, he was paralyzed, unable to finish pulling in the breath he had begun a moment before, certain that even his heart had been frozen in midbeat.

And the cramped ship's compartment vanished from around him.

For a moment, there was nothing but the harsh intensity of the streaks of light, now enclosing him like a cocoon.

And he was in the place that, seconds before, had been only an image on the monitor screen. The creature that called itself Worf stood before him, looming over him like a demonic colossus. At one side, Shar-Tel stood stiffly, unmoving, unblinking. Around them, enveloping them, was the ocher haze, dulling the patterns of lights on the panels that filled the wall behind the creature. The heat was stifling, the air filled with a totally unfamiliar but pungently unpleasant odor.

And he could not move, either forward or backward. He could turn his head, move his arms, but his feet seemed rooted to the floor.

A gasp, then another, came from behind Lyn-Pron. Jerking his head around, he saw the men from the other five ships, their eyes wide in shock. Behind them were more of the haze-obscured panels. Nowhere was there evidence of a door or opening of any kind.

"Welcome to my den, creatures!" the bass voice rumbled. "Is there anything you would like to see?"

Pausing, Worf looked from one to another in mock interest, then smiled, and for a moment it seemed that the tiny head suspended from the chain around his neck bared its fangs in a grotesque parody of a smile.

"No? Then let me show you something of my own choosing."

Another gesture, and one of the blocky patterns of lights on the panels behind the creature shifted and changed.

And in the hazy air, an image of Lyn-Pron's ship appeared, three-dimensional and seemingly solid enough to touch.

Another gesture, this one barely more than a flick of a finger, and a glowing beam of light stabbed at the ship. A moment later, the ship began to glow itself, then it flared and was gone.

"I will perhaps allow you to keep the others," the creature said, laughing. "If you do not prove *too* annoying."

"What do you want of us?" Lyn-Pron, the only

one who seemed to have regained the power of speech, asked. "Why are you here?"

"I came because you had the misfortune to invade what was mine. I remained because your antics amuse me." Another laugh rumbled up from deep in Worf's chest. "The one who called himself Shar-Lon was an endless source of sport, particularly in his egotistical delusions that he was acting of his own free will."

"Then he *was* possessed!"

"Of course—though he called it being 'chosen.' His delusions were almost as amusing as your own frantic scurryings in response to his actions."

"But why have you shown yourself to us now? After fifty years—"

"After fifty years, you were beginning to bore me, even annoy me with your petty plots. Therefore, I have decided to take direct control rather than act secretly through one of you. For your sake, I hope I am not disappointed in the results. Not everyone is so privileged as to have a second chance! Be thankful that, in those early years, you amused me as well as you did. Otherwise, I might simply have departed, never to return."

"Do it, then!" Shar-Tel almost shouted.

Worf looked down at Shar-Tel for a moment, a hint of amusement in his hooded eyes. Then he stepped back and lowered himself into a thronelike chair, its arms covered with miniature versions of the lighted patterns on the wall panels.

"I may," he said, "if you become *too* boring or *too* annoying. I do not believe you would be happy with the results, however." He paused, his eyes briefly touching each of the six. "Remember," he finished with a smile, this one definitely mirrored in the tiny head that rested on his chest, "I do not *abandon* my possessions."

"You would kill us?" Lyn-Pron asked in horror.

"In time, perhaps, unless, without any help from me, you kill *yourselves*. That, of course, could conceivably sustain my interest in your little world for some time to come. Planetary suicide *is* an intriguing phenomenon, and I—"

"Then why did you destroy our missiles fifty years ago? Why—"

There was a hint of a shrug as Worf said, "It seemed like a good idea at the time. And it did give me decades of diversion that I would not have had if I had allowed you to simply turn your world into a cinder. So, no matter what you think of my methods or motives, you can at least thank me for several years of planetary existence you might not otherwise have had." He laughed again. "Perhaps you can show your gratitude by accomplishing your self-destruction in as interesting a fashion as possible. I could arrange for some of the more exotically destructive 'Gifts' to be distributed among certain of your leaders—"

"Damn you!" Lyn-Pron exploded. "This is our world you're talking about! We've no interest in destroying it—not with your Gifts, not with our own weapons—not at all. You act as if this were a *game!*"

"But it is, little creature, it is. Do you not have similar games on your world? I believe I have seen them, games in which lesser creatures are set upon each other, and you cheer them on, urging them to kill and mutilate each other?"

"Just a sick few enjoy such things! Not everyone—"

"Who is to say who is sick? Perhaps it is more widespread than you think. Perhaps you, who set out to purposely murder more than a thousand of your fellow creatures, share in this so-called sickness."

Worf waved a hand dismissively. "But I weary of this. I will return you to your ships—those of you who still have ships to be returned to. You—" His eyes gripped Lyn-Pron. "You, I may retain for a time. You seem more spirited than the others."

Lyn-Pron shuddered but did not flinch.

Then, a moment later, he suppressed a start. *Something* was forming in the haze behind Worf's massive chair. At first, it was as if the haze itself were thickening, but then he saw that it was independent of the haze. It was pale, almost paper white, and it grew gradually more distinct.

Until, suddenly, it came into focus.

Nearly a meter high, hanging two meters above the deck, it was Shar-Lon's face!

302

And, though Lyn-Pron had managed to keep his face from betraying the image's presence, the others had not been as successful. Worf turned in his chair.

For just an instant, he appeared startled, but then he laughed. "You are more persistent than I thought, oh Chosen One. What is it you have to say?"

"Lyn-Pron," the ghostly face said, "if you are seeing and hearing this, I have succeeded. Now it is up to you and Shar-Tel and the others, and you must hurry. You must concentrate all your thoughts on Shar-Tel. Give him your strength, quickly. This monster *can* be overcome."

"That is enough!" Worf growled, pushing himself erect and striding through Shar-Lon's face, as if to prove it didn't exist.

But even as he passed through it, Shar-Lon's voice continued.

"This creature is *not* invincible. It is a rogue, an outlaw, even among its own kind. It was able to trap me with its Gifts because I was naive. It was able to control me because I was alone. But even so, I have not been totally helpless. I was able, before my death, to—"

At the panels at the back of the room, Worf stabbed roughly at one of the patterns of lights with his gauntleted hand.

But the face, though it suddenly froze, remained.

And, a moment later, began its words again, from the beginning.

"That is enough!" Worf almost shouted, but at the same moment, Shar-Tel lurched backward, as if breaking free from whatever had held him.

"Lyn-Pron!" he grated. "This is our only chance! Our *world's* only chance! You *must—*"

"Mindless savages!" The words erupted from Worf as he grasped at a small, jagged-edged weapon holstered at his waist. As he drew it, it expanded as if by magic into a meter-long scimitar. It slashed through Shar-Lon's outsize face but disturbed only the haze that still filled the air.

An instant later, he turned on Shar-Tel, his roar drowning out Shar-Lon's disembodied voice.

And Lyn-Pron was released.

Whatever had been holding him motionless suddenly released him.

Lunging forward, he leaped at Worf's back, his hand grasping for the hand that held the blade.

And then another was released, and another, and then all five were lunging forward, grasping Worf, clinging to him desperately as, together, they forced the blade back until its glittering edge touched the giant's grimacing face.

A deafening roar erupted from Worf's throat, and then he fell.

And vanished in a crackling display of transporter energies.

Lyn-Pron and the five collapsed in a heap.

304

"It is gone!" Shar-Tel gasped. "We have won! Now hurry, I must make one last use of the Gifts to return you to your ships. In a few minutes, now that the creature and his control are gone, the Repository will *truly* be destroyed! That is something else that my brother was able to accomplish."

Without waiting for a reply, without even waiting for the six to untangle themselves and scramble erect, Shar-Tel jabbed at one of the panels.

Shar-Lon's face, still speaking, vanished.

A moment later, Lyn-Pron felt a tingling and was enveloped, along with the other five, in the energies of the *Enterprise* transporter system.

Shar-Tel, as they vanished, breathed a massive sigh of relief, then turned and waited for the imitation Repository—in reality, a mixture of images from a half dozen sources, including the bridge of a century-old Klingon battle cruiser—to fade and the holodeck doors to open.

He stepped out into the halls of the *Enterprise,* leaving behind the last of his world as it had been—a world of dictatorships and petty jealousies, of war and constant struggle—and strode forward into a future filled with hope. Peace would come to his world, not through "superior firepower" or sleight-of-hand from above, but rather through the cooperation of all nations and peoples.

Two minutes later and ten thousand kilometers away, where the Repository would have been if it

305

had not already been destroyed, a photon torpedo flashed for all the world—and the five remaining ships—to see.

From a safely undetectable distance, the *Enterprise* watched as the five remaining ships approached the habitat.

"Too melodramatic!" Picard had protested, almost wincing as he watched the performance. "They will *never* believe such an unalloyed villain!"

Even Worf, though he obviously enjoyed his first "dramatic improvisation," had his doubts about its effectiveness.

"No Klingon would ever be so foolish as to turn his back on six enemies, no matter how well they were supposedly restrained," he complained with a faintly wistful look as he removed his Klingon battle garb and donned his Starfleet uniform with its token sash. "My 'defeat' was utterly implausible."

Troi, who had monitored the emotional state of the six pilots and relayed the results continually to Worf to serve as a guide in his improvisation, was the only one who had appeared to be confident of the results.

"No matter what they say, Jean-Luc, they *want* to believe," she reassured him at one point. "No matter what their grievances against Shar-Lon and the Peacekeepers, they do not relish the thought of murdering a thousand helpless people."

And with each passing minute, with each new broadcast that Yar intercepted, the more it appeared that Troi was right. Worf's demise, and the "final destruction" of the Repository, had been accepted almost without question.

All those on the Peacekeepers' World—with the possible exception of Kel-Nar and his inner circle, who, upon awakening, had found themselves confined and under guard—were themselves being viewed as victims of the Builders, not the elitist tyrants they had seemed to be for decades. Already there was talk that, someday soon, the habitat itself would become what many had originally thought it had been designed to be—the first major step in the world's space program.

Finally, the five ships came to rest, and their pilots emerged. Lyn-Pron, his ship destroyed, had been transported directly to the habitat with Shar-Tel, and now the two emerged from the habitat airlock to greet the five ceremoniously.

Picard, apparently finally satisfied that the situation was indeed under control, settled back in the captain's chair.

"It appears we've managed to undo the results of our unplanned interference—and set the planet back on its natural course of evolution," he said.

"Yes, sir." Riker nodded. "I expect they'll be venturing out into space soon enough—in their own time and manner. Perhaps we'll meet them again."

"Perhaps we will," Picard agreed. "Without the need to be anything but ourselves—correct, Mr. La Forge?"

"Yes sir," Geordi said, turning in his seat to face the captain. Picard had already made it quite clear to him how important it was to keep the Prime Directive in mind when dealing with emerging cultures. Even though he'd based all his decisions solely on a desire to save lives, his decision to impersonate one of the Builders had been the root of all their subsequent involvement. This time, everything had turned out for the best. Next time . . .

He shook his head. The Prime Directive was a complicated thing.

Picard smiled.

"Resume course for Starbase fifty-four, Mr. La Forge."

"Course laid in, sir."

"Engage."

And the Peacekeepers' World vanished behind them.

A few minutes later, when Picard had retired to the Ready Room to contemplate the report he would have to make to Starfleet, Geordi turned to Data at the ops station.

"Commander Riker tells me that it was you who came up with the idea that saved the day, Data."

"I suggested only the basic framework of the idea. It was the others, particularly Lieutenant Yar, who developed it into a workable solution."

"Nonetheless, Data, the original idea was yours." He smiled and leaned closer, as if he were telling a secret. "I don't want to upset you, but that idea sounds an awful lot like plain old intuition to me."

Data shook his head sadly. "Thank you, Geordi, but I fear it was simple logical extrapolation. Among the stories collected by the Ferengi were no fewer than three in which massive explosions in space—presumably orbiters self-destructing—produced virtually identical long-term positive results. The people on each of those planets, though none had yet developed space travel, were constantly warring among themselves, squandering their planets' limited resources on weaponry. But the explosions in space, coupled with the effects of the radiation on the planet's surface, made them aware that something was out there—something that made them realize how petty their own differences were. The current situation seemed similar—in fact, the people of Shar-Lon's world appeared more than ready to institute world government, to rid themselves of their self-destructive nationalism and the arsenals it engendered, once they had eliminated the Peacekeepers. So the solution seemed obvious: to bring the Peacekeepers and the rest of the population back together, a 'common enemy' was needed. And since we had already been told that there were those who had believed from the beginning that Shar-Lon had been 'possessed,' it was only logical to make use of that belief in the solution. Indeed, from all accounts, Shar-Lon truly was influenced by some aspect of the Builders, by something that was inherent in the mental-control device in the Repository. In a sense, therefore, we were simply informing them, in a somewhat distorted and dramatic fashion, of what really did happen to Shar-Lon."

"I know," Geordi said, laughing. "It's all perfectly clear in hindsight. But, then, that's the way intuition works, too. Whenever someone comes up with a brilliant idea, someone else always says, 'Why didn't *I* think of that?'"

He paused, shaking his head. "Maybe the only difference is, for mere humans, 'intuition' happens in our subconscious, where we can't see what's really going on, so we call it a hunch and let it go at that. But you don't *have* a subconscious, so the process happens right out there in the open where you can keep an eye on it."

Data brightened, but looked at Geordi questioningly. "Do you really believe that this is possible? That I do possess a form of 'intuition'?"

"I do, Data." Geordi nodded, smiling. "But, then, it's only a hunch."

STAR TREK®
THE FINAL NEXUS

Uncounted centuries ago, an unknown race from
beyond our galaxy created a series of interstellar
gates - shortcuts across our universe - and then
disappeared, leaving behind no clues to their fate, or
the operation of their system. Twice before, the
Enterprise has used the system to traverse the galaxy,
and returned each time no wiser to the
gates' operation.

Now it is imperative that they find out. For the gates
are breaking down, taking the very stars in the sky
with them. The fate of the galaxy rests in the hands of
the *Enterprise* crew, and their ability to communicate
not only with creatures from another world - but from
another universe as well.

For a complete list of Star Trek publications, please
send a large stamped SAE to Titan Books Mail
Order, 19 Valentine Place, London, SE1 8QH.
Please quote reference NG2.